Jade C. Russel

CURSEBREAKER

When Love is a Curse

novum ◢ pro

This book is also available as e-book.

www.novum-publishing.co.uk

© 2017 novum publishing

ISBN 978-3-99048-964-2
Editing: Louise Darvid
Cover design, layout & typesetting: novum publishing

www.novum-publishing.co.uk

To my family, my heart, my rock, my lovely curse.

PROLOGUE

William.

I was comfortably sitting on a sofa, smoking a cheeky cigarette – that I wasn't allowed to smoke officially – while I distractedly listened to some of my friends discussing the score of the match they watched the day before.

I smiled catching some people's disapproving stares at my lit cigarette, they could stare and complain as much as they wanted, no one would ever even dream of saying a thing to me, I had something they didn't have: power.

I, William, had the power to shut everyone up with my money or simply by saying my own name. My name, like a feared brand to bow from.

The famous Black family.

Generations and generations of perfectly reckless rich human beings who owned the city we built centuries ago.

From father to son, our legacy of money and power didn't go to waste.

We were an utopian species, genetically programmed to rule.

Every Black family member had two purposes in life: to keep the business – ergo the money – running and find a worthy wealthy wife to breed other Black offsprings who would one day do the same. No room for mistakes.

My father, as the perfect Black, was a legend, one of the richest and most powerful bank owners in the UK and soon-to-be mayor of that shithole they called a city.

Flawless.

Idyllic.

As for me, I was just uninterested with all that crap. I would eventually comply with what was expected of me but I was just totally and utterly disinterested in the meantime.

Too bored not to have another drink, I stood up and went downstairs, ignoring the alarmed stares from my mates.

"I'm thirsty," I simply said. I knew that without me they'd be kicked out of the bar for they were all underage.

I almost smiled, my father's bank gave a mortgage to the owner of the place, so I was treated better than a God in there as one word from me and the place might fall in ruin.

What did I say? Yeah, power.

I sat down on the stool at the main counter; a skinny bartender saw me and asked me what I wanted to drink.

"I want a Bloody Mary. Drown me in gin."

"Right away."

I smirked, the guy didn't even bother to ask for my age, I liked him already.

You earned a good tip, mate.

I looked around me, the place was packed, the particularity of it was that it was mostly dark. Like the only lights were in the dance floor, all the rest, the bar and the tables were in semi-darkness, only lit by the fluorescent glasses full of alcohol.

I loved it.

With the corner of my eye, I saw a movement; a girl sat a few feet from me.

With little interest, I tried to look at her but it was too dark to see her face.

"Can I have a tonic, please?" she ordered.

Her voice was nice but I couldn't quite place the accent she had, it was like a weird mix.

I was curious now.

"She's having gin with her tonic," I said imperious, just to catch her attention. Girls those days were so easy to get a hold on that I liked to try new ways every now and then.

She turned to look at me, surprised and vexed. "No, I shall stick with my tonic." She looked at the bartender. "No ice, please."

The girl was ignoring me. I was almost amused, she was clearly from somewhere far away to have the guts to contradict me.

Or, most likely, it was too dark to recognize the features of my face.

"Why are you in a bar if you are not drinking?"

"I'm underage," she simply said, clearly meant to end the conversation there, but she had no idea who she was dealing with.

"So am I." I raised my newly arrived drink to make a point.

"I don't drink alcohol."

"Why, are you a nun?" I didn't even know why I kept on talking to her, she seemed to be a know-it-all self-righteous kind of girl.

"Yes, I am. Now, enjoy your illegal drinking." She faked a smile and grabbing her drink, she turned to leave.

Not quite ready to let you leave, babe.

I was surprised by my own thought; I usually avoided any kind of interaction with girls who seemed to be frigid to death.

I grabbed her wrist. I could touch the shape of a bracelet, a spiral themed bracelet. "What if I wanted you to stay?" I was taunting her.

"You could go to hell. Now let me go." She seemed to be calm.

I couldn't even see her face properly, I couldn't tell whether she was attractive or not, her body was concealed by what seemed to be a huge jacket.

So why was I playing with her, now?

"Make me." I was definitely amused.

In the darkness, I could detect a look of anger but then all of a sudden she smiled; in a second I felt wet and sticky.

She had splashed her tonic – all over my face.

Everything fell silent, with the corner of my eye I saw the bouncer flinch but not make a move.

With just a look, I intimated everyone to keep on doing what they were doing; apparently she was the only one who didn't know who she was dealing with.

Then I turned back to her, my own eyes like flames.

"How dare you, you little lousy girl?" I was still holding her wrist. I could easily break it if I only gave in to the rage, just a tiny bit of pressure and her bone would be in pieces. She felt so fragile in my hands, just like a doll.

I'd never hit a girl. I thought I was better than that, but that little savage horse deserved to learn a lesson; she had to be tamed.

"You do not touch me," she hissed. A cat ready to attack.

"You're gonna apologize *now*." I articulated the sentence like I was speaking to someone with mental problems.

"What if I don't?" She was being dangerously cheeky.

"Then you're having the worst five minutes of your life."

"Let me go or I..." She seemed to be strangely calm.

"Or you *what*?" I faked a laugh; it sounded too phoney even to my own ears. I was still too enraged.

I slightly increased the pressure on her wrist, I wanted to scare her just because I knew I could, make her bow like everyone else always did.

And then chaos exploded, it all happened in less than a blink, with the fluorescent light of my glass, I saw her close her eyes and murmur something I didn't get.

Behind me the cracking noise of broken glass. I instantly let go of her and checked what happened. Hundreds of bottles were broken on the floor, I turned back to face her but she was simply gone. Disappeared into thin air.

What happened to those bottles? Why did she look kind of pleased before closing her eyes? And most important of all, where was she?

"What happened here?" I interrogated the skinny bartender.

"I don't know, sir. One moment I was shaking a drink, the moment after, the disaster happened."

"Have you seen the girl that was with me not long ago?"

"What girl?"

"The girl who ordered the tonic with no ice."

He gave me a weird look. "Sir, no one has ordered a neat tonic for years in this place."

New school, new life

Jayne.

I looked around me, the big hall was empty, I had to admit I liked that school; it had something about it that was elegant and Spartan at the same time.

I knew though I'd better not get attached or even used to it, I might be on my way soon.

That was my golden rule, my lifestyle, never to get attached to places or people for I was destined to live my life as a hermit without resting.

"Honey, whenever you travel, you don't let anything touch you deeply, it's less painful if you consider them as transitory," my mum always said.

Not that I ever had the chance to get close to people, Mum.

I never had real friends, boyfriends or a family even, because of *what* I was. And in the end, it almost didn't hurt anymore, the wall I painfully raised between myself and the world was stronger than ever.

I would not let anyone in, I would always stand tall and alone, I learnt that I didn't need anyone else but myself.

Not those hypocritical and mean people, not a lousy home not anything. I just didn't get why I had to always try and pretend to be normal when I was clearly not.

I checked the paper the principal gave me that morning, my first class was Art and I was already late.

I sighed before knocking on the door. I felt a bit nervous at first, but then I remembered how many times I'd done that before so I pushed the door open.

"Guys, here's our transfer student from Aberdeen, Scotland," he smiled, "Jayne Frost."

I half smiled nervously. Everyone was staring curiously, and even though I'd done it a million times before I still hated the attention, I was far too used to it.

11

I walked to an empty desk and smiled politely to everyone, until the teacher caught everybody's attention to the daily lesson again.

I wasn't particularly interested in the subject but I tried to pay attention anyways, enjoying those few moments of normality I could have.

He was explaining something about the Mona Lisa, nothing new to me as I had seen the painting myself during the brief period I spent in France.

Eventually, the bell rang so I collected my stuff and went to leave the classroom, when the teacher held me in a moment.

"I expect you to keep up with your classmates, Miss Frost. I expect nothing but the best by my students."

"I will try my best indeed."

"Here are some chapters you have to catch up with in the next couple of weeks." He passed a book full of bookmarks.

"But, sir, those must be like three hundred pages!" I was truly horrified.

"Then you better get started." He winked at me. *Winked.*

That's what I hate about normality: school.

"Right." I surrendered.

"Oh, Miss Frost?" I turned to look at him. "Welcome to Nostradamus High School," and I left with a forced smile.

Let's try and survive the second class, this time if they try and give me stuff to catch up with... I will probably explode!

I was on time for this class, Ancient Latin, so I didn't have to be introduced that formally. The teacher just mentioned my name distractedly and then started with his teaching.

That's the way I like it.

I knew Latin like I knew English, I grew up with it. My parents taught me that old language when I was only a toddler. It was part of who I was.

Since the professor wasn't saying anything I didn't already know by heart, I let my mind drift. My eyes check the classroom and my new classmates.

I looked around and noticed that I had caught many people's attention. A great part of the class was in fact staring at me for some reason. When I met a dark blond guy's eyes, he smiled softly while I turned away uncomfortably.

You wouldn't smile like that if you only knew.

Next class was French, easy peasy as I knew it already. Foreign languages were my strong point as I'd travelled everywhere in Europe and outside my whole life.

I'd always liked learning new languages, it helped me camouflage myself and become accustomed to the new culture.

The only thing I found hard about that class was finding the classroom. That school was way too big for my tastes and, after finding myself in the same spot for the second time, I knew I'd got lost.

I sighed and checked again the little map the headmaster had given me that morning, trying to find a sense of orientation I hardly ever had, when all of a sudden I bumped into something.

"Look where you're going!"

Or someone, judging by the irritated voice of a guy.

"I'm sorry, I..." I looked at him and I couldn't quite finish my sentence. Words just refused to come out.

The guy I'd bumped into mustn't have been a student, he must have been a model or a Hollywood actor. He was tall, perfect alabaster skin, dark-haired which seemed to be messy on his head on purpose, just to give him the "I just got out of bed" sexy look. But what truly enchanted – and I gotta admit kinda startled – me really were his eyes, his big grey eyes that seemed to pierce my very soul.

I realized he was the most handsome person I'd ever met. I blushed.

He smiled, pretending to adjust the fancy clothes he was wearing.

He seemed to be aware of the effect he had on girls, – are you gonna get out of my way any time soon or wanna still stare for a bit? I can give you an autographed picture if you want. He had such a cheeky smile that I cursed myself mentally for being that silly.

Apparently, he didn't only look like a hot model but he also had the attitude of one.

"I didn't see you," I said collecting my books from the floor. To take my eyes off him required more effort than I dared to admit.

"Clearly." He was amused, he walked passed me with a grin.

I glared at him while he disappeared in the hall, he hadn't even bothered to help me.

What an idiot.

Eventually I found my class.

The lesson went smoothly; I already knew half of the stuff I had to catch up with my classmates so I felt a bit more relaxed.

At least being a stupid hermit who travels continuously pays off.

On lunch break, I hurried to buy some food — a slice of pizza and an apple — to find a nice empty table to sit in peace. I usually chose the most isolated one and I didn't make an exception this time.

The pizza didn't look nice, it seemed one of those frozen ones you keep in the fridge till the end of time and it tasted like an old boot. Disgusted, I let it drop on the plate.

I thought this was a posh school.

"Hey, may I sit?" A friendly voice.

I turned and faced the dark blond boy who'd smiled at me during Latin class, I was quite surprised he had found me there.

"Yeah, sure," even though I wasn't very convinced.

"My name's Gabe Benson." He took a seat just in front of me.

I shook his hand. "Jayne Frost."

"How do you find it here?"

I watched him biting his pizza; he didn't seem disgusted by it like I was. I wondered if it was just me.

"It's still early to have an opinion." I smiled and thought of the guy I'd bumped into earlier that day, and I hoped not all of the students were like him. Gabe didn't seem like it.

"Hope we made a good impression, though. If you need anything, I'm here for you." He winked at me, and I thought he was really handsome with his young features.

"Right." I forced a smile uncomfortably, I knew that kindness would disappear as soon as he found out *what* I was.

"Would you like a tour? This school is quite big so you might get lost." He smiled.

I hesitated and he smiled reassuringly. "Sure, thank you."

In all fairness, I only accepted as I thought I might really need a tour as I didn't want to get lost again before a lesson; it's not nice to be scolded by a teacher on your first day.

After a bit, I decided I liked Gabe, he seemed to be an easy-going person so it wouldn't hurt anyone if I came out of my Fortress of Solitude for once, would it?

He showed me a great part of the school, the auditorium, the garden, classrooms and so on, then, as a great finale, he brought me to the library.

It had loads and loads of shelves full of books, all divided by topic, author in alphabetical order. I must admit I totally loved it. I had always imagined my own dream house with a big massive library.

On the left there was a light wooden counter, behind it an elderly lady with white-grey hair and little glasses was having a nap.

"She's snoring," I thought out loud, amused.

He smiled and took a picture of her with his phone. "This will be of use next time I take a book and forget to bring it back after three days," he explained.

I laughed. "Do you usually do that?"

"It happens." He smiled. "She's very annoying, when you don't bring it back after three days she goes to the principal and there's disciplinary action."

"She sounds evil." I nodded.

"She is indeed!" He laughed. "So when you borrow a book from here, you better bring it back right away or she'll have you gutted!"

I'm not planning on staying here for long anyways.

I forced a smile and after waving at him, I walked to my next class.

THIS EERIE STRANGER

William.

"William, are you listening to me?"

"Yes, you were talking about the food in the cafeteria," he answered bored.

"Yeah! It sucks! We should sign a petition or something to make it right."

I nodded distractedly, I wasn't really interested. I had to admit I hardly cared about anything lately, everything bored me to death.

I really hoped I wasn't becoming like that amoeba I called a father. In fact, I had never seen William Jonathan Black I being bothered about anything or anyone that wasn't work or his good name.

Not his money, not his cars, not his houses, not his family.

He seemed to be born for his job, a stupid Stakhanovite that was only living when he was in the office and just surviving when at home with his wife and kid. Maybe that was even a torture to him.

I had always promised myself that if I ever became like my *beloved* parent, I would point a gun at my temple and pull the trigger without hesitating. Actually, I would do it if I became like *either* of my parents.

"This girl is proper hot though."

Those words brought me back to reality, curious to know what my friends were talking about.

"The transfer student, she's in my Art class, she's hot."

"What are you on about?" I asked horrified. The only transfer student who was in his class was an ugly duckling.

"Check her out!" He pointed at the yard, where a girl was focused on her studying.

I immediately recognized the girl I bumped into a couple of days ago, and I was gutted to admit she was hot indeed.

I'd noticed she had a nice face on a good body, but looking at her now... there was something about her, something beautiful and charming I couldn't quite catch before.

She was focused on her reading, her face was thin and she didn't wear too much make up like all the other girls in school. She seemed to be from another world.

Her hair was something strange as well, it wasn't quite blonde but it was not brown; it looked like chestnut, rippling down her shoulders.

She had something eerie and mysterious in her look.

Like she's not like every one of us.

That thought hit me hard and I couldn't help but laugh at myself, I definitely had to stop watching vampire-zombie horror movies.

"Wasn't I right?" my mate insisted.

After a moment, she felt observed and raised her head, her eyes. Those strange light green eyes locked with mine for what seemed to be a long moment.

Then, after centuries, she looked annoyed; she must have recognized me.

I smiled in mockery at her.

An eerie beauty.

As if enchanted, my legs started moving towards her direction. I only realized I'd gone to her a few seconds later when I found myself facing her.

"So have you learnt how to walk without bumping into every single person in this planet?" I teased her.

"I've only bumped into you, once." She didn't even raise her eyes from her book.

"Should I consider myself special?" I smiled amused.

"Whatever you wish."

Her accent was odd, it was a mix of loads of different ones; it reminded me of something I couldn't quite place.

"Where are you from?" I asked genuinely curious, the amusement gone.

"Aberdeen," she answered automatically, she didn't even seem to pay much attention.

"No, it's not a Scottish accent. Or at least not only that, there's more." I realized I really thought that.

There is more.

She finally looked at me, kind of surprised. "I have foreign friends so I must have picked up many accents." She clearly meant to end the conversation but she didn't know I was more stubborn than that.

"Why don't you sound Scottish?"

"*I am* Scottish."

Now, I considered myself a master in the art of lying, I lived a lie. The perfect family, the perfect life, the perfect kid lie, so I could understand right away when someone was not being honest. Call it a gift.

"Liar." I wasn't even amused anymore. I was annoyed, I didn't even know why.

There was something about that girl that I couldn't quite wrap my head around and that bothered me more than I cared to admit.

"I guess it takes one to recognize one." She challenged me quite casually.

I realized that she may have seemed a kitten but she was a lioness.

I looked surprised. What had she understood? What did she know?

"Is everything ok, Jayne?"

Cavalry arrived apparently...

I looked at the guy who just interrupted us, Gabriel Benson, a stupid scholarship kid who used to worship me years ago. A nerd.

"Yeah, we were having fun." I took the liberty to answer for her.

"I said *Jayne.*" He looked serious yet a bit nervous.

The little nerd is showing his teeth now for a girl, that's interesting.

"I'm fine." She smiled. "Are we going now, Gabe?" She stood up and dragged the Nerd away without even looking back.

It's not over. For any of you.

The rest of the school day went quick.

As usual I didn't pay attention to any of the classes I attended, I was one of the most brilliant students in the school but even in case my grades ever dropped, I knew it would be very easy to fix that with Daddy's money.

After the last class, I walked to my grey Mercedes and started wandering the streets in town. I wasn't quite ready to go back home.

Home.

I laughed mentally. When had I ever considered my house a home? When was the last time?

Everyone thought of their homes as their safe place, to rest their head and bodies with beloved people who understood them.

My home?

A huge cold manor with a butler and two cooks, where my mother was having her daily doses of cocaine or whatever she was into at the moment, possibly with a younger lover. Oh and an absent father, always away for "work trips".

I thought of normal families I saw in movies, where you confide in each other and support each other, and realized I had never had that. No one had ever taught me how to ride a bike, no one had ever kissed better one of my wounds.

My own father simply filled my pockets with money to end his guilt, if he even felt it.

My mother, well, she was always too drunk or too high to even acknowledge my presence.

The closest thing to a family I had was my butler and yet, he was paid to take care of me, so I was my family, I was my home.

Once I arrived, I parked and went in the house. My mother was sitting on the long table, she hadn't touched her food. "William!"

At least she acknowledged me this time.

"Mother." I waved.

She was definitely high on something. She looked pretty relaxed, her eyes mirrored mine, same colour and same shape, but the pupils were dilated.

Hello, Mother Cocaine.

I sat on the other side of the table, the butler served me dinner and I started eating.

"How was your day, son?" She seemed euphoric. Too much euphoria to sound genuinely interested.

"Fine. Yours?" I answered politely.

"Amazing!" She laughed at some good memory she seemed to recall.

That comment got on my nerves. How could she do that? How could she let her own child seeing her like this?

"Have you had a good sniff?" I was so irritated, I'd lost my appetite.

"Why do you always have to do it? Ruin everything?" She started crying.

"Get a grip, Mother!" I'd once again lost my patience.

"Why do you despise me? I should be the one despising the Black offspring!" She was screaming.

The butler showed up and, expecting the worst, he stayed there, observing, ready to intervene like many times before. Like the silent guardian he'd always been.

"Calm down and get something to eat."

"I hate you!" she cried.

She started convulsing right after saying it. I flew to her side, trying to protect her head from hitting the glass and iron table. "George, call Doctor Kim!" I shouted to the butler who promptly dialled a number on his cell phone.

I thought the butler must have had his number on speed dial by now.

"Get them out! Get the bedbugs out of my skin!" she cried.

"It's okay, Mother, there's none."

"Get them out!!" She was hysterical.

"Okay, okay, calm down. Doctor Kim is coming. He's on his way." I held her till the convulsions and hallucinations were over, while thinking how unfair it was, I should have been the one to be protected and shielded.

By the time the doctor arrived, the woman was in her bed still screaming. The doctor had to give her a stomach pump.

"I can't reach your father, I've been trying for the past few weeks," he told me when my mother's crisis was over.

"He's on a work trip somewhere." I was massaging my temples, exhausted.

"Do you know when he'll be back?"

"Do I look like I do?" I glared at him.

"Your mother needs help, William, she needs rehab."

"I know, dammit."

"I know about this clinic, they can help her."

"My father will never approve her going public, I tried to talk to him about it." My voice was flat.

"There might not be another choice; your mother is a danger to herself and to others at the moment."

"He will never approve it," I repeated tiredly. "He'll never agree, it would be a scandal. It's easier to hide everything under the carpet if she stays here."

"Try and convince him, she needs help." I nodded knowing already it was a lost cause. "I will spend the night here, if that's okay, so I can monitor her," he continued.

"Thanks, Doctor."

Once I went to my room, I slammed the door shut and tried to call my father a couple of times, but as usual, it went straight to voicemail.

Uncaring bastard.

I put on my boxing gloves and started punching the sack.

First punch was for my father – "*absent moron*". The second one was for my weak-willed mother – "*coke head*". The third one was for that cheeky new girl – "*eerie bitch*". Fourth for that ugly-faced nerd Gabriel – "*damned meddler*".

I kept on going like that until I couldn't feel my arms anymore, then I went for a long shower and to bed. Praying for that day to be over as soon as possible.

I woke up early as usual and, after checking on my mother, I went for a swim in our private swimming pool. I had always liked swimming, it was somehow chilling.

Everything seemed so little when I was underwater, there was no sound of the world outside, nothing could touch me as long as I was down there.

When I thought I was relaxed enough and all dry, it was already time to hit the road for school, so I jumped in one of our family cars and drove to school.

First class for the day was English Literature, one of my favourites; I loved how disturbed and unhappy people put all their pain and sickness in paper.

I swam, they wrote.

The lesson had already started when a shy knocking was heard. A girl's head popped in and shyly apologized for being late and asked for permission to still attend the class.

"Yes, come in, Miss…?"

"Jayne Frost."

"Miss Frost, for the future I don't like when people are late. So since you're new for this time you can still follow this lesson, next time you're out. Please sit."

She nodded, embarrassed and sat on the first chair available.

Jayne Frost, that's your name. I still prefer "eerie bitch".

"So as I was saying we'll be studying William Shakespeare's life and plays in these first months. At the end of these three months you'll have an important test about him. Who can tell me who he was?"

"A dorky loser who had nothing better to do than torture himself and others with his sadness." I cleared my throat. "'To be or not to be…'" I mimicked what I thought was the old poet's voice. Everyone laughed.

I didn't really mean it, I actually thought this Shakespeare guy was really cool. I'd read a couple of his works and I'd quite enjoyed them but I liked to be at the centre of attention. In my defence I could say that I came from a family of junkies: my father was addicted to his job, my mother to cocaine, and I personally was addicted to attention. That was my own drug.

"Thanks, Mr Black, that was enlightening!" The teacher was slightly amused, I shrugged in response. "Who else can tell me something about him?"

"He was an English poet, playwright, and actor, widely regarded as the greatest writer in the English language and the world's pre-eminent dramatist. He is often called England's national poet, and the 'Bard of Avon'. His extant works, including collaborations, consist of approximately 38 plays, 154 sonnets, two long narrative poems, and a few other verses, some of uncertain authorship."

Everyone in the class turned to look at the new girl surprised.

"Miss Frost, have you already studied this author?"

"Yeah, I find it fascinating." She smiled enthusiastically.

It was almost cute how her eyes lit up talking about it. *Almost.*

"Nerd." Everybody laughed and she blushed.

"Good. Good for you then, less work on your shoulders." He smiled and talked to the rest of the class. "So as Mr Black quoted, we'll start with Hamlet. Hamlet was a Danish prince who..."

He kept on explaining Hamlet for a couple of hours. When finally the bell rang, everyone flew out of the classroom. Everyone but Jayne, who seemed to take her time collecting her stuff.

"So you're not a stupid as you look," I teased her, pretending to be impressed.

For some reason, I wanted her attention on me.

"And you're exactly as I thought you'd be."

In truth, I hadn't really thought she was stupid but it seemed to please me quite a lot to get on her nerves. It could easily become my new hobby.

"And how's that?" I didn't need to fake interest this time.

"I can't tell you, I don't want to damage your big huge ego." She smiled.

"Big huge ego?" I asked back, all smiling myself.

"Precisely."

"How did you understand so much about me?" I faked shock.

"I'm quite a good observer."

What is it you're hiding?

Again that thought struck me as lightning. Why was I doubting her? Was I being absurd?

All the amusement was gone.

"So you spend all your time on depressing authors?" I asked just to shake those thoughts off my mind.

"What can I say, I had a complete education." She smiled slightly.

"Oh yeah, you seem to be quite the nerd."

"I had much time on my hands."

She didn't look like the typical bookworm; she was too beautiful and she seemed to be fun. She could reply to all my provocations just as well.

Besides, she must have a flock of guys ready to die for her.

Then why does she claim she has had all that time to study?

Again that mystery, and that accent, it was starting to bug me for real. I had to know, I never liked unsolved puzzles.

"Where is your accent from?"

"I said it's from Scotland," she insisted.

"I do not like liars. It seems to me there's more to you that meets the eye."

I saw her flinch slightly but never lower her eyes. She looked straight at me with the strength of a lioness. "You don't know anything about me, you're just a spoiled child." She turned to leave the class.

I almost admired her for it, so much strength in those green eyes. And a spark of something else I didn't quite recognize.

"Frost?" I called, serious. She turned to look at me. "Neither do you."

Jayne left without answering.

MEET THE FROSTS

Jayne.

"Aunties, I'm home." I shut the door behind me and dropped my school bag on the side. There was a strange smell coming from the living room.

"Honey, dinner's not ready yet, why don't you go and cook something? You're way better than us," a tall woman with chestnut brown hair all held in a ponytail said, smiling.

"That's fine, Aunt Maisa. What's that smell?" Only then I noticed a cauldron boiling and fuming. I glared at my aunt who pretended not to notice my disapproval.

"I thought we weren't allowed to do it in the house, if Aunt Kora found out…"

"But she won't unless you snitch." She smiled all innocent.

"What about our neighbourhood? What if they all noticed?"

"Oh please! They wouldn't know what's going on even if it hit their long nose!"

I almost smiled, but I tried to refrain from doing so. They should be more careful with those things —what if they did? "I thought you liked this city," I insisted.

"We do, we like this house, don't we Sybil?" she called after her sister.

"Yes," another woman, way shorter and weedier with the same hair colour showed up from the kitchen, "and we're planning on staying indefinitely." She smiled.

"Then you shouldn't probably have invited me over," I muttered.

I personally wasn't planning on staying long, a couple of months maybe a bit more, but at some point I knew I'd have to leave, I knew I couldn't stay too long.

"Don't be daft, we're glad you joined us!"

I smiled brightly. I hadn't doubted that for a second. We've always been fond of each other but since I lost my parents, I had chosen to stay on my own; it'd been safer for all of us. Years ago, I made the decision to lay low and change place every few months.

My amazing aunts had understood it, they've always let me make my own choices and be on my own, that's why I was quite surprised when I got Aunt Sybil's call on my new Italian number one day.

It was a good morning and I was sunbathing in my yard when my new phone rang. That was odd, I had thought, I had only bought that phone the day before, I hadn't given anyone my new number.

"We want you to move in with us," Aunt Sybil had said.

"You know I can't."

"We'll be expecting you in a week," in her voice a smile.

"I just moved to Florence, haven't even started school here yet..."
Too late, the call was already over.

After that phone call, I had thought a lot about moving in with them, fact was, I knew I shouldn't but in the end, I still decided to give it a try.

"And anyways, my dear, I've been making potions since I moved in, no one ever noticed anything. You know how commoners work, they see something *weird* they think they imagined it." She winked at me.

"Until they know," I pointed out.

"It'll be fine." Sybil nodded.

I've always noticed a huge difference between me and my aunts. I had spent my whole life trying to hide and run away from my *condition*, to fit in once and for all, whereas they seemed to be very proud of it.

The gift, they called it. I called it *The curse*.

"How was school, Honeypot?" Sybil asked.

"Great." I only noticed my answer was dry as soon as I said it.

"What is it?" Maisa looked at me.

"Nothing, it's just... I don't understand why I have to do it. Go to school and all." I threw myself on a green armchair, massaging my temples.

"Here we go again." Maisa rolled her eyes.

"I'm serious!" I jumped.

"You need to have a proper education. We talked about this already, that was our deal, remember? You go to school in every place you move to and you can do whatever you want."

"What's the point though? They'll find it out sooner rather than later. I will be marginalised, teachers will not want me to attend class and all! Been there done that so many times already!"

"It doesn't mean it's going to happen again. The past is in the past," Sybil said, then she closed her eyes. "One day, the world is going to accept us, all of us."

"Us freaks?" The word just slipped out of my mouth before I could stop it.

But it was true, we were all freaks.

"They will accept us," Sybil repeated.

Hearing that from Aunt Sybil was kind of comforting in a way. I knew that if Sybil said something, that was going to come true.

I just didn't know if that *one day*, I was going to be still around to see it.

"We are *gifted*, young lady," Maisa scolded me as usual.

Gifted... I almost laughed out loud. I never asked Santa for this present! The chance of being a freak.

Every night since I was a kid, I would pray to have a normal life as an ordinary teenage girl.

What wouldn't I give up to be able to only worry about clothes, guys and homework?

I sighed, thinking that would never happen. "What potion is it?" I asked just to change the subject.

"Love potion." She smiled.

They were in some kind of business, based on word of mouth, where their customers paid to get this kind of potion or to have their future revealed.

Maisa would take care of potions and Sybil would read her customers' future using her special *gift*.

The ability she had was incredible. She had the second sight; she could see the whole life of a person by simply touching their hands.

Funny how she would read and tell a stranger's future but still had a strict code; she would never reveal her family's future. Never. Nonetheless, I've always thought she carried a heavy burden.

"Who buys this crap? To have their hopes up for a month or two?"

"Desperate people." The room fell silent.

I've always thought I was part of that category but still, I would never pretend pink bubbles for a short period of time, it wouldn't feel right.

I guessed everyone was different and people might be truly desperate sometimes, so who was I to judge?

"How's Aunt Kora?" I changed the subject once again.

"She called this morning, she says hi. She might be calling tomorrow but she's not sure as the jetlag is driving her insane, apparently."

Kora was the eldest and wisest of my aunts, she was some kind of manager and she was always travelling around. She was not gifted like the other two but she was the most important member of their family; the one who made all the important decisions. *That* was her power.

Dinner went smoothly; I talked about my day in school, my impressions and all the things I thought they would find interesting and amusing, pretending to give a damn about anything around me.

"What about classmates? Have you made any friends yet?" Sybil asked.

I stopped and wondered why she'd ask such questions if she knew the answers already, or anyways, she could get them by simply touching my hand. I guessed that was her way to pretend normality and deal with her power.

"Well, I kind of did, this guy, Gabe seemed alright." *For the time being.*

"Anyone else?" she insisted casually.

For some reason, I couldn't bring myself to mention the other guy, the disruptive and annoying one. I just didn't want to sound like a frightened kid who comes crying to Mummy when things go wrong. No, I would deal with him myself, like I'd always had.

"No one worth mentioning." I smiled without looking at her while finishing my mashed potatoes.

When the meal was over, I excused myself and went to the upper loft, where I knew I would find the peace and quiet I needed to train.

The room was empty except for a few candles and an old tea table, the perfect place to release my powers.

I positioned myself in the middle of the empty room, I closed my eyes and tried to focus.

Suddenly, I stopped thinking, the world faded around me.

I knew I was whispering Latin words, the language of magic, but my voice wasn't my voice and my mouth wasn't my mouth. It was like someone else was directing me, controlling my actions.

And there was nothing else but this energy pulsing through my veins, the very essence of my powers filling me.

And I felt light as a feather and heavy as lead, and I was all and nothing, dead and alive, until this energy was tingling my skin needing to be released.

I felt the scorching heat of the fire I knew I generated all around her, circling me, challenging me to do better or to burn in it.

How easy would it be? Just to give up, to let my own power consume me, to burn my skin and my very soul with it.

No more fighting or hiding or running. Just nothingness.

No more pain.

No more fear.

Would there be peace? Could I finally rest my head?

I realized I was so tired and fed up with running, I just wondered if it wouldn't be easier to just give up, to surrender.

I was sweating, the heat was too much.

The energy it took to keep the fire alive was draining me, leaving me weak. I was nauseous.

I felt my heart slowing down ever so slightly and I wondered if that was what it felt like dying.

I felt it missing a beat and fear overcoming me.

I knew I could burn this house to the ground, I could burn myself senseless or I could just carry on and keep on fighting.

What's to choose, though?

What's to fight for?

And I knew I was just about to give up, to find that so called eternal peace... when I thought of my aunties.

They had always looked after me in their own strange ways but they did.

But especially, of my father who kept on loving her even when his beloved wife sacrificed herself for that little toddler that I once had been.

Of all the efforts to hide me and protect me.

Was I really willing to throw all that in the bin?

I opened my eyes and the fire was out. Black–gray smoke was all over, I gasped for air opening the door.

"What a mess you've made." Aunt Sybil was looking at me disapprovingly.

She probably knew what was going on, how close I had been to just giving up on my existence. She had a sixth sense for those things.

"I'm sorry..." I coughed and we both knew those apologies were more for what we both knew was about to happen than for the mess I'd made.

Sybil tossed what looked like a chocolate bar and left. "I hope you clean it up, Jayne."

I couldn't know whether my aunt was annoyed about my thoughts, about the temptation that had hit me a few moments ago. I suddenly felt so ashamed.

"It's never easy, Jayne. It will never be, that's how you know you're alive. But, kid, you keep on swingin'," she once had said.

At the time I hadn't understood what she had meant, I was only a kid with all the things one could ever dream of, loving parents, a place to call a home.

No, the meaning of those words had hit me a few years after, when my entire world had broken into small pieces.

I managed to rise from the floor slowly, the smoke was still thick around me.

I ate the chocolate bar greedily, getting all the energy I needed from its sugar, and with a snap of my fingers the smoke disappeared as well as the ashes of that old tea table I hadn't noticed I had burnt.

Note for self: buy a new one.

I went to my bedroom once I felt better. Jumping into bed I could still smell the fire. And the shame was stinging my very heart, but I tried not to think, abandoning myself in a reinvigorating sleep.

I opened my eyes slowly, still half asleep I checked the time on my alarm clock, 7.57 a.m.

I closed them again, I still had time.

...

Wait, what?? 7.57 a.m.??

School!

I jumped out of bed, I could not be late for school again, they would have me gutted this time for sure.

I had the quickest shower in the history of showers, wore my uniform in a messy way and put my hair up in a long ponytail.

I looked at myself in the mirror, I definitely looked as scruffy as a homeless person. I breathed, I snapped my fingers and suddenly my hair and clothes looked tidy and well pressed. I smiled a lip gloss smile.

I biked fast to school, which thank goodness wasn't too far away, and when I arrived I could hardly breathe.

I'm so unfit, I should start going to the gym.

I knew that would never happen anyways.

I ran to my first class and sprang the door open, the teacher gave me an evil look and commented with a hint of nastiness that I finally honoured them all with my royal presence.

Everyone laughed. I blushed.

Fair. Low, but somehow fair.

"I can pick you up in the morning if you want from now on," Gabe whispered after I sat down.

I almost jumped. I wouldn't want anyone to see my house, know my location. It could be dangerous information to hand out; one day they could all pester me at home.

"Oh no, thank you but I've got my bike." I tried my best to smile but my tone came out quite wary.

"If you change your mind." He smiled. He didn't seem bothered by my refusal so I decided I really liked him.

The day went on slowly, lesson after lesson. I tried to focus on what those teachers were talking about but I found my mind drifting away more often than I cared to admit.

On lunch break, I once again sat on the table with Gabe and a couple of his friends I already forgot the names of. They were talking and teasing each other about something that happened in their past. I wasn't really paying much attention.

I never had the luxury of having friends of my own, and again, all I could think about was how envious I was of all those normal people around me. Their laughter, when their only worry was school and popularity. As for me, I've always had a death sentence on my head. A Damocles' sword.

I was different from them, normality was a luxury I couldn't afford.

Whatever I did or wherever I went, there always seemed to be a line drawn on the sand, between me and everyone else. Normal people.

"…Jayne, believe me, he was so scared he pissed his pants," Gabe was saying while one of his mates was blushing.

I laughed at his facial expression, the guy seemed to be unimpressed and embarrassed and was ready to retaliate, when my attention got caught by something else. A pair of gray eyes so light and hard they seemed to be made of pure ice.

He was staring at me like I'd found him doing quite often lately. He hadn't approached me again after that afternoon and I was grateful for that. He seemed to be different from everyone else, suspicious and clever. It seemed like he knew exactly what was going on with me, like he knew I wasn't telling the truth and that intimidated me a bit. I'd tried my best to hide it from him but it did indeed.

His glance seemed to be burning ice, smouldering my skin, burning my very soul like the fire I created just a day ago.

I shivered while wondering if it could kill me too.

'I know and I'm watching you', it seemed to be saying.

I really hoped that my own glance said back to him: *'watch away, I do not care'*, even though it was a lie.

"So, Jayne, are you in?"

Gabe's voice interrupted the moment. I broke my eye contact with that mysterious guy to turn to my friend.

"Uh?"

"This Saturday, to the pub," he breathed. Whether he noticed where my attention was I couldn't tell. "Are you coming?"

I opened my mouth, ready to make up an excuse but then I shut it back. For once, I thought, just for once I would pretend to be an ordinary girl who goes into a pub with other ordinary people.

"Should I pick you up around nine?" Gabe insisted. He had probably noted my indecision.

Why not?

"You can pick me up in front of school if you like?" I smiled.

"Sure."

Call it an experiment, call it boredom but I would try and have fun as long as I possibly could.

Why not?

•••

NIGHT OUT

I looked at my image reflected in the mirror, I almost didn't recognize myself.

For the first time in a long long time, I thought I looked decent, nice almost, wearing a tealgreen dress. Nothing too dashing but not too informal either.

It had taken me a good thirty minutes to decide what to wear but, in all fairness, I had never bought anything to go on a night out. My clothes were all jeans, hoodies and informal dark tops.

I had left my long hair down, curling the ends of it with magic. I'd worn a thin line of eyeliner and some of that strawberry lip gloss that made my lips look bloody and full.

I had to admit, I was a bit nervous, it was the first time I was truly going out. I just didn't want to be either overdressed or underdressed.

I kissed goodbye my snobby ginger cat Gary, who had been looking lazily at me from my bed the whole time I was getting ready, took my father's leather jacket and left the room.

"Look at you! You look so pretty, dear. So much like your mother." Maisa clapped her hands nodding with approval.

"Thanks, Auntie." I smiled.

"Do I need to tell you to be careful?" She interrogated me; she genuinely looked confused.

I couldn't help but laugh. "I will be, you know I will. I will not be back too late." I closed the door behind me.

When I arrived at school, Gabe was already there. Waiting for me, leaning on his car and checking something on his phone.

When he saw me, he gave me a big smile. "you look stunning."

I blushed with pleasure and smiled back, "So where are we going?"

34

"Wherever you want to go, miss. You just pierced my heart."
He theatrically put his hand against his chest, right where the
heart is.

"You little lying rascal." I giggled and jumped in the car. Tonight I could giggle; tonight I was just a normal girl.

"I was not lying," he said after he turned the engine on.

I smiled. "I'm curious to see this pub everyone's speaking about."

"You could have asked for the moon, Jayne. But pub it is."
In his voice a smile.

After parking and queuing, we finally got access.

I looked around, the place was huge, there were loads of couches and tea tables and comfortable armchairs, the bar counter was
long and there were at least five fashionable bartenders.

The dance floor was crowded, at each side two pretty girls
were dancing around a pole.

They all seemed to enjoy themselves, all with a drink in their
hands spilling it everywhere they danced.

Was that what people my age did for fun? It didn't look bad
to me.

"What do you want to drink?" Gabe asked in my ear, the
music too loud to be talking normally.

"A lemonade, please."

"Coming right up." He left to order.

I looked around once more. I liked that place, it was a good
chance to let myself go for once.

I was going to laugh, let my hair down and dance until my
feet were sore. And that's how Gabe found me when he came
back with my drink in his hands.

His friends joined us and we spent what seemed to be an infinite time dancing all together. I thought that was fun, real fun.
I wondered why I'd never done it before.

Strange enough, I kept on finding drinks in my hand as soon
as I finished them. I couldn't tell who gave them to me but I felt
way too happy to care, I drank it all.

Bottoms up.

The music was so good, for once it seemed like that was my place, with those people, in that bar, with laughter in my ears and mouth. I felt free, euphoric, invincible. And light-headed.

All the noises seemed to be echoing in my head. I noticed I was sweating and when I touched my hair, I found it was wet. It was way too hot in there.

At some point, the euphoria suddenly faded.

I was gasping for air, I felt the room closing up on me. I couldn't breathe.

I needed air; I knew I needed to get out of there.

"Are you alright?" Gabe's voice seemed to come from far away.

"Yes, I need to refresh myself." I left him there while running to the doors.

I didn't even know where I was headed, until I touched the cool handle of one of the doors.

Someone asked me if I was alright, I nodded, I needed to get out.

I found myself sitting on the stairs of the cathedral in front of the pub, while thinking how odd it was for a cathedral to be in front of the pub area of the city.

To save the damned nightly souls?

I felt my head throbbing, I was gasping for air once again. Like a fish out of its natural environment I just couldn't seem to breathe.

I found my hands trembling while massaging my temples, my clammy and sweated skin having goosebumps in the chilly night air.

What's wrong with me?

I felt nausea rise up my stomach, I turned to throw up all I'd had all over the stairs while feeling ashamed for desecrating that holy place.

Suddenly, a strong hand was holding my hair back and another was caressing my back in a smoothing calming movement.

I felt alarmed, I hadn't heard any movement and now, someone was touching me, holding my head. I tried to get free.

"It's okay, get it all out." The soothing calming voice was like a balm for my nerves.

I thought I would have to kiss Gabe to thank him for that. I wouldn't know how to explain vomit all over my hair to my aunts.

Why couldn't I just fit in? Why did it have to end bad the only time I let myself go?

I almost sobbed.

"Easy easy, I believe someone has spiked your drink," the far away calming voice said. It didn't sound like Gabe's though, now that I listened to it.

Gabe's tone of voice was pleasant but kind of acute, this voice was deep even though it was a mere whisper.

It sounded like they knew exactly how to say something to calm someone down. I did bet that voice could make a savage animal relax.

You're safe, that movement seemed to say.

When I finished, I fished in my purse for a tissue. Luckily finding a semi decent one, I finally looked at the person who'd helped me.

I was surprised to find the Icy Guy, as I had named him, standing a few feet from me, ready to help me out once again if I needed.

The Icy Guy, the one I'd bumped into on my first day of school, the one I had a class with, the one who always stared at me.

"Someone what?"

"Did Benson give you that drink?"

If his voice was soothing and low before, now it was filled with what seemed to be cold rage.

As cold as his icy eyes.

I tried to remember, but my head was still hurting. "No, he... he was in the toilet when I got that drink."

"Do you usually take drinks from strangers? Mummy never told you it's dangerous?" Again that mocking tone together with unmasked rage.

"My mother died." I regretted saying it the moment it came out of her mouth. Why had I even said that to him?

Silence.

"Well, you shouldn't accept things from strangers especially in a bar." He hadn't apologized.

I hadn't expected him to.

"Why do you even care anyways?" I blurted.

"Puking in the stairs of a holy cathedral is falling low even for someone like you." He was teasing me now. There was an amused light in his light eyes.

"Someone like me?" I raised my eyebrows.

"Someone who lets others see her with someone like Benson." He was smiling.

I really did try and look annoyed but I found myself laughing hoarse. Only this guy could say something that mean and get away with it. Even make it sound funny.

"Are you laughing?" He looked quite surprised. He certainly hadn't expected that reaction from me.

"You could get away with murder, couldn't you?" It wasn't a question. And maybe because I was still a bit high, I didn't find him as unpleasant as I had previously thought.

"Of course, I'm a God," he said with a twisted smile.

"And I'm a witch." The word came out of my mouth before I could even think about the implications of it.

I opened my eyes wide, waiting for him to have a reaction. I only noticed I was holding my breath when he smirked.

"Stand up, I will take you home." It wasn't an offer, it was more of an order.

"I shouldn't accept things from strangers, especially lifts home." I smiled clever, using his words against him.

"Yes, remember that next time." He sounded quite amused once again.

He started walking, confident I would follow.

"I don't want to go home." I knew I sounded like a whining little girl and I hated myself for it.

"You're still high." He almost smiled.

"I can't leave Gabe..." He'd brought me here, I couldn't...

"You really want to stay because the guy who possibly spiked your drink would get offended, if you left without him?" He knew he had a point, we both did.

I just was so damn sure Gabe had not been there when that some-one had passed me that drink. I was certain he had said he was going to the bathroom.

I must have looked as confused as I had felt because the guy insisted. "I do not bite. Unless asked." He smiled, his perfect white teeth showing as if to state just the opposite.

"I don't even know your name." I objected weakly but I was already standing up.

I found it difficult to even walk but he didn't notice, he wasn't looking at me.

"We have a couple of classes together, of course you know my name." He was already walking again, hands in his pockets. A casual pace in the dark alley.

I wondered how he could look so careless, fearless even walk-ing in a deserted place with just a few lights to show the way.

"I know your surname, not your given name," I pointed out while starting following him.

His confidence was reassuring, even though somehow, some-where inside me, something was begging me not to do it, not to trust that mysterious stranger.

Somewhere inside me told me to just get as far as I could from him. An ancient call.

Like an ominous feeling.

"That is enough, isn't it?"

"As far as I know you could have been the one who spiked my drink," I said without thinking and he stopped.

Had I offended him?

When he turned, he had half of a smile on his face. "Do I look like I need to drug girls to get them wrapped around my pinkie?"

No, I'm pretty sure any girl would go to Hell and back just to be looked at by him.

"Precisely." His smile was wider as if he had read my thoughts. I muttered a curse back at him. "Such a wicked mouth for a lady!" He mocked me while jumping in his car.

He saw me hesitating. "Are you coming or not?"

Or not. But for some reason, I got in the car, ignoring that thought.

The ride was silent, I had my window open so fresh air would help me get rid of the headache I still had.

"Where is it I'm going?" he asked halfway.

Don't give him that information. Information is power.

"Leave me at the school." I closed my eyes.

"Don't be silly, I'm not dropping a possibly drugged girl in the middle of the street." He sounded genuinely disgusted at the thought.

When I didn't say anything, he insisted without ceremony. "I don't know what idea you have of me but I'm not leaving you in the middle of nowhere just because..." I turned. He'd sounded and looked... *pissed.*

"Fine! Fine!" I breathed and told him my address.

He drove silently for the rest of the short journey. He parked in front of the front door.

What to say now?

I opened my mouth to say something but he was quicker. "Get out of my car or I will indeed show you I'm not trustworthy." He had spoken without looking at me.

Again, I went to say something but my mind was emptied. Why was he mad at me if I was careful who I gave the power of information to? What right did he have to insist or even worse, to get angry?"

I got out quickly and slammed the car door. The movement cost me. I was about to throw up again but thankfully, I didn't, I managed to keep my dignity this time.

While walking to the front door, I felt his glare burning my skin.

I wondered if it was the drug in my drink to give me this kind of hallucination.

Just before turning the keys in the lock, I finally found the courage to surrender the temptation to turn and look at him.

I instantly regretted it. His eyes... they were indeed burning me. Me, my clothes, my skin. They pinned me there where

I was, and some part of me ordered me to run from and to him at the same time.

I give him the finger instead.

I almost flew to my room and I jumped into a restoring hot shower. When I thought I had scrubbed my hair and skin enough, I got out and was sick in the toilet.

I cleaned my mouth. Without even drying myself, I abandoned myself in bed.

Between sleep and wake, I thought I felt myself smiling.

FATE

William.

I parked the car and, once I collected my school stuff, I walked in the school hall.

As usual, I noticed all the admiring and envious stares from my schoolmates but, as usual, I just ignored them.

There was not one glare I cared about. Well okay, maybe one or two.

I saw a shadow entering the toilet, I made a twisted smile and followed suit.

Gabriel Benson was washing his hands when I'd entered. The other hadn't even raised his head.

Big mistake.

In a fast and fluid movement, I grabbed the collar of his jacket and pushed him violently against the wall. "Hello, Benson." I breathed viciously in his ear.

"What do you want, Black?" He tried to break free in vain.

I got you exactly where I want you, stupid bastard.

"A little bird told me you're such a loser, you need to spike girl's drinks to enter their graces." My voice was cold, almost disinterested. My usual perfect act.

"I don't know what you're talking about." He looked genuinely surprised.

And for the first time, I felt proper hatred for him.

In the past that nerd guy was nothing, not much better than a mosquito in my life, but now I had noticed for a while, every single time I saw his face, my fists would shut closed, and my body would ready to hit him.

I also noticed that feeling was just getting worse and worse each time I saw him talking to that eerie new girl, the one that actually pissed me off so much just a few nights ago. I hadn't dared to ask myself the reason.

But now that I knew – suspected – that piece of crap had spiked her drink… somehow, for some reason it seemed to me that he had signed his death sentence.

"Right, listen to me very carefully, if I see you again…"

The door sprang open; an insisting coughing made me turn. From the mirror I could see it was one of the teachers; someone must have snitched on me.

"Mr Black, I advise you to let Mr Benson go, unless you both want to spend the next hour in the headmaster's office."

Annoyed, I looked at the guy still in my grip and slowly, very slowly, I let him go.

Never mind, we shall finish our conversation soon enough.

Benson theatrically coughed a fake cough. I smiled. It would take so much more effort for me to be in any trouble at all.

Amateur.

"We were just having an exchange of opinions."

Before leaving the toilet, I gave one last look sideways at him. My eyes full of promises of silent threats.

From the look on his ugly face, I understood my hatred was returned. My twisted smile grew wider.

Good, there'll be more fun in that.

I entered the classroom and sat at my usual desk; the last one close to the window. I liked looking at the nature outside whenever I was bored.

A few minutes later, the classroom was filled with students. I saw her without even needing to search for her; her bright hair colour seemed to be screaming compared to all the other dull hair colours.

I seemed to be driven to her no matter what I did. No matter how I tried to ignore her, her presence seemed to sing to me, a pretty siren who wanted me to fall into her trap.

I would actually *feel* her before seeing her. Somehow.

It had happened two nights ago too, when I was flirting with some girl, and I had automatically turned when she had got into the bar. My attention had been irremediably caught.

I'd tried to ignore her, not to look at her – which I regretted now because I missed seeing who spiked her drink – but when I had noticed her going out alone, I hadn't been able to stop my feet from following her.

Something about this girl had been dragging me to her ever since the beginning, when I first bumped into her in the school hall, something weird and inexplicable.

Let's not get this wrong, I was still pretty *pissed off* at her for not trusting me enough to tell me her home address that night. What was she thinking, that I was some kind of crazy stalker?

Or even for the fact she had accepted that spiked drink that easily, she was so naïve that girl...

And yet so wary with me.

"Very well," the teacher was saying, "last night I was trying to think of the best way to torture you, guys," he paused theatrically to create suspense, some laughed, "and I came up with an idea. You'll be divided in groups of two and each group will be assigned a topic. You'll have three weeks to prepare a presentation together. This will determine thirty percent of your final grades so I advise you put your heads into it." He took a little old baseball hat from his suitcase. "I will randomly divide you into couples, fate will decide."

The classroom fell silent. Everyone was hoping to end up with the nerd in charge.

"Sanders and..." he took another name out of the baseball hat, "...Baker."

And that's how the nerd has been already taken... I sighed looking at the newly made couple; one looked as happy as Christmas day and the other like at his dog's funeral.

"Black and..." he took another name, "...Mcbride."

"Mcbride is at the hospital due to knee surgery," I commented bored. It wouldn't have been bad to be matched with the guy; he was known to be quite clever.

"Oh right. Then Black and..." he took another piece of paper from the hat and something inside me reshuffled. Somehow I knew exactly whose name it was going to be. "Black and Frost."

Fate, uh?

She slowly turned to me, giving me an evil glare and I almost burst out laughing at her facial expression. "I knew you'd be a happy bunny but this is just overwhelming, please contain yourself." I couldn't resist but mock her out loud. Everyone laughed.

"Shut it you," she snarled then turned to the professor. "Is there any chance you could fish another name for me?" she pleaded.

I told you, girl, I only bite when asked. I smiled.

"I'm sorry, Miss Frost, fate has decided."

"Stupid fate," she muttered not too quietly.

Now everyone was waiting for me to fire back. I could feel the tension in the classroom, everybody seemed to be holding their breath.

I smiled wider than before. "I shall make sure I give you a very *very* fun time," I had said. The drawl in my tone made me sound malicious.

The classroom laughed again relieved. They were expecting an explosion of cold rage as was my style, but they seemed to be pleasantly surprised.

Before she could shout an answer, the teacher caught everyone's attention again, creating new matches.

When everyone had been assigned a partner, Mr Laurent assigned each of them a topic and gave his permission to start working on them.

I watched the girl drag her chair to my desk like she was dragging a huge heavy rock behind her. She sat as far away as possible from me and, glaring at her, I noticed she didn't look impressed.

"I was serious when I promised you a fun time." I hid my smile.

Why had I never had this much fun with any other girls?

"Right, I don't like you and you don't like me but..." she started calmly.

"Oh, I think you do like me." I interrupted her, just to piss her off.

"*But* you're forced on me like a bad allergy so let's get through it as quickly as possible." She ignored my comment.

"Like a bad allergy?" I almost smiled in amusement.

She nodded. "The ones that comes with rush and spots."

"Eww, you're vile." I had to admit it required more effort than I expected not to laugh out loud at that.

She smiled. "While I have the chance I want to have good grades..." She stopped surprised by what she'd said.

While I have the chance?

"'While I have the chance'?" I asked disoriented. "Don't tell me you're planning on leaving the school; I could be a happy bunny then."

"No, I mean ... I care about grades ... and I ... I'm not planning on leaving or ... I just ... It just didn't come out right?" She looked in a panic; her explanation so confused that I wondered if she was feeling alright.

"Are you still high from Saturday?" *Maybe the drug was very strong and it hadn't worn off...*

"What?! No, of course not!" She looked at me breathlessly.

"It seems to be so."

"Shut up," she breathed.

"And anyways, I don't like you either," I said just to annoy her.

"Perfect, now that we can bare that in mind, we can..."

"You're also incredibly ungrateful. I brought you all the way home and you didn't even bother to thank me for it." I wasn't too annoyed about it but I just wanted to get a reaction.

She looked at me, our eyes locked for a long moment, then she said, "Well, to get me to thank you, you are gonna need to be nicer than that. And try not to piss me off while you try."

Looking at her, I couldn't help but realize how beautiful she was with her determined expression.

"Girls these days, so demanding." I mocked her just to say something.

She muttered a curse at me but before she could say anything else, Mr Laurent gave us the piece of paper with the topic we needed to write an essay about.

I watched her read it and flinch violently. I looked at the paper. In tidy handwriting there were a few words: *Salem's witch hunt.*

She raised a hand and waited to be given permission before talking in a feeble voice. May we ask for another subject?"

"Why?" I asked her, I was confused. What was wrong with it? With her?

She ignored me and spoke to the teacher. "Please?"

"I'm sorry, Miss Frost, that's your topic. You may start." He dismissed her request.

"What's up with you?" I asked, curious.

"Nothing." She wasn't looking at me, focused on a spot on the floor.

I could see it wasn't nothing, something was up for sure. "Do not offend my intelligence, what's wrong with our topic?" I insisted more curious than ever.

"I don't like it, it creeps me out and..." she glared at me, "... and it's none of your business."

"You are completely insane," I thought out loud. I really did believe that.

"Right, I will find text books and testimony..." she started.

"Testimony?" I interrupted her, confused. "Girl, the witch hunt happened centuries ago, you can't find testimony."

"I meant written documents, of course you can't find testimony..." She smiled a bit nervously. "You can search and make an essay about the city of Salem."

"Quite bossy, aren't we?" I smiled in mockery. "No, we'll do all that together. You won't give me the boring part."

"Fine, whatever." She snorted.

"So... my house or yours?" I gave her a leer, my tone more malicious than ever.

"What do you mean?" She blushed to her ears. I actually fought not to laugh.

"You weren't thinking of doing this presentation just in the classroom, were you? We need extracurricular time." I winked with malice.

"But I..."

"*I* wouldn't let you have all the fun on your own," I blinked again, "we'd probably end up having a bad grade for it, you're not too bright, are you?" I was being sarcastic.

The girl looked like she was about to actually punch me in my guts. "And I should see your cheeky face even out of school?!"

"I'm afraid so." I acted like I was sorry while writing something down on a piece of paper that I left on the desk just as the bell rang. "I will see you today at six o'clock."

She looked at the paper. "Is that your address?"

"Don't be late." I smiled, leaving her there.

LIAR, LIAR

Jayne.

I breathed collecting my books, then with a horrified look in the mirror, I saw my hair was too messy to be left down so I decided to braid it with care.

I didn't even know why I cared about that, I was only going to do some research with the guy but... somehow I wanted to look as decent as I could.

Perhaps, because every single time we'd talked, he had looked like he just got out of a fancy perfume advert and I... I always looked like I just got out of bed with the wrong foot.

I had to admit that he intimidated me, with his perfectly handsome looks, with his witty answers and banters... and the most absurd thing ever was that he seemed to have some power over me, like I was bound to tell him the truth all the time.

"And I'm a witch."

Why had I said that?!?

Had it been the drugs in my system? Or what?

I couldn't seem to explain that to myself.

Why for the first time in my whole life I had said *the* one word that had tortured me in forever to *him?*

Thankfully, he had thought it was a joke.

I had to be careful from now on. I would have to think twice before saying anything at all to him.

"Wish me luck, Gary!" I looked at my cat who, again, was loudly snoring on my bed.

I had no idea where his house was and I was running late already, so I called a taxi.

To his credit, the taxi driver didn't make any comments about where he was about to drive me. He'd only studied me and my clothes for a few seconds, probably trying to understand what kind of business a girl like me could have in that place.

The house seemed to be in the countryside, so it took us a good half an hour to get there. I'd never seen that part of the city so I stared out of the window for the whole journey, sometimes glaring at the numbers on the taximeter which were already too high.

Eventually we arrived at the house or, better, at the *manor*.

I swallowed hard while paying the expensive fare due and getting out of the car, thinking that later on I'd have to walk all the way home as my wallet was sadly empty.

I stopped to observe the big dark gate. Their family name was written on it, big and intimidating letters that formed the word *Black*.

With great surprise, I noticed my hands were shaking when I rang the bell before the gate. I cursed myself for being that absurd. Why would I be afraid?

"Yes?" a formal but polite voice asked.

"I'm Jayne ... I'm here to see ...?" I started a bit nervous.

"Please, come in." The gate opened automatically.

I followed the path, a long elegant way of little pebbles and candles all around, to the front door which was made of painted glass and pine wood. I knocked again.

The door opened revealing a tall, slim elegant man in his early fifties maybe, his hair, streaked with grey, gave him a smart look. "Please come in, he's waiting for you." He led the way to the big hall and I followed him.

I looked around while walking, taking in every detail. That place was full of vintage and expensive looking furniture, the paintings, I noticed, were original artworks from famous painters. All the ornaments were Swarovski, silver and gold.

I could have asked for one of them as compensation for the expensive taxi fare.

The man, I guessed he was some kind of butler – if they even existed still – led me all the way to a big massive library. My eyes almost watered while taking in all the bookshelves and the smell of paper pages. That was paradise.

"You're late," William greeted me.

I turned to him, he was sitting on a dark leather sofa in front of the fireplace, a laptop on his lap; he looked quite bored.

"I couldn't find the house," I justified myself, not moving an inch.

He lifted a hand to the twin sofa in front of him and dismissed the butler, asking him to bring some tea.

"Please, sit. Unless you want to study from there, but don't expect me to stay turned towards you all the time. I wouldn't want to have a bad neck for you." He gave me half of a smile before turning his attention back to his laptop.

I bit my tongue not to give him a witty answer, and sat on the other sofa, which I had to admit was like the most comfortable thing I've ever sat on my life, just like a fluffy cloud.

I put my old backpack on the tea table in front of us, emptying it. "I found some books about it and..."

"So did I." He smiled voluntarily interrupting me. "As a family heritage apparently we have some documents of inquisitors that were there at that time."

Whether he noticed me hide a shiver I couldn't tell.

"How do you have them?"

"I don't know, apparently it's something we've always had for some reasons." He shrugged.

"That's just..." *creepy,* I looked at him and faked a smile, "... interesting."

He smiled and his smile seemed to be concealing something, it was the smile of someone who knew more than he'd let on. My heart skipped a beat.

Could *he* know?

Impossible.

Tea arrived. When the butler, George, served it, I grabbed it in a feline movement, holding it tight like it was my only saving. The steamseemed to relax me ever so slightly.

"Shall we start?" I asked a bit on edge.

"Dig in, girl." He gave me a half smile.

I read and read and wrote notes after notes, always aware of his presence just a few feet from me. *How could you forget?* I didn't actually find anything I didn't already know. I'd heard those stories first hand but I had to look as normal as possible.

I had let Icy Guy have the Inquisitors documents, I couldn't bring myself to even touch those wicked diaries. Only thinking about it could make me shiver with disgust.

We stayed silent for a time that seemed like ages. At some point I felt his heavy look on myself, so I turned to meet his icy eyes. "What?" I asked disoriented.

"I'm bored and hungry," he said simply.

"But we have to finish it…"

"Relax, girl, we got three weeks." He stood up and went to the door. He smiled at my confused expression. "I'm hungry." He asked George for dinner.

I checked the time on my watch. I was surprised to find out that it was past dinner time, it was actually quite late.

"Right, I'm going." I started collecting my stuff quickly, trying to think which way was best to get home at this time.

Taxi was out of question, I couldn't possibly afford that.

Maybe I could ring Maisa? She had a car.

How could I explain how to get here though, if I had no idea myself?

"Where have you parked your car?" he asked me casually.

"I don't have a car, I don't have a driving license."

"How did you get here then?" Genuine surprise written all over his face.

Is it that bad not being able to drive? To be way too poor to own a car? "Taxi?" I said tentatively and he burst out laughing. "It's not funny."

"Stay for dinner and I will drive you home." He was still laughing.

"No, I'd rather walk my feet off." I was offended. How dared he?!

"Penniless people and their *rich* pride." Again that hoarse laugh.

"Hilarious." I muttered a not too nice curse at him, still collecting my stuff and passed him without looking back.

I suddenly felt a grip on my wrist a heartbeat later.

How had he managed to move that fast and as silently as a cat? I didn't know.

He was serious now. "I will drive you home."

Something in his icy eyes, in his voice made me understand he wouldn't have given up that easily, not about that so I just nodded. The hold on my wrist released and I felt my skin burning where he'd touched me. I was sure it was not for pain.

We sat down again and dinner arrived a few moments later. I heard my stomach grumble when I smelled what looked like some delicious chicken with peas and potatoes.

It smells so nice!

Indeed, that was the most amazing food I'd ever tasted in my whole life and he noticed it.

"What? You don't get fed in your house?" he asked seemingly innocent.

"We don't have a butler." I hadn't even looked at him.

"I also have two cooks," he pointed out amused.

"Stupid spoiled child," I muttered.

We ate in silence. There was so much food on the tea table, I wondered if that was how they treated guests or if they were their usual meals. If it was so, I wondered how he managed not to gain as much weight as a dirigible.

After we finished, he asked me — *ordered* actually — to follow him and we went to what seemed to be a huge garage. There were at least seven or eight different types of cars, all in different colours and shapes. I saw him pick up distractedly a pair of car keys from a counter, and walk confidently to what looked like a dark very — *very* — expensive car.

"You really are a spoiled child." I was shocked by all the money they must have had.

And I can't even afford the taxi back.

He gave me half smile from the driver's seat, gesturing for me to get in the car as well. I did.

"They are family cars, not just mine. They were personally chosen by my father," he explained a few minutes later, while opening the big gate with a remote in the keys.

The formal and cold way he'd said the word *father* made me turn to him.

"What's your family like?" I was curious. Now that he had mentioned it, I remembered I hadn't seen any of them in the house that day.

He hadn't looked at me. "Like all the others I guess," he said in a monotone ages later.

I studied him, his voice, the way he hadn't turned to me. There was something that told me it was not the whole truth, that it was like a standard answer he'd give to anyone who asked.

Typical behaviour of someone who's used to being popular and couldn't afford bad gossip or simply some kind of protection from the world?

"Liar," I whispered still looking at him.

He glared at me. "As you once said, it takes one to know one, Miss *Scotland*."

I almost jumped in my seat. Why was he insisting so much on that point? Why couldn't he just drop it like everyone else had before?

I was used to curious people asking me about my strange mix of accents; I always gave the same answer I thought was safest. They would either accept it or insist a bit more but not as much as he was. He seemed to be so stubborn about it.

"I'm not a liar." I turned and stared outside the window.

Liar.

"How did your mother die?"

"Car accident," I said automatically without looking at him.

Liar.

He nodded. "Is that why you don't have a car?" In his voice a hint of a smile.

"I don't have a car because I'm poor and because I never stay in places long enough." I breathed.

Why are you not lying anymore, Jayne?

"Why?" He was looking at me now.

His icy eyes seemed to be burning my skin, scorching my very soul like he could read me directly from there.

"I'm not good at staying, I spent my life running." I granted him a slice of the truth. "I wouldn't even know how to stay."

What bad could it do? I was just so tired of all the lies and hiding and deceiving.

"Running from what?" Again that curious yet understanding look on his face.

"You wouldn't get it." I turned away again.

Who would? Or even want to?

"Because I'm a rich spoiled child?" He was serious now.

I could feel the rage building up in him.

"Because it's complicated." I looked at him and for a second, just for one, I just wished I could tell him the truth.

I desired someone to talk about it to, I wished I could just let myself spill the beans and be free of my many secrets.

To be honest for once in a lifetime, just to see what it felt like to have someone to share my problems with, somebody ready to listen to every single crazy word coming out of my mouth and not thinking about locking me up in an institution.

For once, I wished I could just share the weight of the world I carried everywhere I went.

I breathed again. "My life is a mess," I admitted softly.

My world is insane.

"Whose life isn't?"

And judging by the look in his icy eyes, I knew he too had his share of pain and loneliness, he too had his problems, he was just as good as I was at pretending.

Pretending that nothing touched him.

Maybe that was what had seemed to be drawing me to him so much, maybe somehow we were kindred spirits in a strange and complicated kind of way.

"Some people are just better than others at hiding it, aren't they?"

"A penny for your secrets, Jayne Frost," he said after a few moments.

"I'm not *that* poor!", I had to crack a joke. The tension between us was visible.

Clench your teeth, Jayne. Keep the lie going.

He didn't answer, perhaps he understood that I wasn't ready to share my cogitations and he respected that.

We spent the rest of the trip silent.

"Well, thank you, I guess." I started awkwardly when we were in front of my house. I turned to leave.

I had already opened the car door when his voice stopped me.

"If you ever decided to tell me your secrets..." I turned to look at him surprised, "...I might as well teach you how to stay." He was staring at me now, piercing my skin with his eyes.

Would you really?

"I shall keep that in mind." I gave him a soft smile and got out of the car. I felt my cheeks burning for some reasons I couldn't quite understand.

"I'll pick you up after school to study, don't make me wait." He drove off with half of a smile.

And when I closed the front door behind me, I understood something: there was so much more in him than met the eye. I just wasn't sure many people knew that.

For the fourth day in a row, I was sitting on that soft leather sofa in his house. My head was pounding. I'd been reading and taking notes for the last couple of hours, now I could really use a break.

I raised my eyes to the handsome figure in front of me; he was studying quietly, not paying me any attention. I noted his tense shoulders and thought that maybe, just maybe he too had his burden to carry. I just wondered what that was.

Not that he would ever tell me, we weren't friends but I was glad at least to know that, despite our first few bad encounters and different opinions and ways of seeing things... well, we couldn't call each other foes either.

In all fairness, I was kind of starting to like his company. William was the oddest person I'd ever met, he could say the nastiest thing ever and make it sound funny without even trying. He was stubborn and somehow protective, I still remembered how he had gotten mad at the thought of leaving me at school while I was on drugs.

The way he had calmed me down that night, that had been incredible.

It was like he was used to doing it, to try and take care of people, but that went against what everyone else said about him, all the rumours. Those rumours had him being an insensitive and selfish person who used people for his own advantage.

Danger.

That's all he was radiating, like danger indeed was his very essence, I knew that. I'd understood it the first time I'd lay eyes on him and yet, he'd helped me whenever I silently needed it and I could sadly say, it was the closest thing to friendship I'd ever experienced.

Don't you ever trust him. If you were wise, you'd stay out of his way. He's insane.

That was what Gabe had told me about him one day, when he had noticed the looks we'd exchanged and I had bought it as very true.

That guy with those icy eyes capable of freezing you to the bone was never to be trusted.

Nevertheless we seemed to never be able to escape each other, our paths would inevitably cross no matter what. And I had to admit, I didn't mind that.

"If you keep on staring at me like that, eventually you'll pierce a hole in my forehead." His distracted voice was sudden, he'd spoken without raising his head.

"I wasn't staring at you," I blurted, regretting getting caught.

"Sometimes I think," he finally looked at me, "you're the best liar I've ever met." He smiled at me and I flinched slightly. "Other times I think you're just an amateur."

"You should make up your mind about me, you know," I said with all the nastiness I was capable of.

He looked thoughtful. "I really should but you confuse me," he admitted.

"How?" Why was I even blushing now?

"I really don't know." "His icy eyes seemed to be studying me like I was a rare lab experiment. "I can say without lying that you're a complete mystery to me."

I moved in my seat uncomfortably under his look. I wondered whether it was wise to ask him to explain himself after that affirmation but I decided it was best to just drop it. It was dangerous ground.

It might have led to questions I could not answer.

"Where is your mind, girl?" he asked curious a few moments of heavy silence later.

I picked what I believed was the least dangerous thought in my head. "I'm thinking that stupid spiked drink ruined my night. I still wanted to dance and have fun." *And feel normal.*

With a twitch of his hands he shut the book closed on his lap. He stood up and went to that vintage record player I hadn't noticed before; a heartbeat later Frank Sinatra's voice was filling the room softly.

"Not quite the music that was in that place but..." He gave me a half smile and reached out his hand for me to take it.

I thought that a clever girl would smile, decline his invite to dance with him and formally collect her stuff and leave to never come back, 'cause the situation she was in was too messy to let herself go like that.

A clever girl wouldn't have felt her heart skip a beat.

A clever girl wouldn't have accepted his hand and wouldn't have started dancing close to him.

Like I just had.

You'll regret this, Jayne. You'll burn for it.

I ignored those thoughts in my head and just let myself go for once, trying not to think about the consequences of tomorrow.

It was just a dance. Just him and me.

And I could just be normal and fit in just there in his arms, only this once.

We danced for an infinite time, until the record player was silent, until what felt like a lifetime.

You're lying to him. Lying to yourself, if he only knew the truth you wouldn't be here.

The thought hit me like a painful jab.

Suddenly, I was the one to stop and disentangle myself from him, not really able to place the disappointment I felt rising in my chest.

"What's wrong?" he was confused.

"I can't," I whispered.

"What do you mean? Why can't you let yourself go with me?" I hadn't looked at him but his voice sounded almost hurt.

"I got to go." I started collecting my stuff distractedly.

"Why?" He grabbed me by my shoulders, making me look at him. "Why can't you let yourself go with me?" he repeated loudly. "Tell me!"

"Because I can't do that with anyone," I busted out, "ever!

William stared into my eyes for a long moment before asking, -why?"

"It's complicated," I breathed, my eyes pleading him to let it go.

He finally released me, wearing his mask of indifference. "Collect your crap, I'll drop you home."

Saying I was surprised would be using a euphemism. After all that had happened, he still wanted to drive me home?

Did I really deserve this kindness?

The car trip was long, made of awkward silence and embarrassment. It was like no one wanted to be the first to say anything. Maybe for fear of being vulnerable or maybe there was simply nothing left to say.

When we arrived, I grumbled a shy *thank you* and almost ran to the front door, not willing to break down in tears in front of him.

The morning after, I woke up early, had a long shower to calm my nerves down and took my time for breakfast.

I had made a decision, from that moment on I would avoid that guy like the plague. I wouldn't let myself walk in that minefield again.

It's okay, nothing I haven't done before.

"Good morning, honey." Aunt Sybil greeted me cheerfully. "I made you a latte."

She probably knew for once I would join her for breakfast.

I smiled, accepting the mug from the woman. "Where's Aunt Maisa?"

"Sleeping in, she's just so lazy. She was shaking her head in disapproval.

"I wish I could sleep in," I mumbled.

"Were you late last night? I didn't hear you come in."

"No, it was actually the earliest I've been the whole week," I admitted not looking at her.

But you know that already.

"Is everything okay with you? It feels like we haven't spoken for ages," she started.

"All perfect." I gave an attempt of a bright smile.

"If you ever wanted to talk about it..."

"Maybe another time," with a gulp, I had downed my drink, "I'm late for school." I kissed my aunt's cheek and left.

Biking to school that day felt like climbing a mountain, the strangely hot day made me sweat like at the gym, I cursed myself for not having a car.

In the parking lot, Gabe was waving awkwardly at me. I breathed in distress; we hadn't spoken since the incident on Saturday night.

I hadn't replied to his texts or even listened to the voicemails he had left for me, asking me what had happened and all, I had been a proper piece of...

"Hey, Gabe, how are you?" I almost had to run to reach him.

"I'm not bad, thanks. How are you?" His voice was tense.

I felt guilty and awkward about it. "Listen, I'm sorry about Saturday night and for not getting back at you... I've been very busy and," I breathed, "I'm really sorry."

He seemed slightly relieved. "What happened on Saturday? One minute you're having fun with us and the other I can't find you anywhere. I got worried," he admitted.

"Someone had spiked my drink and I felt really sick." Just remembering the taste of the sick made me want to throw up all over again.

"Really? That's awful!" He opened his eyes wide. "Were you okay afterwards?"

"Yes, the aftermath the day after wasn't the best feeling ever but I survived." I smiled.

"How did you get home?" he asked quickly. He appeared genuinely concerned. I felt bad for doubting his good faith.

"I jumped in a cab."

Liar.

I didn't know why but I hadn't felt like telling him the truth, not that I was ashamed or anything but, but it just didn't feel right.

"Thankfully nothing bad happened to you!"

His voice so filled with pure relief that I felt like I was drowning a kitten. He couldn't have spiked that drink, he was the good guy.

If he was the good guy though, what was William Black in all that?

I dropped that thought.

"Would you like to come to dinner with me this Friday?" he asked nervously after a few moments of hesitation.

I have to admit, he caught me off my guard. I was about to make up an excuse when I remembered that I owed him that much, owed him an apology and whatever else he had asked.

Who knew, maybe he was that much of a good guy that one day he might have accepted my real nature.

Maybe.

CHECKMATE

William.

I had never noticed how small that school was before trying to avoid that damned girl.

I kept on seeing her and bumping into her everywhere I went, at some point I had even started thinking that she was doing it on purpose to make me find her with that pest she called a friend.

Or should I call him "her new stupid toy boy"?

Yes, I'd heard they were going to go on a date that weekend.

Yes, I was extremely annoyed about it.

One thing was being rejected because of some silly frigid afraid-of-men girl problems but being rejected for that spotty face of a Benson? Unacceptable.

I had to admit I was caught by surprise when I'd heard the news, I never knew that rascal was game.

I'd thought I'd scared the guy that day in the male toilet.

I'd thought she'd be out of his way for what he – my instincts said – had done to her drink.

I was completely and utterly wrong.

And now, not only was I to bump into them – chatting cheerfully and laughing together – all the time; not only had I to witness him giving her lingering eyes, but I'd heard he'd booked a table in *my* favourite restaurant of all time. Together with a room.

Yes, the crook was expecting to have the most exquisite dessert apparently.

And no matter how many times I swore to myself I did not care, that I shouldn't have cared…

The whole thing got in my nerves.

Maybe it was because I was pretty sure that *she* was not aware of the web that spider had prepared for her, she was so naïve and defenceless…

I had tried to repeat to myself that it was none of my business, that she could deal with it by herself but I just couldn't seem to let go for some reason. It felt like it was my job to protect her.

I laughed at myself mentally, I must have gone completely insane.

Maybe not being with a girl for all that time had damaged my brain.

Or maybe it was my testosterone so to speak.

Perhaps I just wanted that strange girl *safe*, instead.

I don't know.

I just know I have to think fast.

An idea suddenly struck me like lightning.

A dark smile twisted my lips.

What was life but a chess game?

Benson had made his move.

Now it was my turn and I knew exactly how to destroy his game.

I checked that everything was ready to go according to plan, turned off the laptop and waited. I had sent a driver to pick the girl up from her house. I was too busy setting my plan in motion to leave.

An irritated knock disturbed my thoughts. I smiled giving permission to come in.

Perfect timing.

"I am not some kind of parcel, pick, sign and deliver." She was raging.

"Please sit." I gestured the couch with a hand.

I stared at her while she did it, she was wearing a pitch black top under what looked like an old-fashioned leather jacket that covered half of her back, tight jeans on her slim body seemed to highlight her perfect curves.

Her chestnut-ginger hair was up in a severe straight up ponytail; her light green eyes were looking daggers at me, her red lips tight with rage.

She didn't seem pleased.

She looked utterly delicious.

"I don't want your driver picking me up," she articulated.

"My apologies." I smiled clever. "I was busy with something, *babe*. I will pick you up myself next time." I misunderstood her on purpose.

I was definitely in a good mood now.

"That's not what I meant. And do not call me *babe*." She didn't look impressed.

"What did you mean then, *babe*?", I asked faking innocence and candour.

I enjoyed irritating her so much.

Again, she looked daggers right at me. "This will be our last session, let's get it over with."

"What are you talking about? We still have a bit less than two weeks." I was genuinely confused now.

"I decided this will be the last extracurricular meeting between us two." She spoke seriously, looking at me straight into my eyes.

Why?

True, we've had their little argument and differences of opinion, but jeopardizing the thirty percent of our final grades just for a few quarrels was too much.

Unless...

Unless it had been that idiotic less-than-a-human-being of Benson to suggest it to her.

Maybe he was too jealous and told her to stop seeing me.

"I hadn't taken you for someone who took orders." My voice came out colder than I'd planned it to be. Glacial.

Now it was her turn to look confused. "What are you on about?"

"So if your dearest boyfriend tells you to do something, you just comply? If he tells you to stop seeing me, you obey? I thought you were better than that." *I thought you were strong willed.*

I had tried my best to hide my disappointment behind layers of icy resentment and anger. I just hoped it had worked.

"He never said anything like that." She looked horrified. "just thought..."

"You thought wrong." I interrupted her abruptly.

I would not accept that. Never.

"You can't tell me what to do." She pointed.

"Watch me."

We scowled at each other for a long time, a fight of will, two savage animals who would not let one tame the other, not one of them would back down, not one of them would accept defeat.

"I have to," she admitted, her voice feeble like the fire on a candle.

"Give me a good reason…" *why I should let you go.*

"For me, I have to do it for me." She opened her mouth to say something else but then thought better of it.

"That doesn't make any sense whatsoever."

"Please," she pleaded.

No.

"I'm not letting you go." I understood I had thought out loud only when I saw the shock on her face.

Too late now to hide my hand in my pocket, the stone had been cast.

So I repeated with a steady voice, "I'm not letting you go."

Her confused expression disappeared, replaced by a challenging look in her light eyes. "We'll see about that."

You're playing with fire, kid.

I had thought Jayne actually was walking a dangerous line, the thin line of my patience . She was trying to focus on what her date was talking about and completely and utterly ignoring me, while we were at my favourite Italian restaurant, the day of the *damned date.*

I had booked the entire place – except for the *happy couple's* table – and messaged half of the school to attend the celebration.

No one had been left out of my invite, I'd thought the more the better. Everyone had to witness the celebration of my victory, as I'd called it in my mind.

If I focused, I could still see the mad expression on her pretty face, her eyes looking me daggers. But what I had enjoyed the most was the Nerd's raging face when he'd understood that I, William, had done a remarkable checkmate.

I was gloating in my glory. My schoolmates were being loud, very loud just as I'd predicted and both the love birds were having a hard time even hearing themselves thinking. All was going just according to plan.

I smiled but suddenly my smile turned into a sneer when I saw the Nerd — *how dared he* — leaning in her ear whispering something that made her smile.

Right, game over, Benson.

"I spy with my little eye, something repellent, something vile," I half sang out loud.

The restaurant fell silent following my eyes' direction.

I was glaring at them. Heaven knows I had tried to sound as mocking and ironic as possible but I myself admitted there were hints of rage in my voice, anger that I couldn't manage to hide. They turned slowly towards me.

"William Black," the guy greeted, "I smelled the devil in all this."

Prepare to go to Hell.

"And I smell corpse." I gave him a harsh smile.

I felt like a rattle snake, my foe, my victim would hear my nasty comments first like some rattles and then, he'd taste my sour poison.

"That's enough," she intervened staring right into his eyes. She seemed to be half pleading him and half ordering him to stop.

"Is it now? But we are all having so much fun together."

"Why don't you guys continue with your dinner then and we go on with ours?" With a look in my direction, she understood that was never going to happen so she breathed, "May we have the bill?" she asked the waiter who looked a bit intimidated by the whole situation.

"Where do you want to go next?" Gabe asked her, giving his back to me.

"Home, I'm just very tired." She collected her handbag.

Good girl. I smiled.

"No, I don't want him to ruin our night." He touched her hand, caressing it slowly.

That's it. You crossed the line now.

My saccharine smile was still on. "Certainly not, he had other plans, didn't you, *Gabe*? Why don't you tell us all about the room you booked for tonight? Late check-in, such class."

The restaurant had a chorus of *Ohh!* and someone was laughing, others started mocking the guy. And I knew in that exact moment, Gabriel Benson's social life had been ruined forever and so had his chances to be with that beautiful girl who now looked at him with a nasty and shocked expression.

"Is that true?" she asked with a harsh voice.

Gabriel was cringing.

William was triumphant.

"Of course not, he's lying. That's what he does best, he lies all the time," he begged.

"The only liar I see here is you, Benson." I smiled viciously.

The joke's on you, mate.

"Do not listen to him!" He grabbed her wrist, a desperate attempt to make her stay while she was leaving, utterly disgusted.

Now you're really done.

"Benson, you and I. Outside this shithole. *Now.*" I stood up.

I saw Jayne in shock, her eyes begging me to leave it, but I waited for Gabriel to let go of her and follow me outside, in the darkness of the alley. Everyone tagged along behind us; we were going to offer quite the show.

"Has anyone never taught you not to touch other people's belongings?" I hissed at him solely, in a way only he could hear.

"She's not yours, she despises you." The other looked on edge.

My smile widened. "Perhaps," I got closer to him, "but I like to think there's some kind of justice in this world, and I'm now the hero. And you... I think a cat has more chances of getting anywhere with her than you do."

"I will kill y..."

"Enough! Both of you!"

I turned towards her. She looked so raging and so... beautiful, looking like a vindictive Valkyrie in her pretty blue dress.

"You!" She pointed at me, I raised an eyebrow amused. "*You* stop interfering with my life, stop provoking people and stop trying to be a freaking fire breathing dragon guardian. Let him be." She turned to the other guy. "*You* don't speak to me ever again, you do and I will fry you up and eat for dinner."

Feisty little girl, I like it.

My smile only faded when she started walking away. "Where are *you* going?" I asked confused.

She's certainly not planning on walking home alone, is she?

"Home. While you were being stupid out here, I called a taxi." As if to show the truth in her words, a cab showed up immediately after she finished.

I watched her jump in, she was still pissed. I wasn't too worried though, I was planning to make it right somehow on Monday or even earlier than then.

Something in her last glare told me that if I had indeed gotten into a fight with that ugly being standing a few feet from me, she would never forgive me for that so I turned to him.

"It must be your lucky day, I'm not beating you up," I smiled viciously, "but bear in mind, if I see you even looking at her or at me, you're as good as dead." With a look, I had everyone dismissed. I started walking off.

"Where the hell are you going?!"

"I'm still hungry." I closed the restaurant door behind me.

KINDRED SPIRITS

Jayne.

How dare he?

Who had he thought he was dealing with? Had he thought I wasn't capable of defending myself?

Why would he care so much about trying to save this damsel in distress?

I had suspected something was going on, I'd felt it like a tangling feeling at the back of my head, an alarm but I'd thought I'd enjoy the dinner, without too much thought and then reject him swiftly for whatever he had planned after for me. That was my idea.

I wouldn't have needed a Knight in a Shining Armour to save me, I'd have survived using solely my strength like I'd always done before.

And yet... yet, the thought that he'd done all that just to save me the embarrassment of rejecting him, just to show that indeed he wasn't letting me go. All that gave me an unknown warm feeling right in my chest.

A feeling that I certainly couldn't allow to live and bloom or it would have been the end of me. I would keep on avoiding every contact with him and so, at some point when it'd be safe...

A beeping sound interrupted my thoughts. It was my phone, I got a text message.

Hey Valkyrie girl, I liked that explosion of rage tonight. It would be a delicious thing to watch, if you showed the same fire in other moments.

I knew who it was, I had somehow known it when I'd heard the phone ringing, but just to piss him off a bit I texted back: *who's this?*

Valkyrie...

He'd called me that, I almost shivered. Valkyries were creatures to be afraid of, ever since I'd seen one when I was young, I'd always tried to stay away.

I will show you the Valkyrie when I see you again. I smiled.

Another beep and I thought my heart skipped a heartbeat when I read: *the one who's not letting you go.*

The insistent ringing of my phone woke me up. I'd forgotten to turn it off the night before. I'd fallen asleep staring at that last text.

The one who's not letting you go.

I could still shiver thinking about it, wouldn't he really? Even if he'd known the truth about me, about my life, about my *condition*?

I honestly doubted it.

And yet, I couldn't help but hope. For the first time in my life I hoped my instincts were utterly wrong.

I hoped miracles existed for people like me.

You never learn, girl, do you?

The phone was still ringing when I decided to pick it up. "Hello?" I still had my eyes closed.

"Honey! Good morning," a high pitched voice was trilling.

"Auntie Kora! How are you?" I rose from my bed.

"I'm fine, thanks. Are you okay, kiddo?"

"Yes. I go to school and eat my vegetables." I smiled a bit.

Why did I feel... disappointed?

Why did I hope someone else was calling me? I breathed.

A genuine laugh. "Good. What about your schoolmates? Are they behaving? Are you making friends? Maisa sent me a recent picture of you, girl, you grew to look absolutely gorgeous just like your mother."

I felt guilty for hoping it wasn't her to call. I loved my aunt, she could be absent but somehow always present in my life. She had that ability, that *magic power* and she'd probably known it whenever she accepted her role of livelihood of the family.

Kora had left a couple of years before I was even born to pursue the American dream, as she had said, but I knew deep down she'd done it because she was the only one in the family born without any magic in her veins. Therefore I thought she'd felt like some kind of burden and decided to contribute financially instead. She'd send large amounts of money to her sisters, and most of the time to me as well, every single month.

"They are alright... for now," I breathed.

The one who's not letting you go.

"Oh don't worry, child. Everything's going to be just fine eventually."

"I'm just so scared," I whispered, closing my eyes.

The one who's not letting you go.

"I know, I know... but I have a good feeling this time." She was trying to make me feel better, we both knew that. "Try not to think about it, live your life."

I smiled a bit. "You're the best."

We spoke a bit longer and then Kora had to hang up, apparently it was late night wherever she was.

After a bit, I heard a shy knocking at my door. Aunt Maisa came in my room smiling, with a coffee mug in her hand.

"Good morning. I thought you'd appreciate some coffee since selfish Kora woke you up this early." She snorted.

"You're a star." I smiled back holding the cup in my hands. The strong smell of coffee filled my nostrils and I sipped it.

"How about you and I go to the loft and exercise your magic? When was the last time we did it together?" she asked.

When my father was alive, after my mother passed away, for a brief period we had moved in with his sisters. Maisa and I used to snick out in the loft all the time. The woman would teach me how to defend myself and all I needed to know about my particular abilities.

She'd been a terrific teacher, the best I'd ever known. It was thanks to her that I knew all my strong points and weaknesses, where and how to restore drained magic and what to eat or drink to regain energy after I'd felt one word away from collapsing.

"Ages ago," I admitted.

Maisa nodded. "Finish your coffee and meet me in the loft."

A couple of hours later, we were still training. I was a pool of sweat, Maisa looked fresh and rested like a rose.

We literally had destroyed the loft, the once white walls were now black with burns and smoke, we'd even broken the Venetian window with a ball of lightning.

Yet, I'd enjoyed myself; it had felt like being a kid all over again, when I had my father looking after me too.

Oh, I missed my dad like I'd miss a leg if they cut it off.

Every single day, I'd long to see his eyes full of unconditional love even just one more time. Sad but true, I'd known since then that he'd be the only man on earth capable to ever love me like that.

I knew I was the only reason that had kept him going, *alive* after my mother's death, he'd held on solely for my sake.

Since he passed away four years ago, my life hadn't been the same.

"Focus, Jayne!" my aunt scolded me.

"I'm drained!" I coughed blood in my hand.

Oh great.

I hated the taste of blood in my mouth.

I tried to rise but my legs were like stuck on the floor. I felt knackered.

"Deal with it!"

"I am done, Aunt Maisa," I said glaring at her.

"You're not close enough to be strong to..."

"I said *enough*."

My power exploded, the other window cracked open, millions of little pieces of glass everywhere on the floor, the woman hit the wall violently.

"Finally, Jayne!" A smile. "It's no use when you contain your power."

"I'm done for today." I stood up. My legs as heavy as rocks, threatening to give up any moment, and dragged myself to my room where I fell into a restoring deep sleep.

An insistent beep from my phone woke me up. With one eye still closed I checked the text messages:

Has no one ever taught you not to ignore nice people?

And another one that said he would check if I'd died, if I didn't reply again.

I typed quickly and smiled at the screen while sending my answer.

Maybe I did die of boredom. You're not as funny as you want to believe.

It took him longer than I'd expected to reply. I only noticed I was waiting for it when I heard the beep.

Maybe I should come in and ask whoever you live with for their opinion.

I jumped out of bed, was he there for real?! Had he witnessed the windows breaking with magic?

I checked the time. No, that was about three hours ago. I relaxed a bit and texted back: *no way!*

Another beep: *Come down, looking at your house is not as interesting as hearing your moans and nonsense.*

I muttered a curse and, after snapping my finger to straighten my hair and clothes up on myself, I ran down with my heart pumping in my ears.

A car was indeed parked there. I cursed at him in a low voice.

"I thought you promised me you'd never stalk me." I hid a smile when I saw him, comfortably sitting inside.

"I would never make such a promise." He faked indignation.

I almost laughed. "What do you want?"

"Take you for a ride." He blinked maliciously.

I faked hilarity that sounded nothing like real. "You wish! Goodbye, Black."

I turned to get in the house, thinking that in the end it was better off like that.

I have to. It's probably the wisest choice.

"I meant it when I said that I'm not letting you go," he called after me.

I froze where I stood.

"What do you want from me?" Enough games, I just wanted to know.

"Maybe I want to show you I'm better than you think, or I want to be seen with yet another pretty girl, or I'm just bored. Choose the one you like the best but get in the car."

I looked undecided towards the house, what to do now?

Perhaps that would be the first and last time something so un-expected happened to me, the only time I'd get to be crazy and careless enough to get in a car with that dangerous guy who I didn't quite understand. And, as much as I hated to admit it; the guy who had such an effect on me.

Be wise, Jayne.

Ignoring that thought, I got in, texting my aunts I'd be back later on.

The car roared under me after he turned the engine on with a swift movement.

I had no idea where we were headed to, I decided I'd just enjoy the feeling of freedom I felt inside me for the first time.

I put my head out of the window, fresh air hitting my face. I undid my ponytail to let the wind blow my hair all around it.

I smiled, weren't those little moments happiness itself?

Close your eyes and pretend you're safe.

William drove all the way down to the coast, he entered a narrow hidden road that I wouldn't have noticed normally, and parked after a few minutes.

I got out of the car, and what I saw was one of the most beauti-ful landscapes I'd ever seen. The sun was setting down, colouring the sand around them with a bright orange-pinkish colour. The dark water seemed to be full of shining yellow diamonds of light.

He took his shoes off and walked in the sand, waiting for me to follow him. Maybe he knew already I would, perhaps he knew all that was too beautiful not to try and be part of it.

I took my shoes off as well and walked on the fluffy warm sand to the seashore, where we sat in silence admiring the sun-set for a few moments.

"This was where I used to run to when I needed to escape when I was little. It's always been my favourite place in the city." He spoke without looking at me, his eyes lost looking some-where far away. "I even tried to build a little house once, the strong wind destroyed it after a couple of hours." He smiled at the memory.

I looked at him, his eyes were lighter now, they looked like liquid silver. His handsome face appeared even prettier in that light and somehow peaceful, like this very place, just being there could relax him for real.

I had to turn away, it was almost scary how much he looked like an angel at that moment, maybe one of those who had joined Lucifer on their crusade against God.

"How many girls have you brought here?" I swallowed hard, waiting for his answer.

Do I really want to know?

"This is my safe place, my secret." A smile in his voice. "I've never brought anyone here. Until now."

And somehow I believed him, I couldn't help but do it.

"Why have you brought me here?" I asked with a half voice.

"I don't know," he had sounded the most honest I'd ever heard him, "maybe because I feel you need peace too."

I almost flinched, how could he have understood so much about me?

"It's beautiful." I saw him smile softly.

"Tell me about your life, Jayne Frost." I opened my mouth to protest. "A secret for a secret."

Is this a trap?

"You don't give up, do you?" I breathed.

"Never." He gave me a half smile.

"What do you want to know?" I asked carefully.

"Whatever you want or need to say out loud." He looked at me.

I'm not letting you go.

Are you really not?

"You were right, I lied about something."

Among the other things.

"Tell me."

"My mother died when I was five years old. She was murdered in cold blood just in front of my eyes." I turned to look at the sea. "I don't remember much of her apart from that."

"So no car accident." He nodded. "Who did that?" He sounded horrified.

"I don't know," I whispered without looking at him.

Liar.

If you choose to tell him a secret, do it properly, Jayne.

But I knew I couldn't, I could never reveal the truth without exposing myself and *what* I was as well. I'd never told anyone outside my family what I had witnessed.

"What about your father?"

"He died a few years after her in a car accident; that is true."

I tried to hide the frustration in my tone, I still struggled to believe that someone like my dad, as powerful as he was, had died in a stupid common car crash.

Perhaps life has a weird sense of humour.

"I'm sorry." He sounded genuinely displeased.

"It was a long time ago." I hadn't looked at him.

"Is that why you never let anyone in?"

My heart had skipped a beat at that question.

That and so much more.

"My life is… a mess, seriously. I've always felt like Cinderella, you know. I always have to run from everything but no one bothers to bring my shoe back to me," I confessed gravely.

He seemed to be studying me carefully like a scientist would study a newly discovered species. I looked at him and again, our eyes locked for a long moment. I was stunned, his eyes were the most magnetic and strange I've ever seen, it was like I could get lost in them. Get lost and never find myself again.

"Why don't *you* let anyone in? Because of your family too?" I asked just to distract myself from him.

"My parents are still alive but it's like they aren't." That was all he said, not really an answer to my question but enough for me to understand him a bit more.

There was no sadness, no rage in his voice just… just what had sounded a lot like loneliness.

And in that moment, in that instant I knew why I'd thought we were kindred souls: loneliness. We were both fighting our own battles so utterly alone. Each of us in our own way and our own personal different struggles, but both of us in solitude.

"I'm sorry." It was my turn to say that.

And I wondered if that strange guy with those glacial icy eyes capable of freezing you to the bone like the cold winter wind, with his witty provocations and his cheekiness... had only been a facade to hide a tormented deep soul.

I wondered if he'd only dropped the mask he was wearing, because he too had felt that we were similar. If he'd noticed too that we were somehow bonded by the things we hid to the world, and the suffering that came from them.

And in that exact moment, alone with him I felt a bit less lonely.

"You haven't asked me whether I beat your *friend* up last night." His voice was lighter with a hint of a smile in it.

I completely forgot about that, I'd forgotten that I was supposed to be angry at him, that I had been the night before at some point.

"Do I want to know?" I asked him tiredly.

"I didn't." He gave me a half smile, proud of himself. "I figured I'd better stay in your graces."

"Why? Why do you care?"

And for a moment his tormented eyes told me that not even he knew the reason, that he was as confused as I was by all that, by our weird inconstant love-hate relationship. His eyes mirrored mine.

"I've never liked him." Ice in his stare. "I've always thought he was sly and had to pay for it."

"Who voted for you as Defender of the Weak?" I teased him.

William looked at me with a serious look on his face. "I don't think you're weak," now he smiled a bit, "I just think you're naïve."

I can prove you wrong.

"I knew he had something in mind, my alarm bells were already ringing before you *saved the day*." I smiled thoughtful, remembering the day before.

"Why did you go then?" he looked confused.

I shrugged. "I just wanted to see what it was like to be normal. I definitely didn't need you to save my sorry ass, I've always saved it myself."

William studied me for a long moment before declaring, "You're a weird girl, Jayne Frost." And that particular time, from that particular person, the word *weird* hadn't seemed as bad as it had been before.

"Said the creep who stalked the girl and convinced her to follow him into a beach in the middle of nowhere." I smiled.

A mischievous light in his icy eyes, a second later I was in his arms while he was carrying me towards the sea, I was laughing and screaming at the same time.

"Put me down, you piece of..."

"You definitely need to wash your mouth!" He was sneering.

Certainly he wouldn't...

In a swift movement, William dropped me in the freezing cold water, a few feet from the sea shore and started laughing out loud mercilessly at me.

"I... you..." I was gasping, shivering from the cold mid-March wind.

"I thought you wanted to freshen up." He was still laughing.

I gave him a look of pure hatred, then an idea hit me, if he insisted on playing games...

From underwater, careful not to be seen, I made a quick twist with my hand, and suddenly he fell down beside me.

It was my turn to laugh, he was soaking wet and was wearing a shocked look on his handsome face.

"How the hell?!" he busted out while pulling his wet hair back from his face.

"That, my dear, is called karma." I giggled amused.

Or magic.

He splashed water at my face, he definitely wasn't impressed. My expression must have been hilarious because he started chuckling.

"Your face... you looked like a fish gasping for air." He couldn't stop his titter.

I was just about to give him a witty answer but then, I looked at him.

He almost looked like a completely different person when he laughed, so handsome and *warm*, his icy eyes somehow seemed to reflect sunlight. And I realized that was the first time I'd seen him really laughing.

"I can't remember the last time I've seen you like that."

"Like what?"

"Truly laughing."

His smiled faded a bit. "I can't remember the last time I truly laughed," he admitted slightly confused. He rose all of a sudden and started walking off.

I tried to hide my disappointment while following him to the beach, I started shivering violently as soon as I left the water. Definitely not the kind of weather for a nice swim.

"What's wrong?" I couldn't help calling behind him.

He didn't seem to have heard my question so I repeated it louder.

"I'll take you home." He hadn't turned while speaking to me, still walking to his car.

I felt stupid and confused, why was he acting like that now? What was up with him all of a sudden?

Still looking confused at him, I got in the car, he was already getting the engine started.

William must have noticed how cold I felt as he kept one hand on the steering wheel, and with the other one he grabbed a black jacket from the back seat. He tossed it to me.

"I don't need your pity," I muttered.

Now I was in a mood too.

"Just take it," he breathed while turning the heating on in the car, "we don't want you to get a cold."

"I don't need such deep concern, thanks," I bickered.

I was ready to pick up a fight.

"I am not concerned." His voice was flat, he spoke without looking at me.

"Indeed, I was just being sarcastic." I turned to the window.

Why that change of spirit all of a sudden? Had I said something? *Well, whatever.*

I decided I had enough on my plate already, I didn't need to worry about his loony behaviour.

The drive seemed longer than it had on the way there, not one of us spoke a word. The silence was starting to annoy me the closer we got to my house.

As soon as he stopped the car in front of my house, I turned to him ready for a battle. I could feel the rage building up inside me.

How could I have felt such a connection before? He clearly wasn't friendship-or anything else-material. I had opened my heart to him and he had... he had been just like everyone else.

I took the jacket he'd given me off; my clothes and hair were still humid and I dreaded getting out of the car without that but still I tossed it back at him. "So much fun being around you, let's do it again," I commented dryly. I was clearly sarcastic.

William simply looked at me, he opened his mouth to say something but then shut it back right again.

When leaving the car, I slammed the door shut just to make a point.

•••

ABOUT THE LAST TIME

Sunday came and went; I had spent it with my aunts just chilling in their house. Aunt Sybil had been particularly insistent in wanting to know who I went out with the day before, but I had succeeded in avoiding telling them the details.

I had tried not to think about that weird Icy Guy and his moody behaviour but with not much success. I just still couldn't explain his sudden change.

I had told myself I didn't care.

I had lied to myself.

I hadn't been able to wrap my head around it and that was driving me insane. I'd tried to type a text message to send to him but I'd always ended up changing my mind; my pride fighting against it.

Monday morning in school had been boring and very lonely, I'd seen Gabe but he hadn't attempted to approach me and I was glad. I couldn't deal with him too that day, it would just be too much.

It was okay though, I was used to being alone, so it hadn't really make a big difference to me. I had always known everyone's company was temporary as usual.

I'd also seen William a couple of times but he'd avoided acknowledging me, like I hadn't existed and that had hurt. Hurt so bad.

Now, I was sitting on my bed, catching up with homework after I'd trained with my Aunt Maisa and sweated like a camel, when I'd heard a beep coming from my phone.

I will pick you up in ten minutes. I hope you're ready, I hate waiting.

I felt the rage building up inside me and typed: oh, *so now you speak to me again?*

How could he expect me to keep on working with him, when he was being such a fickle child ignoring me and all?

No way. Not ever.

Apparently I do, he had replied.

I wrote a curse back to him quickly, I didn't need his moodiness. Another text, it said he was waiting for me downstairs in his car.

Go away, I wrote back, then decided I wanted to tell him in person, I wanted to look straight into his icy eyes and advise him to get lost.

I ran down the stairs and to his car. He opened his car window, he wasn't smiling.

"Whoever taught you those manners should get spanked," he greeted me, "repeatedly."

"We must have had the same teacher," I bickered, bracing myself for a fight.

A hint of a smile. "Jump in."

"I thought you made it clear you didn't want to see me again," I said flat.

"You thought wrong. Now, would you please get in the car?"

"No!" I turned and started walking away.

"I meant it when I said I couldn't remember the last time I laughed," I froze, "and it bothered me the fact that a lousy little girl would have such an effect on me." His voice was almost a whisper.

It was clear that this admission had cost him, his pride had probably fought against it and lost.

"And now it doesn't?" I half turned to him, ignoring the insult like a lady.

"It still does but I decided to ignore it," he confessed.

"I don't like moody people, I don't like not to know what to expect."

"Tough. Now, please get in the car."

I breathed, it was probably the closest thing to an apology I could expect from him.

Looking at his fine clothes, I realized I was still wearing gym clothes and stunk a bit. I blushed, suddenly self-conscious.

He seemed to have read my thoughts and said while chuckling, "You can have a shower at mine. I'm not waiting in here while you try and look decent." He noticed the plumber's truck parked opposite to him. "Besides, I think you do need to use my shower."

I was tempted. That morning I hadn't been able to wash up as apparently in my aunt's house there had been some problem with the pipes, the water had come out brown.

Maisa had forbidden us to fix it with magic. Sybil and I had suspected something odd was going on, and our speculations turned out to be true, when we saw the handsome plumber and the lingering look she'd kept on giving him, and as Aunt Sybil had said his visit was almost a weekly thing.

We even suspected she'd kept on breaking stuff on purpose, to see her crush.

Certainly, there would be nothing bad in having a shower at his place, would there, anyways? It wasn't like I was going to shower in front of him.

The other option would be to fix myself with magic, but how would I explain that to him afterwards?

"Fine, let me go and get some clothes." I ran back into the house.

"Hurry up," was his dry answer.

I picked some dark jeans and a purple tank top from my closet, I took my father's old leather jacket, shoved everything in a bag and left.

The drive was silent. When we arrived at his house, he parked the car and guided me through a long hallway.

On the way, we met an Asian man who asked to speak to William. From his face it must have been important news. I wondered who he was and what he was doing in that house.

William brought me to a wide room, where there was a canopy king size bed with navy curtains and beddings in the middle of the chamber. On the left a mahogany desk with a laptop on it beside a door – I supposed it was a built-in wardrobe – leather couches in front of a big fireplace. In front of the bed, attached to the wall there was a massive television, and a few feet from it a big window with a balcony.

I realized it must have been his bedroom, I started getting nervous.

"Beautiful room, let's go to the study." I tried to smile.

Why had he brought me here?

He smiled maliciously and gestured for me to follow him; he seemed to have noticed my anxiety and he was basking in it.

William opened another door I hadn't noticed before, and revealed an enormous en-suite bathroom with a spacious Jacuzzi.

Oh yeah, the shower... I thought he... Clearly, he's better than that.

While I was looking around delighted, he ran the water and then tossed a big white towel to me. "Try not to drown, little girl," he said teasing me.

"Just get out, you moron, before I try and drown you." I showed him my tongue.

"I would like to see you try, maybe I should join you in there so you can get your chance." He looked at me mischievously.

I gave him the finger and literally pushed him out; I was looking forward to experiencing a Jacuzzi for the first time.

As soon as he closed the door behind him, I locked it, got undressed and as the bath was filled with steamy hot water, I entered.

That was just paradise!

The spurt of water against my skin seemed to massage my tensed muscles; the hot water seemed to have a soothing calming effect.

I felt like nothing bad could happen to me as long as I was there, in that Jacuzzi, in his house with him so close.

I almost flinched at the thought, I couldn't think like that.

I was never safe anywhere and I would never be.

I was destined to fight my way into this world, to struggle for a place in this life.

I breathed and closed my eyes, since I was there, I wanted to chill out a bit, so I had to empty my mind.

Of course he's always relaxed, he has in his bathroom the best invention humans could make, I thought.

I flinched when I realized that his naked body had probably been a million times just where mine was. I shivered but not for embarrassment. Something inside me reshuffled.

Chill, don't think about it.

I washed myself with care just to distract myself. When I thought I smelled enough of amazing coconut, I closed my eyes again and left my thoughts go adrift.

I could stay in here forever...

After a time that seemed like ages, I woke up to the noise of violent punches against the bathroom door, his voice came in furious and far away. "FROST, OPEN THIS FUCKING DOOR, NOW!" he was shouting.

I jumped, I got out of the Jacuzzi and covered myself with the towel, then I opened the door.

I was surprised to see him with his face red with rage, he was gasping. His icy eyes more glacial than ever, he looked daggers at me.

"Do you want to explain why you spent the last forty minutes without answering while I was calling your name?!?" His voice was feral.

Forty minutes?

"What are you talking about? I was only there for five minutes maximum." I frowned.

He showed his expensive watch with a graceless movement. "Forty freaking minutes!" he roared.

I looked down at my bare feet, ashamed. "I'm sorry, I must have fallen asleep and lost track of time."

His eyes were wild and beastly, his face still red but in his voice now I could hear hint of what sounded like... worry?

"I thought you might have died in there!" he barked.

"I said I'm sorry," I repeated slowly, still not daring to meet his eyes.

"Get dressed and meet me in the study," he ordered dry and left.

While he was closing the door behind him, I thought I heard him whisper with anger, "See if I had to fall for a stupid lousy girl!" but it was so soft I might as well have imagined it.

I *must* have imagined it. William Black could have never fallen in love with me, no one in this world could or would.

I dressed and admired myself in the big mirror in the bathroom. I looked a bit more relaxed than before, but my hair was damp and looked very messy, I braided it with care.

When I joined him in the study, after strolling around lost in his huge house, I found him writing some notes in a notepad on the floor just in front of the fireplace.

He turned and studied me, he looked from head to toes. I blushed, uncomfortable, and sat on the floor a few feet from him. After he finished scrutinizing me, he focused again on his notepad.

I was curious. "What are you writing?"

"A first sketch of our final essay for the research." He hadn't risen his eyes to look at me.

I stared at him for a long moment and thought that unlike his peer teenagers, he must have really cared about his grades.

"What?" he asked looking at me questioningly.

"Nothing," I said quickly.

"Indeed, just do some work for a change instead of looking at my amazing self." He gave me a half smile.

Another swing in his mood, for Heaven's sake. I might end up with eternal headaches like this.

"Are you still not working?" he asked me sarcastically.

I snorted at his Stakhanovism, but started reading some other book for the homework and wrote some notes in another notepad.

"Try and write decently, the last time I checked your annotations I got nausea," he said just for the pleasure of pissing me off.

I muttered a curse back at him. "As Your Majesty commands," I bickered sarcastically and kept on reading and writing.

We spent the following hours in silence, each of us focusing on their papers without paying much attention to the other, then William ordered dinner from his butler, which was served shortly after.

When I'd finished my portion of Italian style tortellini with white cream and mushrooms, I lay down on the floor, touching my belly.

"I'm so full!" I declared, almost in pain. The sweet pain of being satisfied.

"Of course you are! You ate with the voracity of a dragon," he mused solemnly.

I laughed, I couldn't deny it was true, I'd always had a great appetite.

"I wonder how you can eat so much and manage to stay skinny." He pretended to be thoughtful.

"I don't know but I don't really care, my destiny stays the same whether I'm fat or not." I only noticed I'd said too much when he looked confused.

I cursed myself mentally, how could have I been so stupid?

And above all, what kind of power did he have over me that bound me to always hint at my deepest secrets?

"What do you mean?" Bewilderment written all over his face.

"Nothing, just that I don't do diets and stuff." I smiled uneasy.

William inspected me for a few more moments, whether he'd bought that explanation or not I couldn't tell, then he emptied his glass.

"It's quite late, do you mind driving me back home?" I asked still a bit tense, when we finished eating the chocolate dessert.

He nodded and rose, I suddenly felt bad for asking it that cheekily. "Or I can call a taxi," I muttered awkwardly.

"Don't be daft." He made his way downstairs not waiting for me to follow him.

When we arrived down to the Black's car park, he chose a nice grey car.

As soon as he started the engine, I remembered about the clothes I left in his bathroom. "Wait, I forgot my tracksuit!"

"That's fine, if George hasn't already burnt it, I'll bring it to you one of these days." He smiled meanly, while getting out of the big gate of his house.

I faked a laugh. "Very funny."

That was supposed to be the last time we had to work on the project together, we'd finished so I felt relieved in hearing that he was indeed planning on seeing me again.

I'm not letting you go.

Maybe he'd meant it, maybe he was really going to stay no matter what, no matter how much of a freak I was.

And what if I told him all the truth about me, about my life and *curse* now?

I'd never thought I would reveal my reality to anyone ever, but perhaps... perhaps, it was time I'd entrusted someone with it, maybe it was the moment to share the weight of the world with someone.

I opened my mouth while he parked in front of my house, that compared to his seemed to be a Wendy house.

I was trying to think about a way not to sound like a crazy psycho while confessing the truth but he spoke first. "You don't have to feel awkward, this is not the last time I'll see you," he reassured me.

I felt relief inside of me, the butterflies in my stomach moving fast.

"It's not what I meant to say," I breathed a bit frustrated.

"What was it then?" he whispered softly.

"I...," I started.

"Yes?" He smiled and somehow he was closer to me, his face a few inches from mine.

My heart was pounding, we'd never been this close, I could even smell his masculine – probably expensive – perfume.

I felt intoxicated by his scent, by the way he looked at my eyes and my lips, by his being so close I could almost feel the heat of his skin.

I forgot what I meant to say, there was just him and me and the rest of the world just faded away.

He smiled again, noticing the effect he'd had on me and leaned to finally kiss me. A slow sweet kiss, like we had all the time in the world to enjoy our tastes.

And I died and was reborn, I felt alive for the very first time. I felt like everything was just as it was meant to be, I felt my heart beating its own rushed rhythm, the blood flowing in my veins.

It felt so natural to kiss him back, to wrap my arms around his neck, to caress his soft hair that I was almost shocked by those reactions.

It was a unique kiss, it felt like he was trying to convince me that he was there for me and he was not going anywhere. He wasn't leaving me.

After an eternity, I was the first to break that contact. He leaned his forehead against mine, still with his eyes closed.

"You'll drive me insane," he whispered softly, it sounded more like a confused confession than a statement.

And I realized I couldn't bring myself to tell him the truth about me, to ruin the enchantment of that perfect moment that I was determined to cherish until my dying day. I couldn't tell him.

In that case, I would have really driven him insane.

I could never be with anyone and I knew it. I accepted it for a long time, then he arrived and I hoped, but I knew my hopes were vain. I knew I had to let go.

Even if it killed me, I had to let him go.

It was not fair on him to, even if he accepted the truth about me, ask him to endure all that would bring.

He was smart, brilliant even, he had an amazing future ahead of him, I just couldn't ruin it.

I wouldn't, because somehow I had started to care about him and I couldn't bring myself to be selfish. Not with him.

So I opened my eyes and with death in my heart, I declared, "I'm sorry, I can't."

Please let me go.

He looked at me confused and a bit irritated, "What?"

"I can't, this... this was a mistake, I'm sorry." I didn't look at him.

I couldn't, I knew if I looked into his eyes I would surrender. I'd beg him to take me back into his arms. I knew he deserved better than my crap, than me.

"A mistake?" He was raging. "What are you talking about, our kiss or the fact that you have feelings for me?"

I almost flinched. "I can't be with anyone." I finally looked at him. "I don't want to be with anyone."

I'm doing you a favour, trust me.

I saw him opening his mouth to say something but I was faster. I opened my car door and I ran out of it while muttering an apology. Not quick enough as he was behind me in a heartbeat, grabbing my wrist, his face a mask of pure fury.

"Why are you running away? Why are you being a coward now?"

"Just let me go, it's better off for everyone, trust me…" I tried to get free but he was too strong for me.

"I am not…"

I never knew what he was about to say as all of a sudden confusion was written all over his face. He was staring at my bracelet.

"Where did you get this?"

"You're hurting me!" I complained.

"Answer me!" His grip was lighter now.

"I've had it since I was a kid." I couldn't understand the reason of that bewilderment. "Why?"

"You're the girl from the bar, the one who had a tonic." His voice was a mix of confusion, rage and amazement.

Was it him? The guy who'd made me do something I'd never done before: use my powers in public.

"I don't know what you're talking about," I denied.

"Don't lie to me, I touched this bracelet just like I'm touching it now." I felt his gaze on me and almost flinched. What to say now?

"There must be thousands of the same bracelet," I lied.

I knew it was not true, as far as I knew that was the only existing one. My father had crafted it for me when I was a kid, he had done it just for me. It was magic, it would warm up every time danger was close.

"It's you, I know it is," he stated incredulous, "your voice, your accent… this bracelet."

"You're wrong, I really don't know what you're talking about." I tried to buy time to think of a way out, an excuse.

How could he even remember it? I thought I took care of it.

"I don't, I'm not, just… How did you manage to disappear into thin air?" His facial expression told me he wouldn't give up, he wouldn't surrender until he'd had a satisfying answer.

What now then?

"Jayne?" A female voice behind me.

We turned, Aunt Sybil was looking at us, her dark blue eyes full of concern and something else I couldn't decipher.

Her slim figure was wrapped into a grey nightgown, her shoulder-short black hair down.

"Are you okay, girl?" she asked observing William for a long moment, then she turned back to me.

"Yes, I was just about to come in." The grip on my wrist was way weaker now so I snapped it out of his hand.

Saved by the bell? No, saved by the seer aunt.

I turned my back on him and started walking off. I knew, if I looked at him now I'd only see rage and disappointment. I didn't want that, I wanted to remember him as he looked at me in the car just before he leaned to give me the most amazing kiss I'd ever experienced.

I shut the door behind me and leaned on it. I heard the engine start and drive off, he was out of my walkway. Out of my life.

I felt something break in my chest, something I knew could never be fixed no matter how much time passed. I'd just have to learn to live with it.

This time wasn't like all the other times, it was deep and painful like I'd never experienced before, it felt like the end of the world and in a way it was actually. It was the end of my world.

In that moment, I knew I'd always think with regret about this handsome guy I'd sent away, I knew it would always be my unfinished business. I didn't need Sybil's gift to be aware of that.

"Are you okay, Jayne?" my aunt asked and her voice sounded miles away.

I hadn't noticed I was sobbing, with my own trembling hands I touched my cheeks, they were soaking wet.

I fell into Sybil's arms and cried there for a time that seemed endless. My tears were for my complicated life, for my condition, my destiny and for that guy I knew I'd have to try and forget.

How could he have got in that deep in so little time?

The woman was caressing my hair, whispering reassuring words in my ear but my weeping seemed to know no end and I felt ashamed, I hadn't want anyone to see me like that but I just didn't know how to stop.

When I finally managed to get a grip on myself, I disentangled myself from my aunt and after thanking her for her support, I ran to my room.

I started sobbing all over again as soon as I lay down on the bed, burying my face in the pillow.

I knew I'd done the best thing; I'd made the best choice both for him and for myself.

Then why did it have to hurt so bad?

CATCH ME IF YOU CAN

William.

I looked at her while she wrote down some notes on her notepad.

Heaven, she was extremely beautiful when she didn't know she was being observed.

I felt like a bit of a creepy stalker at the moment, but I could not help it.

It had been a week since that night, since that kiss.

That kiss that still kept me awake at night, the one that felt like it was the most right thing I'd ever done, like all my life and all the steps I'd made had led inevitably to that perfect moment with that stunning girl.

And gosh, she kissed like an angel and the devil. The gentle brush of her lips against mine and the sweet taste of her mouth, mixed with the voluptuous way she'd grabbed my neck... that was an explosive cocktail I was determined to have again.

I didn't care if she was being a coward, if she wanted to deny the attraction and passion there was between us two, if she was too scared to admit it even to herself, I still couldn't help but want her.

I realized I desired her soul and body.

Yes, I was clever enough to understand when a battle was not worth fighting and I knew when to accept defeat, so I'd stopped denying the truth to myself and surrendered to the feelings I knew I now felt for her. Feelings I'd never felt for anyone else ever.

But damn, she's making it so hard for me.

The day after that night, we went to school and presented our work to the teacher. He had loved it and had given us quite a good grade. And I'd thought I'd get a chance to speak to her about the night before.

Clearly, I'd thought wrong.

Apparently when this girl wanted to avoid someone she was the best at it, an artist.

After class I'd looked for her everywhere, but with not much success. I'd tried and searched for her on our lunch break but to no use.

And the few times I'd seen her ever since, had been when loads of people were around or between us so when I could finally make my way to her... she'd be already gone.

I've always felt like Cinderella you know, I always have to run from everything but no one bothers to bring my shoe back to me.

Then give me a chance to make you stay, girl.

All that was so very frustrating for me, I still couldn't manage to understand why she'd have to be so... complicated.

It had almost become an obsession for me.

I had to talk to her.

I had to taste those soft red lips again, hold her in my arms and never let her go again.

I knew I wouldn't have peace ever again, if I couldn't have her.

I had even tried to distract myself with other girls, with sport... even swimming hadn't given me the usual peace.

Every single time my traitorous mind would always find a way to think of her, that unusual strange girl who was contradiction made person.

Yes, because she was hot and passionate but somehow cold, clever but at the same time so very naïve, that I just felt like I wanted to protect her from this cruel world, cheerful but had something sad in her eyes.

I'd noticed that every time Jayne thought no one was looking at her, she would stare out of the window with a grief-stricken look on her face, or she would observe people careful, always her guard up like she was expecting to be attacked or something.

And I didn't know why, but all that intrigued me so much. I was literally dying to know the reasons behind her behaviour, what she hid to the world.

In all fairness, I was dying to just *be* with her.

When did I become this pathetic? That I didn't know, I breathed almost sorrowful.

I just knew I had to have her in my life, I wasn't ready to let her go just yet.

My eyes met hers and for a moment we looked at each other. A battle of will and power, then the moment was gone and she turned to stare elsewhere.

Why are you torturing me, girl?

I kept an eye on her for the whole day, I would wait for my chance and then talk to her, she owed me more than one explanation.

First of all, she had to explain the night at the bar, when she'd disappeared into thin air.

Secondly, she had to open up and tell me why she was acting like that, avoiding me and denying what there was between us.

Jayne had so many tales to tell me, apparently.

If she thought she could get away with it against me, William Michael Black... she'd soon find out she was dreaming. And reality would catch up with her earlier than she'd think.

In fact, one second of distraction, I grabbed her wrist and dragged her behind the lockers, she was looking at me lividly.

I almost smiled, a bad reaction was at least better than no reaction at all.

"Finally, I was starting to think you were avoiding me." My voice full of sarcasm.

Jayne looked like a little mouse trapped in a stranglehold by a cobra; my ego enjoyed it a bit. Finally, I felt powerful and in control again. I had missed that feeling.

"Very clever," she hissed.

"Why are you trying to avoid me? You don't answer my texts nor can I ever find you anywhere to talk. 'Cause, baby, we do need to have a little lovely chat," I hissed back, trying to conceal the irritation in my voice with sarcasm.

"There's nothing to tell!" She looked daggers at me. "That kiss was a mistake, everything was a mistake I just want to forget."

"Maybe if you say it once again but with more confidence you'll believe it too!" I almost shouted coldly, now I was *pissed.*

How could she act like this? I *knew* for a fact that kiss had meant something for her too, I had seen it in her eyes and felt it by the way she responded to it. Such an ardent passion and sweetness.

"What do you want from me?", she asked tiredly.

Everything in her seemed to shout to leave her alone because she was exhausted, tired by this whole situation or the demons she seemed to carry everywhere she went.

"I want you to look into my eyes, and tell me that you didn't feel like I felt when we kissed, to tell me that I am a dreamer to think you have feelings for me just..." I breathed, "just as I do."

I saw her open her eyes wide and then find her composure again. When she spoke her voice was calm and somehow cold and she looked straight into my eyes. "I do not have any feelings whatsoever for you, that kiss meant *nothing* to me."

Ouch.

That hurt me more than I would admit, how could I have been wrong? The signs were there but this coldness... I didn't like it, it reminded me so much of... of myself before meeting her.

"You don't mean it," I tried.

"I do. Now, if you don't mind I would like to be left in peace." She turned to leave.

Peace?!?

She had some guts to talk about peace after she'd entered my life like a hurricane and left a mess in my life, my soul and mind behind her.

And suddenly, an evil thought, a malicious idea to get some revenge over this cowardly girl who had hurt me so much with such coldness.

I smiled mischievously, she had no idea what kind of devil she was dealing with, but she was bound to find out soon enough.

"By the way," I said loud enough for everyone to hear, "I still have your clothes in my room, you should come and get them." My voice was malicious.

I saw the girl freeze where she stood and slowly turn towards me. Her eyes were a dark pit of pain and humiliation that soon evolved into pure hatred, while every other schoolmate around them was laughing and whispering.

Get burnt, girl. Feel what I feel.

She raised her head and walked away without saying a word. No matter how people were laughing or muttering in disapproval, she just kept on going her way with the pride and strength of a lioness.

And once again, I couldn't help but admire her, the way she would rather break than bend.

I breathed, realizing that I'd succeeded in hurting her, but that wouldn't get me anywhere close where I wanted to be: with her.

Damn stupid impulsivity.

"What are you all looking at?" I barked to the crowd which had stopped to study me.

I noticed one hurt look in the further corner of the hall, two dark eyes which had followed the exchange and were now full of pure jealousy, I ignored it.

Nothing mattered if she wasn't with me.

I had tried to call and text her, to find her in school but no one seemed to have seen her anywhere, it was like she'd disappeared into thin air. Again.

I breathed thinking that if that girl ever decided to start a serial killer career, she'd be the best one and get away with it.

If she ever became that, I'd be her first victim after today.

For the two following hours, I'd searched for her between classes, with not much success. So when I thought I couldn't wait any longer, I'd decided to go exactly where I knew she must have been.

I turned the engine of my car on and set out for her house. I'd talk to the headmaster the day after and tell him I'd felt sick.

As soon as I got there, I parked and ran for the front door. I had to speak to her, I felt so guilty I couldn't wait any longer. I knocked.

When after a bit still no one answered, I started banging on the door.

"Frost, open up! I know you're there. I need to talk to you." My voice was loud and clear. "I'm sorry, okay? I'm a moron," I breathed.

Again no one at the door. With all of my strength and rage and feeling of guiltiness I knew I could easily knock down that piece of wood that looked so fragile, but thought better of it as I didn't want to scare her and make her keep more distance.

"Please, just listen to me, I'm really sorry," I admitted softy, leaning my forehead against the glass frame on the door and closing my eyes. "I'm not ready to give up on you and I feel so stupid and pathetic but I don't care, you deserve to see me begging but..."

Suddenly, the door sprang open.

I didn't fall just because of my feline reflexes. I looked at the person who almost made me lose balance full of hope, but the eerie girl who was haunting my dreams was not what I saw.

A tall woman with a slender figure, long brown hair and dark blue eyes was glaring at me and she didn't seem pleased.

"My niece is not home," she barked, "now, if you're done trying to stress me and my door out..."

Now I see where she got her temper.

"I know she's here," I retorted, "I just need to speak to her for a moment," I said tiredly.

I was tired of running after her, tired of being rejected for her, God knows what, kind of fears. I knew I should just give up.

I also was the first to know I wouldn't.

"I wouldn't have any reason to lie to you." She seemed to realize something. "Actually I would but I'm telling you the truth."

I ignored the not too hidden insult in her words, and asked where she was then.

"Where you should be as well: in school." She scrutinized me carefully.

"She's not," I said with gritted teeth.

That woman... now I knew that Jayne's temper wasn't really her fault, it was a family inheritance!

She looked disoriented. "What do you mean she's not?" For a moment the irritation on her face disappeared, replaced by concern.

"I've looked for her everywhere but she's nowhere to be found." I felt like a dog with his tail between his legs. But I knew I deserved it.

If anything had happened to her because I made her run away, I would never be able to forgive myself for that. Ever.

"It's okay, Maisa. Jayne is fine." A female voice behind the woman; Maisa seemed to calm down instantly.

I've heard this voice before... I just don't remember when or where.

Another woman appeared, this one was little, with short black hair and dark blue clever eyes. I suddenly remembered about her, she was the one who had interrupted Jayne and I, while we were talking after the kiss.

The little one smiled at me and got closer. "You must be William Black," she purred while extending a hand.

I shook it a bit surprised, if Maisa had been cold and on the verge of rudeness, this other one seemed to be quite friendly and easygoing.

While she was still holding my hand, I saw the weirdest thing. Her eyes seemed to turn black and vacuous, like an endless tunnel of darkness where you could lose your mind, if you looked too closely.

And I felt a bit dizzy, my head felt light and heavy, my heart started pounding in my ears for no apparent reason, my blood reshuffled in my veins.

I felt strange and a bit nauseous, I was sweating but still staring at those endlessly dark holes she had instead of her eyes.

Am I going crazy?

As they came, the uncomfortable feelings I had experienced just disappeared as soon as she loosened her grip and dropped my hand. She smiled cheerfully, her eyes returned to their original colour, and I wondered if I'd just imagined it all.

"Sybil!" The other woman told her off with a look full of reprimand.

The little woman, Sybil, rolled her eyes like a spiteful child. "I know, I know, no interferences," she huffed almost bored, "I was just making sure."

What the heck...

"Don't forget it." The little woman nodded and had her tongue sticking out at her. "Goodbye, boy, it's been emotional," and just like that, Maisa shut the door in my face.

"You were very rude," said Sybil's muffled voice from inside.

"I don't like him," the other one justified herself.

"He is the one who…"

"I know, but I can't help it," and the voices stopped.

It's official, the Frosts must carry a crazy gene in their DNA.

I went back to my car and started driving around the city. I looked for her everywhere; shops, bars, cafes but no trace of her anywhere.

I'd also tried to ring her but to no use, her phone was off.

Where are you, girl?

After spending a few hours looking for her, I decided I needed to stop and think.

I was so tired of that whole situation, I just wanted to find her, apologize and convince her to give me a chance. To give us a chance.

I breathed, deciding to go to my safe place, at least I would relax my restless mind a bit. Heaven knew how much I needed it.

When I'd parked the car, I saw something.

Someone sitting on the sand not too far away from the seashore, my heart skipped a beat when I recognized the person.

You're okay.

With feline grace, I removed my shoes and walked towards her, trying to be as quiet as possible.

I couldn't manage to look away from her, like I was afraid she would disappear again.

Not now that I finally found you.

Jayne was looking somewhere far away; she held in her tight grip something that looked a lot like a napkin. I cursed myself mentally; she must have been weeping for my idiocy.

I stopped a few feet from her, not wanting to startle her and whispered, "I'm sorry."

She hadn't reacted to my words, like she hadn't heard me at all.

"I'm sorry," I repeated louder.

"I heard you the first time," she whispered without turning.

I swallowed. "I am sorry, honestly I…," I breathed.

"It's not true." Again that soft whisper.

How could I have hurt something so fragile? What kind of monster was I?

"You have no idea how I feel at the moment." I passed a hand through my hair, frustrated. "I feel like I drowned a kitten."

"I'm not a kitten."

No, you're a lioness.

"I've looked for you everywhere, your phone was off... I even went to your house," I breathed.

"You went to my house?" She turned to me, she didn't sound too happy about that.

I observed her for a moment, her green eyes were red and puffy, her long dark eyelashes seemed wet, the mascara was smudged on her cheeks. Still, she was the most beautiful thing I've ever seen.

"I was worried sick," I admitted. "I think your aunts hate me by the way, or at least one does, the other..." *the other creeped me out a bit.*

"Let me guess, the other shook your hand?" She looked at me with more attention.

"How do you know?" I was surprised.

"She's just a busybody." She almost giggled.

"The tall one wasn't very friendly, I guess I haven't made much of an impression." I gave her a half smile.

"She's just trying to protect me." The girl looked away again.

"I know," I breathed, "if anything had happened to you, I..." I stopped before I could let on how pathetic I'd become.

I didn't mean to hurt you.

"You would have gone on with your life, like you've always done and like you will after me."

What was that in her tone? Melancholy? Sadness? Surrender?

"What?! That's not true! You're being unfair now." I was outraged.

What kind of person did she think I was? Some kind of Abominable Snowman?

"Yeah, you..."

"*You* have no idea how..." I stopped again.

I couldn't expose myself that much now, not after all of her rejections. "If the price to pay to be with you is to accept all your mysteries without asking questions... bring it on, I'm willing to pay it." She looked at me in shock.

I observed her, waiting for an answer. She looked undecided, like she was fighting some invisible demon inside of her, a battle she only knew how to fight.

Jayne turned to stare at the water. "I don't like you," she said flat. *Ouch.*

I held my breath, maybe a bullet into my heart would have hurt less. Perhaps I'd have felt less pain than in that moment with those empty words that I myself had always dispensed freely but had never heard.

So this is what's like to be rejected...

"I see. That explains a lot," I admitted awkwardly.

"Indeed." Her voice cold and far away.

A wave of grit hit me, I wouldn't give up, I would make her admit the truth about how she felt about me or I would have to make her fall for me like I'd hopelessly fallen for her.

"It explains a lot but puts some other stuff in doubt," I said. "The fact you've entrusted me with many of your secrets, memories. The fact that you let me kiss you and the way you responded. I'm no fool, Jayne, I know when someone lies. And I know you're in as much as I am." I gambled, playing with my luck.

The girl stood up instantly like something had burnt her and glared at me. "What the hell do you want from me?" she almost shouted. She was mad, her eyes fierce, ready to fight.

"You know the answer well enough, already," I breathed frustrated, "the question is: what do *you* want?"

"What are you, my personal Jiminy Cricket?! I know exactly what I want!"

"And what is it? Please be so kind to enlighten me."

"I just want you to leave me alone!" She started walking away. *Not so fast.*

"The truth is you're scared, you've always run away from things because you're a coward. I've never met anyone so afraid of living as you are. You're too scared to even admit that we might actually make something good together. And I'm so very tired of following you around, trying to teach you how to live your life and stay for a change." I touched my hair, frustrated.

The girl stared at me from above her shoulder for a long moment, "Then quit doing it," and started walking again.

I watched her leaving me, something inside me ordering me to stop her and my pride roaring against it. What would I say if I even tried to talk to her again? I was so fed up with running after her, so I let her go.

What's there left to say?

I went back to my car and turned the engine on, from the mirror I could see her mount her bike and start pedalling without looking back.

The engine roared under me, just as I wanted to scream my frustration.

Shortly after I arrived in my house, I met the butler, George, who announced to me that my mother had another crisis and she was now with Doctor Kim.

"Where's my father?" I asked almost running to my mother's chambers.

"He said he had a reunion," the man said softly.

"Typical," I breathed. "Bring my dinner into my mother's room, I'm eating there tonight." I entered after a soft knock at the mahogany door.

"How is she?" I asked low to the man I'd known now for a long time.

"Stable, she had a very bad one," he breathed, caressing the woman's hair tenderly and, noticing this gesture and the look on her son's face, on my face, he cleared his throat. "She needs help, William. She truly does."

"There's no way I can even get to see my father, imagine trying to talk to him about it."

"I know but if you could at least speak to her... try and get her to sign her admission to the psychiatric hospital..."

"She's always too high or too sick to even have a proper conversation." I closed my eyes and massaged my temples. I was so tired.

I couldn't remember the last time I'd spoken to my mother, the last time she'd asked me about my day or she'd looked... clean. Clean of the shit she liked to sniff and ingest.

I looked at her, she still looked beautiful with her long white-blonde hair. Time had been kind to her, she looked so young and beautiful like in her early twenties. Just those violet bags under her eyes ruined the picture, they were making her look sickly.

"Go home, Doc. I will watch her tonight." I closed my eyes.

"No, I don't mind looking after her tonight." He was taking her pulse.

"Don't you have a family to go back to?" I looked at him with one eye open.

I've never asked him that, I never really cared.

"Just a mother who wouldn't mind to get rid of me." He smiled.

I know the feeling.

"Go to bed, you look exhausted and you have school tomorrow. I will stay with her, if there's any change I'll call for you," the doctor insisted.

I nodded and stood up. After leaning on my mother's damp forehead for a quick kiss, I left for my own chambers.

I jumped in bed but couldn't manage to sleep. I kept on thinking about that eerie girl and my mother's condition.

I had to find a way to fix both situations, but how would I do that?

And it felt like a bolt struck me, a sudden idea hit me.

I turned my laptop on and typed what I wanted to search.

Hoping; *praying* this would work.

CINDERELLA, THE WITCH

Jayne.

The sun was shining, all that light woke me up, I turned in bed trying to cover my face with the pillow to no avail. I was awake now.

It's always grey and rainy here, and once I want to sleep in, the sun is shining.

I breathed and rose, jumped in the shower and tried to scrub myself almost violently.

I felt wrong and dirty, I just wanted to shake those feelings off my skin.

I'd been feeling that since that day at the seashore, at his secret place.

In his own way he'd declared to me, fought against his nature and curiosity to accept me the way I was, without having to know all my secrets.

And I knew it had been the most difficult thing he'd probably ever said, but still he'd done it for me.

Not to let me go.

And yet, I rejected him, I'd done it to protect him and myself, even if that had killed me inside mercilessly.

I understood it was not fair on him to fool him, to hide secrets or worse tell him the truth, to make him live the life I was forced to live. Always on the run, not knowing what the future would hold for me. Or if I even had a future somewhere.

For once, I had to do the right thing.

That was love in the end, to sacrifice your own happiness to save the other from suffering.

Yes, love.

I'd understood I loved him the moment I'd heard my heart breaking in so many little pieces, when I had to lie and pretend he was nothing to me.

Even though it had almost shattered my very soul.

That day at the beach, while I was biking home, I'd cried desperately, and had understood how important he was to me.

How comforting, his chasing after me was. Even just his presence made me feel good, safe. I was a selfish girl, I knew it, that's why I had to end it.

If I've done the right thing… why does it have to hurt so bad?

Eventually, I got out of the shower and with a snap of my fingers I was dry, my hair braided elegantly around my head like a crown.

The Queen of Misery, I thought while looking at myself in the mirror.

The shape and features of my face were the same but my eyes were different, they were dull and almost lifeless.

I realized it was the first time I'd felt so utterly *hopeless*.

I breathed and left the room, in the kitchen my aunts greeted me with cheerful laughs and words.

Wear your best mask, Jayne. Don't let them see, don't let them worry about you.

"Happy birthday!" Sybil's voice was full of joy.

Oh yeah, it's my birthday today. Forgot about it.

"Thank you." I smiled softly at the two women, they were so different but both lovely people.

"Look at you, older but you still look like a child," Maisa breathed ironically. "tell me your secret, girl!"

"Long walks and amazing relatives." I winked at them.

Sitting on the table, there was what looked like a delicious chocolate cake with my name written messily on it with whipped cream.

"You didn't have to." I smiled.

"Are you joking? Of course we did!" Sybil hugged me and whispered into her ear that Maisa had made the cake, so it was probably the most horrible thing ever.

"Bully," I breathed back at her, amused.

"You'll get our present tonight," said Maisa mysteriously, unaware of the exchange between us two.

"Yes! Kora wanted to be here when we give it to you and she's only coming later!"

"Sybil! It was supposed to be a surprise!" The tall woman told her off.

"Aunt Kora is coming?" That was indeed good news!

"Yes! She would have never missed your birthday!" Sybil sounded so happy, it was almost too cute to stand.

"That's perfect! Let's eat the cake with her then." I smiled at my aunts.

All of us agreed and had a generous English breakfast. I felt like it was one of the happiest moments of my life and I would cherish this memory to my dying day.

If only he was here, everything would be just so perfect...

I shook my head, not wanting to ruin our happy family moment.

After we finished eating, I turned to Aunt Sybil, but the woman was busy trying to beg her sister for something only with her eyes. Maisa was looking serious and inflexible at her.

"What's going on?" I asked curious.

"Please, open it now!"

"Open what?"

"Sybil!" Maisa scolded her.

"She doesn't have to wait to open *that!* Kora can see it opened!" she bickered.

"Open *what?*"

The little woman smiled radiantly and went to fetch a velvet box. "Look inside!" She seemed over the moon about whatever it was.

"It arrived for you this morning, the postman woke me up to make me sign for it." My other aunt sounded a bit annoyed yet amused.

"Who is it from?" I asked dying of curiosity.

"Just open it, already!" Sybil sounded so impatient.

And so I did. My heart skipped a beat when I saw what was inside. A shoe shaped key ring made of Swarovski sparkled in front of me, just on a folded piece of paper.

The writing was regular and elegant; my heart was pounding while I read it.

"For my own Cinderella,
Because I shall bother bringing your shoe
back to you every time you need me to.
'Cause I do care. Really."

A warm tear streamed down my face, he couldn't…

After all the nasty things I'd said to him…

I've always felt like Cinderella you know, I always have to run from everything but no one bothers to bring my shoe back to me. No one seems to care really.

Those were the words I'd said to him some time before, when I'd opened up to him and told him some of my deepest and hidden thoughts.

But what to do now?

You're eighteen now, you're an adult.

Now close the box, give it back to him and leave.

Do it for you.

Do it for him.

"No, you're not…" a horrified Sybil said.

"I can't be with him, not this way," I breathed. Touching my cheeks I noticed they were wet. I was crying. When had I become such a little weepy? I hated it.

"But he really does like you!" she objected outraged.

And I really do like him too, but it can't work.

"You know better than me, it's the right thing to do." I closed my eyes, trying to get a grip.

I closed the box shut, determined to give it back to him in school. Selfishly I decided to keep the piece of paper. I hid it in my dad's old leather jacket's pocket.

I left the house and biked to school. I saw him in the parking lot, he was talking with another guy. He looked as stunning as ever.

Why do you have to make this so hard for me? I breathed.

Securing the bike to one of the railings, I snapped my fingers to erase any trace of my weepy-crying mood and walked to him with a confident pace.

"I don't want it." I hoped my voice had come out as nasty as I'd planned it to be in my head.

He turned to me and dismissed the other guy. "What are you talking about?" He was confused.

"Your gift, the key ring. I do not want it." With a strength I didn't know I possessed, I took it out from my backpack and handed it out to him.

William didn't make any movement to take it. "Why?"

"Because I asked you to leave me alone, because I don't like you and I don't want your gifts." My voice was way too cold and far even to my ears.

It was like a new aloof version of myself had taken over my body, and was now dealing with the guy.

"Why are you fighting it? Surrender to your feeling. Stop running away." His tone was tired but yet irritated, he was still striving for me.

And even though I didn't think it possible, my heart broke at those words. I wasn't even sure I was breathing.

"I don't know what you're talking about. Just take it back." *Please.*

Let me save you from the curse of being with me.

"That's what you do best, when things become difficult, you just run away, don't you?" He sounded so very peeved.

"You know *nothing* about me." I spoke slowly, spelling every single word with care.

"Then teach me." He passed a hand through his hair. He always did it when he was stressed, it was like an automatic gesture. "After all you've said and done to me, I'm still here ready to forgive and forget everything else, because when I say I want to be with you, I mean it." His voice was exasperated. "And I'm still here, fighting for you. Still not letting you go!"

"I'm doing you a favour! You don't want to get mixed up with that mess I call a life!" I exploded.

"Why is it so hard for you to accept that I actually do?!" he hissed back at me.

"Because you don't know what you're putting yourself into!" I closed my eyes, not wanting him to see how rejecting him cost me, not willing to let him see me weep.

Suddenly, I felt his hand caressing my face tenderly, he whispered softly, "Whatever it is, I can take it. I'm not letting you go. I'll fight for you."

And those words killed me and brought me back to life, they were perfect, the words I had never dared to hope to hear.

Maybe, just maybe if I told him the truth about myself, perhaps we could talk about it. I could explain the risks and consequences of being with me. Perhaps, he would accept it.

Possibly, he would run away but at least I could say I'd tried, I'd stayed and fought for once in my life.

Maybe leaving this time wasn't the right thing to do after all. He deserved to know and decide his path for himself.

Question is, could I really be that selfish?

I opened my eyes, his icy ones were so soft and sweet while he was staring at me, so different from all the looks I'd gotten in her past.

No one has ever looked at me like that.

"Before you decide, before you promise me anything, there's something I need to tell you," I started with a low voice. "The truth about me is…" *There you go, breathe…* "I am a…"

"Witch!" A female voice behind me. My heart skipped a beat.

We both turned, a pretty and slender blonde girl was standing a few feet from us. She was looking as beautiful as evil and mischievous.

"What did you call her?!" His eyes turned to ice once again, his voice glacial.

Ready to fight for me.

Amazing how his eyes' colour seemed to change into soft and tender, whenever he was talking to me.

"I called her a witch." The girl came closer, her voice louder. "Witch, freak of nature… whatever you want. Aren't you, Jayne Frost? Or should I even call you that?" She giggled.

"What are you talking about, Alex? You're making a fool out of yourself," he said cold.

"Ask your little *freak* friend for the truth." The girl, Alex, smiled with no trace of amusement.

This couldn't be happening, not now when I had so much to explain to him, that's not the way I'd meant for him to find out.

I felt like someone was stabbing me with hundreds of hot daggers, scorching every single inch of my skin. I felt nude and vulnerable.

William, to his credit, didn't even turn to me.

His faith in me almost made me cry, his voice confident, it killed me how he wouldn't doubt me. "Stop it, now. You're just jealous of her and of me, but enough is enough."

"I might be jealous of *you* but that doesn't change the story I've heard about your precious." She smiled again. The whole school was now circling us like vultures, listening carefully.

"Do you wanna tell our audience, Jayne darling?" Her saccharine smile had the taste of a snake's poison. I almost begged her my with eyes; the girl ignored me. "I will then. Did you know she was attending a school in Ireland a few months ago? The same one as my twin brother." She smiled nastily and I looked at her better, she did look familiar but...

I almost stumbled on my own feet, as I suddenly remembered about him.

Handsome guy with a pretty masculine face but with a horrible temper, a bully really. He'd bullied everyone in school at the time, everybody was utterly terrified of him. Until I'd turned his ears... into donkey ones.

Ignorant bastard.

I couldn't really remember his given name, it was on the tip of my tongue though.

"Jordan told me she'd literally turned his ears into donkey ones! She's a freak who enjoys playing with voodoo crap."

Jordan, yes! Jordan the Moron as I'd named him. Best use of magic ever.

If that whole situation hadn't been that tragic, I would have laughed at her face, *voodoo*... seriously?

"What are you talking about? You're ridiculous." Every line of his face showed how ridiculous he found her story.

Alex wasn't looking pleased about that. "We can't still fix his face... no surgeon would touch it. This girl should burn in hell for what she did to him and probably countless more before and after him! Just at that time she was called *Nora Philips*."

William turned to me, waiting for me to defend myself and laugh at the girl's foolishness, but I was frozen. I didn't know what to say or how to react to that.

"Jayne?" he tried. "Shut her up, say how she's being ridiculous."

And gosh, I wished I could.

I wished I could laugh at her story, turn to him and leave together.

"I've got proof." She handed him two big pictures, one was a photo of Chemistry class.

I knew without looking at it that I was in that, I'd signed at the back as Nora when one of my classmates had asked me. The other one I didn't see, I supposed it to be a shot of her brother.

My heart bled while I watched him flinch and look at me.

"Tell me she's lying. Say that Nora Philips is your twin sister or a lookalike cousin." He was shaking his head; he looked almost in shock.

"I..." I tried.

Heaven, I tried to say something but the words just wouldn't come out. I was frozen by the look of cold disappointment he was giving me.

"Call her whatever you please, William dear; witch, freak, liar, voodoo whore but stay clear of her." She was still smiling evilly; she looked like she was enjoying every bit of it.

"Jayne, say something," he almost begged.

His eyes... I will never forget the pleading in his eyes.

"Think, William, remember all the times when you couldn't explain something she'd said or done," Alex insisted.

Please...

To his credit, he tried and opened his mouth to object but then closed it shut as he seemed to remember something. "Jayne," my name like a plead, "tell her she's wrong, tell *me* you have no idea what she's on about." His voice was broken.

What was the point in denying it now?

Could I even accuse the girl of lying to tell him the exact same things then?

"I'm sorry," I breathed only for him to hear.

For a long moment, William looked so vulnerable and hurt, and I just wanted to disappear there and then, but I stared at him. I would memorize every emotion in his handsome face, as a reminder for the next time. This was what happened when I played with fire, when freaks like me mixed with normal people. Amazing normal people like him.

A moment later, his eyes were dark and glacial. "You're sorry about what exactly? About lying to me? About your name and all the rest. Are you some kind of psychopath? A wanted criminal?"

"I told you to stay away from me..." I said weakly.

"Are my feelings for you even real or are those a lie too?" he barked, his face red with rage.

"I've never done anything to you or your feelings..." I defended myself.

"How do you expect me to believe you now?"

"Believe it or not, it doesn't change the fact it's the truth." I felt like breaking down and crying but I wouldn't do it there.

"Don't you ever dare say that word, you don't even know what *truth* means!"

"Go away, *freak*." It was Alex's nasty voice. "We don't want you here."

A chorus of "*witch, witch, freak*" rose from the crowd like a vicious song just for me.

I gave one last look at William, in his icy cold eyes only hatred for me. Then faking the dignity of a queen, I reached my bike and went home.

I didn't care if my lungs were begging for air, if my legs were hurting, if in my ears I could still hear that hideous song and in my mind could still see *his* facial expression, I had to get away or I would have broken down and wept there and then.

I sprang the front door open and two warm arms were holding me tight. Aunt Sybil's slim body was pointy but somehow soft, she kept on whispering in my ear that everything would be okay.

The sobs were so violent and frequent I could hardly breathe, I tried to speak and explain the situation but the words wouldn't come out.

"I know, baby girl. I know." I felt her head nodding.

I couldn't understand why I felt that way, like the world had just ended before me.

At the end of the day, it wasn't the first time someone had found out about my real nature and the truth about me so what was the difference now? I'd been there, done that a million times.

This time is different because of him. Because of the way he'd looked at me. Like a... freak.

When my sobbing had calmed down a bit, Aunt Maisa handed over a mug full of hot steamy greenish liquid.

"This will help you relax," she explained.

I nodded and gulped the potion with voracity, the warm liquid felt like a balsam to my nerves, the mint flavour that left in my mouth felt very soothing.

I instantly felt better, my eyelids were struggling to stay open, my mind almost empty, the feelings of worry and pain felt far away.

Maisa helped me walk to my room and once in bed, I felt her lips gently touch my forehead. She rolled up the bed sheets for me. "Get some rest, try not to think too much." She closed all the blinds and then the door behind her.

And I tried. Heaven knew how much I tried but I couldn't sleep, my mind kept on ending up thinking about school, about what happened, about William and his expression of pure pain.

How could I keep on living like this? Knowing he now hated me?

Wasn't that what you wanted?

No!

I thought of all the times I could have simply just have told him the truth, perhaps that way he would have understood, he would have accepted.

Who am I kidding? His hatred for me is the best thing that could have happened to him.

It probably saved him.

From now on, I would try and be careful, now that my schoolmates knew, it was only a matter of time before the rumour spread and I wouldn't be safe.

Even taking out the bins for the weekly collection might be dangerous, if provoked, even involuntarily, a witch could become mildly treacherous.

It had only happened when I was a child, a rascal kid had tossed a big massive book at me, I'd turned furious and said, *"Why don't you read books instead, you illiterate pig?"* I didn't mean anything beyond that but after a moment he had a snout where he had a little perfect French shaped nose.

He'd been in therapy for months even though I'd fixed it almost right away.

For that reason, I decided I wouldn't react to my classmates' provocations the following days in school. I'd have them completely ignored, no matter how vicious their words would be. Just like I'd always done.

I stayed like that in my bed for the whole day, lying wide awake in the same position for what felt like ages, without the pressing feeling of disgrace or pain but with my mind full of thoughts.

When I felt like the soothing effect of the potion was wearing off, I realized what time it was and remembered that Aunt Kora had come all the way from America just to see me.

I breathed and stood up.

While going downstairs, I checked my image in the mirror, and I almost got scared, the person in the surface seemed more like a ghost than a human girl.

I don't care. Not anymore.

"Hello, baby girl!" Kora hugged me tightly as soon as she saw me.

"Auntie!" I tried to sound as excited as I could.

I loved my aunt to bits and I knew I was supposed to feel over the moon about seeing her but... I just felt *nothing*. Like my soul and my very heart refused to feel any emotion at all, good or bad as it could have been.

"Happy birthday! How are you?" the woman trilled, she sounded genuinely ecstatic.

I felt like a like a horrible human being, I should feel something... anything!

But it was like I was completely empty, drained of any emotion. Just the nothingness inside of me.

I stayed downstairs with my relatives for the rest of the evening, I'd opened their gifts – a set of earrings from Maisa and Sybil, and a brand new phone from Kora. I'd faked smiles and laughs, I'd blown the candles and eaten the cake. I'd said exactly what I knew they needed to hear, that everything was fine and I'd forgotten about what had happened in school just that morning.

That I'd forgotten about *him*.

I had thought about him while blowing the candles, I'd avoided making a wish because I was afraid it would come true, and if he had ever come back for me, I'd never know if it had been because magic worked its course and granted my heart's request.

When I'd thought I'd pretended long enough, that my performance had been good enough, I'd decided to go back to bed and feel miserable just for a little longer.

Before going, I declared that I wouldn't bother to go to school the day after, no one of them had anything to object to that.

I'd jumped in bed without bothering to change into my pyjamas. I just wished it could turn into a vortex and bring me somewhere peaceful.

TOUGH COOKIE

When I finally had the guts to go back to school, two days after the accident, I had thought the waters might have calmed a bit. Certainly people had much better things to do than remember my humiliation.

After walking a few minutes in the school perimeter, I knew I was completely and utterly wrong.

Not only did people recollect the episode perfectly, but they were acting just as I thought they would: like a frightened crowd.

When I'd walked down the hall, I noticed everyone was staring at me. Some of them seemed afraid, others were shaking their head disapprovingly at my sight, some had gone as far as making up new most *amusing* epithets about me.

Very original.

As for William...

I'd felt his icy eyes on me the whole time, I'd bumped into him every single time I had to change classroom. He hadn't said a word; he'd just looked daggers at me the whole time.

Useless to say, it had hurt like hell.

I'd thought destiny did have a really bad sense of humour, when I'd read in my schedule that my next class was English Literature. With William.

I entered and took a seat in one of the first desks. For once I was early so it took a while before the class was filled with other students. I kept on hearing them whisper and look at me, but I pretended to be focused in doodling something on my notepad.

Somehow, I'd felt something under my skin when *he* had walked in, like I had some kind of sensor inside of me. I hadn't raised my eyes from the paper, but had felt his glare scorching my back.

Please, please just leave me alone.

When the teacher came in, the class fell finally silent. I still felt everybody's eyes on me but at least the murmuring had stopped for the moment.

"So, guys, today we're going to talk about Hamlet. Who knows something, *anything* about it?" Professor Foley had asked.

I knew who Hamlet was, I'd read the story some time ago, but didn't dare to speak. I wouldn't want everyone's attention on myself more than it already was.

The teacher looked at me, like he knew that I did, his eyes seemed to soften for a second.

"Okay then, so Hamlet..." William started. "The whole story is about this Danish prince, Hamlet, who is *betrayed* mercilessly by his conniving uncle Claudius when he double-crosses Hamlet's father, killing him by dropping poison in his ear while he naps." His voice unfathomable.

The way he spoke...

I could feel his stare on me, it was like it was actually touching my skin with scolding daggers. I kept my back straight and my eyes on the teacher standing in front of me.

"It's all about plots and back stabbing," he continued coldly, "but if you want to know more about betrayal, you should ask our *dear* Miss Frost."

I flinched but still didn't turn, that was a low blow even for him. I hadn't expected that.

The formal way he'd said my name almost made me shiver. I felt the urge to cry but I kept my eyes on the wall in front of me. Expressionless.

Professor Foley seemed to have appreciated the provocation as much as I did; he looked like he was ready to scold him good when William continued talking recklessly.

"If it's not true, let Miss *Frost* deny it."

Again, I didn't answer or flinch this time, my heart a hollow stone in my chest.

This time, he'd said my surname like an insult.

It was useless to even bother respond to his provocations, I knew he was made this way. He had to attack and bite like a snake just because he was hurt, but honestly I didn't care anymore, I just wanted this to be over. All of it.

"Enough, Mr Black. We get you're somehow mad at the girl, but no one cares about your little childish bickering," he said with a clever look on his face and I looked at him, stunned and grateful.

"Some *people* deserve public process." His voice sounded the meanest I'd ever heard it.

William was surely hinting at the project we'd done together about the Witches of Salem and their processes, he was suggesting I'd be treated the same way. Public torture and interrogation. Just to be then burnt alive.

Nice one, thanks, pal.

"And you'll deserve detention today, if you do not behave as you're meant to. Again, no one cares about your falling out with people," the professor replied harshly.

William was pushing it, the man looked tense in front of me, he would have got him into trouble if he had insisted a little longer.

I couldn't believe it, this teacher, this man was... actually defending me. Didn't he know? Hadn't he heard the news?

Luckily, William gave up his public crusade against me, and remained silent at that.

Professor Foley started explaining Hamlet like nothing had happened, when he was interrupted by a loud knock at the classroom door.

The deputy headmistress's blonde head popped her head in. "My apologies, Flynn, I need a word with one of your students," she looked at me eloquently, "Miss Foster? Please follow me."

"Frost," I whispered.

It didn't matter anyways, it wasn't like it was my real surname.

I sighed but rose. I left my backpack and books on the desk, counting on coming back on time to get them back before the end of the lesson.

"Please, collect and bring your belongings with you," the woman suggested with a professional voice.

I nodded, getting the feeling that I wasn't probably going to come back at all.

Again I felt nothing, no fear or rage or disappointment.

I left the classroom, and closed the door behind me without looking back.

We walked the deserted hall quickly; it seemed like the chubby middle-aged woman leading the way in front of me, wished to end that little rendezvous as quickly as possible. She looked like she was intimidated by me.

I almost found it funny that a woman almost three times my age would be scared of me.

Once we arrived in front of the headmaster's office door, the woman knocked softly and then opened it, gesturing for me to go in.

The room was big, wooden libraries and comfy couches made it look cosy, the paintings of every type of horse made it look a bit grotesque though.

The Headmaster was a man in his late fifties, his white-grey hair worn short on his head. I guessed he must have been in the army once by his big stature, he was quite a big man.

"Did you request to see me?" I asked just to break the silence.

He looked at me over his little glasses, his brown eyes seemed to analyze the danger accurately before he spoke, taking me in.

"Yes, I did. Please, Miss Frost, sit." He pointed at one of the chairs in front of his desk.

The deputy headmistress went and positioned herself beside him, like his own personal moral support, not that he needed anything like that, he looked strict and confident.

"An anonymous source," he started, "told me a tale. I didn't want to believe it at first, but they showed me proof. They affirmed that you've provided us with false documentations about your identity." He was looking at me with probing eyes.

Anonymous source my ass, it was that girl who ruined my life just a couple of days ago.

"And you believe them?"

"I didn't, I didn't want to at first. But they did show me proof." Was he waiting for me to break down? To admit my sins?

"Then I guess whether I confirm or deny it, that won't change the idea you've made about it." I understood.

I wasn't going to get away with it, no matter how hard I was willing to try, nothing would change his mind now.

"We had great hopes and expectations for you," he looked at his deputy who quickly nodded, "but I already started to get complaints from my students' parents about it." *About you*, it seemed like he meant to say.

"So what's going to happen?" I asked after a few moments of silence.

"I will bring the question to the Council and they will decide what to do. They might have to do a background check on you as procedure requires, until then I can't have you in school," he explained slowly.

Yeah, I expected something like that.

"Then I'm suspended?" I made sure.

"Until they've made their decision, yes. We shall inform your legal guardians when they've deliberated," and with that he'd dismissed me.

"Should I free my locker?" I asked almost bored.

Nothing could shock me anymore.

"It would be appreciated." He nodded.

I rose and left, I'd just reached my locker when the bell rang to announce the end of class.

Great, I gotta do it in front of everyone.

I opened it and started emptying the contents into my backpack, ignoring all the approving glares from my schoolmates.

"Finally someone did something about it!" a nasty female voice said cheerfully. "The area is now freak-free again" I recognized Alex's voice and her giggle.

I pretended not to hear but, apparently, the girls were determined to get a reaction.

I can't even be mad at them. I just do not care.

"So, Freak, are you leaving us for good?" she insisted. "Don't tell me 'cause that would just make my day." She chuckled.

Again, no reaction from me.

Evidently, the girl was not used to be ignored and the fact bothered her a lot, because she quickly got closer to me and pushed me with both hands against the lockers. "Do not dare," she hissed.

I hit my head painfully against the open door of my own locker. With a finger I touched the warm blood that was already streaming down my forehead.

I debated whether to punch her back or just leave it, in the end, that would be the last time I'd ever see that cow.

With all the strength I had, I decided not to pay any further time or attention to her, so with my head still pounding in my ears, I started walking away. To hell with my stuff. To hell with all of them.

"Go, run to that lousy family of freaks you got! But remember, you'll all get what you deserve. Watch your own and their backs, Freak." She giggled.

Have you guys never read stories about witches? Of how it is not wise to provoke them?

To touch the only things they care about?

The only thing that could get them... mad?

I turned very slowly towards her. I could feel rage building up in me, magic roaring to be used, my hands were tingling with it.

The chattering and whispering of my classmate just a white noise for me, now.

I didn't feel pain, I forgot about the gash of blood running down my face.

My mind was emptied.

The only thing I felt was the racing beat of my heart.

And I knew, I was ready to attack.

Just a snap of my fingers, or a movement of my hand, those simple movements were more than enough to erase that evil snare from her pretty face.

So *so* easy to put her back into her place.

I observed her, my victim.

She was a little mouse and I was a lion.

I could destroy her. Wipe her out completely with a blink.

I wanted to.

She had no idea what she'd awakened.

I studied her faded grin; she seemed intimidated now.

Good.

I shall erase your smirk completely, bitch.

She did look like her brother, I'd realized. I would love to make her learn her lesson like I'd done some time ago with that bastard blood of her blood.

"You do not speak about my family. Ever." I fizzed, with a voice that hadn't sounded like my own. It had sounded eerie, cold and threatening.

Almost unaware of everyone's shocked yet terrified looks, I kept on gazing at the girl, Alex, ready to make her regret her pronged tongue.

I could feel the power inside me roaring louder and louder.

I didn't have blood anymore, electricity was flowing in my veins.

It needed release. It demanded it.

And I was certainly ready to comply.

"Her *hands...*," someone whispered, scared.

And I heard it.

I looked down and saw blue sparkles coming out of my hands, ready to hit to kill.

I immediately shut them closed, afraid myself of what I was capable of doing. And what I'd been about to do.

What I'd wanted to do.

Just a mere instant more... and I could have ended her.

Not transformed her.

I had been about to kill her.

That thought almost made me gag. What kind of person had I become?

I knew I wasn't perfect, but I was not a murderer.

I opened my mouth to apologize, just to say something but the words wouldn't come out.

I really was a monster.

For a moment, I met William's icy eyes, they were wide like he couldn't believe what he was seeing, his hands were closed into fists down his hips.

I truly am a freak.

I looked at Alex whose face was bleak and pale, frightened. I collected my stuff and walked away slowly.

As soon as the doors were closed behind me, I vomited violently.

Before going back home, I decided to go and get the clothes I'd left for P.E. at the gym. I was never going to go back to that school of spoiled annoying kids, so I might as well get all my stuff with me.

I could never show my face there again. Not after all this.

I found it almost right away, but I took a moment to collect my thoughts in the quiet of that place.

I made a quick inventory of what I'd done that day in just a few hours.

Being humiliated by the guy I fancy. Done.

Being expelled. Done.

Almost lost it in the hall in front of everyone. Done.

Almost killed a person. I gotta mark this one too.

Doing that in front of the same guy I fancy. Done of course.

Oh yeah, I could be satisfied enough for that day. I sighed.

"You can't say she hadn't deserved to be scared off." A voice behind my back startled me.

I turned astonished to look at my English Literature teacher, Professor Foley.

He was a tall skinny man. I always thought he wasn't good looking but there was something in his expression that was almost charming, maybe his gentle eyes.

His hair was of a rusty ginger colour and the freckles all over his face made him look like a twelve-year-old boy, which was a strange contrast with the serious suits he usually wore. A nasty scar on his left eyebrow made him look a bit bizarre.

"Professor Foley." I was surprised.

"As far as I've heard I'm not your teacher any longer, so you can call me Flynn." His brown eyes were sorry, they reminded me of little coffee beans.

I gave him a smile. "I was expecting it. Been there, done that, Flynn."

He nodded. "People are afraid of what they don't understand, of what they can't control."

"It's hard to be different," I agreed, "but you don't seem frightened of me." It was more of a question than a statement.

"Should I be?" He smiled, his coffee brown eyes lit with an amused light, then he sighed.

I studied him a few moments. The only way he could understand was... either he'd had firsthand experience of supernatural beings or he was one.

He understood that I was waiting for some kind of explanation, though I only noticed I was when he started talking.

"My brother was bitten by a wolf one night, when we went camping as kids together with our parents. No one thought much of it, the animal seemed to miraculously have pity on him and didn't eat him alive. The biting marks healed so fast in the next few days, it was incredible."

He paused a few moments, remembering.

"He said he'd never felt better, just his appetite was... nasty. Bad for a thirteen-year-old, anyways. He couldn't stop eating, red meat especially. Then one night, the first full moon after the wolf had bitten him, he felt weird. Pain all over his body. If I focus I can still hear him screaming in pain even though I was only eight at the time. I tried to see what was wrong with him, trying to calm him down but with a *paw* he sent me flying." He distractedly touched the scar on his face. "My parents weren't home that night, it was just our babysitter and us. The girl ran to see what was going on... wrong time, wrong moment. He sliced her throat by accident, then ran away from the window. I couldn't believe that monster was my big brother, the one I looked up to. And he had killed our babysitter." He paused for a few seconds.

"My parents came back an hour later, finding me bleeding and the girl's now cold body. The police searched for my brother for three whole days, when they'd found him..." he sighed, "they locked him up in a mental institution. They didn't know, they couldn't believe that he... had turned into a werewolf. They thought he was mentally unbalanced, *homicidal*." He whispered that last word.

Oh my Lord!

"What happened to him then? Where is he now?" I pressed, I had to know.

"I helped him escape a few years ago, after spending his adolescence in that shithole. Now he wanders around, never stopping in a place for too long. He sighed again, looking out of the window.

I thought that story had just pierced a hole in my heart, I realized there were worse hells than my own. I was just being a silly girl, crying over a boy.

That guy, his brother... had spent years in an institution.

And I still had the guts to think that mine was an unbearable burden.

"You said you helped him, weren't you scared after what he'd done to you and your babysitter?" My eyebrows narrowed.

"They were both accidents... he's my brother. And he's the best man I've ever met." He smiled warmly.

He must really love him.

"He must be a pretty strong person," I said admiringly.

"So are you. You're both tough cookies." His smile grew wider.

I smiled back, the first true heart-felt smile in days. "I get that you're not afraid of me."

"Just the fact you like Shakespeare says it all." He blinked and my smile grew wider.

"I'm sorry about your brother," I said after a few moments.

About his and your own hell.

"You remind me of him, I got it the first time I saw you in my class. You both have the same disillusioned and sad look into your eyes, like the world has let you down far too many times," he admitted.

And I realized that we indeed were similar, both outcasts, stuck with curses we hadn't ask for, forced to live a half life, always running away. Just his burden was heavier than mine.

I decided, I liked him already, even without knowing him and one day, I'll want to get to know him.

I sighed, realizing that it might be impossible to do so as he was a wanted person.

"Mentally unbalanced and homicidal."

Why couldn't the world accept difference? Why did it have to be so difficult to be diverse?

I felt lucky for the first time in my life though; I had never been locked up in an institution at least. I breathed cold air.

"I've got to go to class now, I will try and speak to the Headmaster again, see what I can do." He rose from his seat.

"I can't..." I whispered, "...you have no idea what... what I was about to do," I admitted without looking at him.

"You were about to make justice."

"No, I was ready to kill her. I wanted to." I looked at him with a look of pure pain. "I don't deserve to be back here."

"Yet, you didn't. She's still alive, she's scared, yes. But she's breathing." He sighed and looked straight into my eyes. "It's not what we think or want to do, it's what we *actually* do that defines us. You didn't hurt her."

"I..." I was speechless.

"Don't condemn yourself for something you didn't do. You deserve better than that." He turned his back to leave.

And I admired him for the first time, he never judged his brother but accepted him, even helped him. He never discriminated him.

He hadn't judged me. Or discriminated me.

"Flynn?" He turned to me. "You're a tough cookie too."

He gave me a sweet smile and left.

•••

THE SHOW MUST GO ON

When I got home, Kora had already left to see a friend of hers in town, Maisa was nowhere to be seen, and I thought I knew the reason, since I'd seen the plumber's truck parked in the driveway.

"How do you want to punish them, kid?" That was how Aunt Sybil greeted me.

"I don't know what you're talking about." I sat on the green armchair in front of the woman.

Sybil made a face. "Sure you don't, now, how do we make them pay?" she insisted.

"Who?" I narrowed my eyebrows.

The other snorted. "The Headmaster and that hideous girl, what's her name again?"

"Alexandra," I answered warily, "but we're not going to do anything to them."

I almost wiped her out from the face of earth already.

"Of course not!" She winked twice and smiled evilly.

"No, seriously, Aunt, nothing at all," I declared severely.

Another double wink from the woman. "Nothing at all."

"Quit it, they would understand right away who did it!" I said alarmed.

I'd be considered more of a monster than I am now.

Sibyl looked offended. "I am not an amateur, I know how to hide evidence!" She was sullen.

"Still no way!"

"But I've done it before!" she debated and then seemed to remember something, she smiled mischievously. "And so have you!"

I almost flinched, one time I'd done it and they had to throw it back at me constantly. I sighed.

"Desperate times called for desperate measures. That once, it's not happening again."

"Why do you have to be such a spoilsport?" she sulked.

"Sometimes I forget who's the adult between us, Auntie." I smiled kindly.

A twitch of lips from Sybil. "Why don't you help me make some potions? You may change your mind by making them. She winked again.

"Doubt it, but I will help you. I've got nothing better to do anyways." I stood up.

What else did I have to do, seriously? I had no life, no school. *No William*.

We spent the rest of the day making, cataloguing and stowing potions. I hadn't minded spending some time with my dear relative; she was good company.

Her personality was cheerful and childlike, she didn't seem to be very mature sometimes, some things she said were very childish, but I always thought it was all a facade.

It felt like she needed to act like a kid to distract herself from the burden she seemed to carry everywhere she went, the ability to see people's future.

A seer, that's what she was.

Real seers were rare, this gift wasn't given to everyone, currently in the world there were three of them, all of them with different ways of seeing what was coming.

She had to touch the person to be able to see. Whenever she felt someone else's skin she would have visions of the time to come, the rest of their life in details.

She often said it felt like it lasted ages, years. Sybil could foresee everything that was coming for them just as watching a never ending movie, but to the person it felt like just mere seconds.

It took a long time to be able to master that power, she had confessed the first few times she'd risked to get stuck in oblivion, to lose sense of reality and believe the vision was life. She had to physically hurt herself to be able to get out a few times.

That was the reason why she always wore long sleeved shirts. I had only seen once seen the nasty scars on her wrists, they'd made me cringe.

And futures were so confused, so much attention had to be paid to the details in order to be able to read them properly, and they were also fickle and uncertain, everything could change any minute.

She explained once that there are two kinds of future, the Fleeting One, which meant that every single stupid action had a meaning, it would bring to someone's future, changing even a second might switch and change it all. And then there was the more important one, the most crucial: Fate. This one was like written in stone, nothing could change it no matter how much a person tried or wanted to.

No matter how hard you tried to escape it, to switch it.

Fate would always find a way to make it right, to catch up. It would always win.

She had the ability to see them both, and she was careful not to reveal too much about what was meant to be, so every word was analyzed before being said. I had always wondered how she could live her life like that.

"Are your eyes jammed in admiring my beautiful face?" the woman asked a few minutes later, after we'd finished writing the last label of the purple liquid.

I shook my head and smiled. "I was just lost in thoughts, don't flatter yourself."

Sybil showed her tongue.

When we'd finished, I retired to my room and emptied my backpack on the bed, I wouldn't need school stuff again.

My attention got caught by a blue velvet box, my heart skipped a beat when I realized he hadn't taken it back, a few days before.

My birthday gift from William.

I opened the box and observed the crystal shoe for a time that seemed like ages, it was so pretty and thoughtful.

He'd remembered my exact words and wanted to show me that he was there, ready to be serious with me.

To make me stay.

And maybe in another time, in another world with no prejudices or differences, we would have been happy together. We would have dated a few years, then married. Had a nice little house with a big garden full of flowers, a few cheerful kids, dogs and a white fence around our nice little house.

In another life, he would have made me stay.

And I would have made him happy.

Perhaps, everything would have been exactly how it should be.

Unfortunately reality is a totally different story.

I sighed. Then made a sudden choice, I took paper and a pen and started writing down.

I realized I should have done that earlier, but I couldn't bring myself to do it. When I was finished, with a snap of my fingers the letter was sealed in an envelope and delivered.

I went to bed, imagining the letter being opened and read.

I woke up early that morning, but since I had no school to attend I lay in bed till late, just stroking Gary, who seemed to enjoy the attention.

It seemed to be a nice and sunny day outside, one of those rare ones of the English summer, but I had no will to do anything but stay in under the blankets for the whole day.

When I felt my stomach gurgle, my Aunt Sybil brought me brunch in bed. I ate my scrambled eggs and sausages with not much enthusiasm.

"Why don't you go out a bit?" she asked me, while I was finishing my food.

"Are you kicking me out of the house?" I smirked, trying to avoid the subject.

"Yes!" The woman smiled.

"Nah, I think I will stay in here a bit longer." I stretched lazily.

What's outside for me anyways?

"For Heaven's sake, kid! You are starting to mould in there!" Sybil sounded exasperated.

"The world is cruel outside this bed." I cracked a joke, but after a moment I realized it was the truth.

Only scared looks and insults were out of that protective bubble that was this lovely and warm cocoon. And that house.

What else was outside for me?

"I'm taking you shopping in thirty minutes, so shower 'cause you stink," she declared all of a sudden and left the room, without giving me the time to object.

Maybe it will distract me from my misery, perhaps it's not a bad idea after all.

I went for a shower, a long warm shower to calm my nerves down.

I was feeling on edge for some reason, which was totally absurd because I didn't take the chance to bump into anyone from school, it was morning and it was a week day. Which one I couldn't tell, I simply lost count since I didn't need to worry about classes.

So I braided my hair on one side, I wore my favourite jeans, a black top and Dad's vintage leather jacket, that felt so cosy and gave me the courage to face the world.

I miss you, Dad.

I met Sybil exactly thirty minutes later. She was always so precise with time, just like a Swiss watch.

The woman was wearing a green cardigan and flower themed leggings. Her yellow raincoat almost made me laugh; she always looked like an extravagant hippie teenager whatever she wore.

"It's not raining." I pointed out after a few moments.

"You never know, girl, you never know." The woman smiled, like she knew more than she was letting on.

Years of knowledge about her special, and in this case handy, ability clicked in, so I nodded and put an umbrella in my big handbag.

We walked to shops and boutiques the whole morning.

I bought cosmetics and books; Sybil extravagant clothes for herself.

I realized Aunt Sybil was right, I had needed that. I'd needed to get out of my dark grey cloud for a couple of hours and feel like life was going on.

Now, my new objective was to find a reason to live and not just survive.

I thought of Flynn's brother, of how they took his life away from him for years... and I just wanted to mould in my bed. I sighed, I could be ungrateful sometimes.

As Sybil had predicted, it started pouring down just a few hours after we'd left the house, I smiled turning to her to make a joke about it, but she seemed to have disappeared into thin air.

I tried to look everywhere for her, but no use.

A strong gust broke my umbrella, I had to throw it to the bin. *Stupid cheap umbrella.*

After not even forty seconds without it, I felt like the rain was soaking me to the bone.

Freezing, I could not feel my face or hands so I immediately decided to get in one of the shops until the storm was over, and then look for my dear relative who'd left me here alone.

When I entered the first shop I saw, I noticed I had ended up in the posh part of the city centre, stunning dresses were exposed on mannequins that looked like real sophisticated people.

Great, I'm in Barbieland.

I breathed deeply and decided not to be intimidated by the luxury, the white leather couches and branded clothes, so after sighing again I started looking around.

My attention got caught by a green long silk dress, but I had to debate whether or not to try it on. I was way too wet and I was afraid the rain on me would ruin the fabric.

I'm also pretty sure they don't have my size; I'm too curvy for this shop.

"There you go, miss," a friendly voice said behind me.

When I turned, a stunning woman in fancy clothes was handing me the whitest towel.

Can't believe they employ models!

"Thank you." I accepted it shyly, starting to rub the water off my skin.

"It's gorgeous, isn't it?" The woman pointed at the dress.

I nodded and sighed, even if I tried it on, it would just be a torture as I could have never afforded it.

"It's for sale, you know. There's fifty percent off on all our merchandise today." She seemed to be reading my mind. I blushed.

Why not trying it on then? a little voice in my head said.

So I smiled and told the woman my size, perhaps I could afford it after all.

When the shop assistant came back with that beautiful dress, I was already dry. I returned the towel, grateful, and closed the fitting room's door behind me.

I put that work of art of a dress on, undid my braid and collected my hair in a French roll, for a moment pretending I was getting ready for prom.

I've never been to one before.

I opened the door shyly and the woman smiled, pointing at the big mirror on the wall. "You look breathtaking." She almost clapped her hands.

I smiled softly at her and looked at my own reflection.

It seemed like I wasn't the only magical thing in that shop, that dress made me feel like I did look good for once, even *hot*. The silk seemed to lay on my figure with grace, the vibrant colour to highlight the curves of my body. That was magic for sure!

And for the first time, I felt pretty and elegant. I almost smiled at my reflection.

"Yes, you do need to have the look for being a conniving enchantress," said a cold male voice behind me.

My heart skipped a beat, recognizing who'd spoken.

My smile turned sour and faded in my mouth.

Please, please not here, I can't cope with this right now.

"If it's just appearance though, we're not allowed to know," he continued.

I turned just to face his harsh icy eyes, that looked at me with despise.

He was there, standing tall a few feet from me, glaring at me with a severe and non-indulgent look on his stunning face.

Needless to say, he hated me.

For a long moment, our eyes locked and it was a battle of will to just look away.

"I will give it back to you," I said to the woman, who now appeared to be confused.

I was determined to ignore him, that way he might leave me alone.

"But, miss, it seems to be made for you," she objected.

"Yes, *Miss*, you can always use it to make more people fall in your spider web." He nodded.

I wish it was that easy.

The shop assistant thought better than interrupting the upcoming fight, so she excused herself straight after to go and assist another customer in need.

"I do not know what you're talking about." I didn't even look at him.

And it all happened in a matter of seconds, without having the time to register his movements, I found myself pinned to the shop's wall. William's face a few inches from mine.

His eyes... they were as dark as winter clouds. The ones that promised rain and thunder.

My heart was pounding in my ears, we hadn't been this close since that kiss we shared what seemed to be like a lifetime ago.

I could smell his particular scent; he was wearing the same perfume he had on the night we kissed.

I felt intoxicated by him, by his eyes, by the mere fact that his mouth was just inches from mine.

I struggled against the temptation to close my eyes.

But I couldn't abandon myself to him.

That would have been the death of me.

"At least have the guts to admit what you did to me," he hissed in my ear. A snake ready to bite to kill.

What about what you did to me?

And I tried to break free but he was far too strong for me, and I was so tired of all this. Of the rage, of the pain.

Why couldn't he just let me be?

But I knew him well enough to know that he wouldn't surrender, he would make me pay one way or another until his rage would be extinguished.

I'm so tired.

So I looked straight into his eyes. "What is it that bothers you so much? The fact that you've fallen for a freak or the fact that you know deep inside you, that I've done *nothing* to make you?" I barked back, collecting all the courage I possessed.

Fire with fire.

The good witch was gone, the kid who kept her head low was replaced by a woman with claws.

"Do you want me to be honest? Fine, I'll tell you the truth, you needed to love and being loved back for once in your sad empty life, *that* I understood the first time I spoke to you. You were desperately lonely and so was I, we were kindred spirits or that's what I thought." The pressure on my hand was light now, his face a mask of shock and cold rage. I managed to break free from him easily. "I was wrong and I'm sorry about that, but you can't say I hadn't tried to warn you," I whispered.

I stared into his dark eyes, shock was filling them.

He certainly hadn't expected my explosion of rage.

William was now looking at me like he saw me for the first time.

"I told you to stay away from me, I *warned you*," I continued after a few moments of silence. My chest felt heavy, I couldn't breathe properly.

Just let me be now.

It's too painful to even look at you.

William's face was marble, no emotion or expression shown by his perfect features. His icy eyes cold and immobile, he looked like a perfect statue of the Greek Adonis.

Let's end it here.

I continued, looking straight at him. "You can't blame me for not opening up to you, for lying to you. I saw your reaction now and I'm glad I never did," I breathed. "Now, please just leave me alone, I'm so done with this crap." I turned and entered the fitting room, slamming the door behind me.

I removed the dress, carefully, I was afraid I would tear the zip or something with the rage I felt inside me.

I looked at the price tag and I decided I would play dirty for once, since everyone thought I was the worst, what did I have to lose? With a snap of my fingers, the numbers on the price changed.

When I emerged, he was gone. *Good!*

I paid to a shocked woman, who couldn't believe the price she was selling that magnificent piece for, but didn't dare to say a word.

Getting out of the shop, I was surprised by two things: the storm stopped, the sun was now shining, and Aunt Sybil was there, smiling broadly at me.

Little rascal, did you do it on purpose to torture me?

"That dress is stunning," was all the woman said.

The price to get it was too high, I'm exhausted after seeing him.

We went back home and I showed the dress to Maisa and Kora. They loved it and made me try it on right away.

They'd laughed when I'd confessed about my little cheating with magic earlier; they'd never reprimand me for using my talents.

At least someone who accepts me.

I thought of Flynn and his brother, I was pretty sure he wouldn't mind now to see him turning into a werewolf.

I felt relieved that at least, he had him just like I had my aunts.

After an abundant dinner, I went to bed and lay awake, thinking about what had happened that day, about William.

I'd finally found the strength to be honest with him, since the beginning I noticed he had that power over me, I remembered all the times I came too close to reveal the truth about myself and my life. About my curse.

I had thought we were kindred spirits, and I still did, a fight wouldn't change reality.

The fact that he now loathed me didn't mean anything, we were similar. Whether we liked it or not.

We were both united by the suffering in our life, different kind of burdens but still both backs bent by the weight of them just the same way.

And even if he disliked me now, even if he abhorred my body and soul with all his strength, I couldn't really blame him for that. I understood and accepted it.

I knew William needed to despise me, he wasn't one for soft emotions, he was all in or out. Black or white. Love or hate.

And he didn't exactly feel love for me at the moment.

But I wouldn't stop trying and live the rest of my life because of it.

I decided I would try and forget all of that happened.

The show had to go on.

And I knew exactly how to do so.

So I rose and went downstairs; I had something important to do.

NOT LETTING YOU GO

William.

When I got in the car, I started the engine with a violent movement. I needed to drive; I needed to stop thinking about that stupid little girl.

A few days had passed since the shocking discovery, since the heart I didn't think I even possessed, broke in a million tiny pieces.

A witch, I had fallen in love with a witch. And a liar.

And no matter how many times I'd told myself that magic wasn't real, that it was just in fairytales and movies, I'd witnessed it.

I hadn't believed the stories about her; I had gotten mad because of all the fake identity matter.

The *Nora Philips* story.

My world was already in pieces then, I didn't need to believe in such a silly thing as magic.

Until...

That day in the hall, when that stupid cow of Alex Lewis had provoked her and tested her limits... that day I'd been ready to intervene, cheater or not, Jayne was still the girl I grew to love so I wouldn't have let that stupid whore treat her like that. Threaten her.

But then, the light had gone out, her hair was dancing crazy around her pretty face and her hands... scary blue sparks were coming out from them, ready to hit. To kill.

I could see it from her eyes, she was about to do something bad.

And Heaven knows, I was ready to intervene.

Not to rescue that Alex girl, no. She would have deserved what would be coming to her without a doubt.

I was ready to save Jayne from making the biggest mistake of her life, one that, knowing her, she would have regretted forever and ever. Not to mention, it would have ruined her whole existence.

Just as I was about to go to her, to try and speak to her, she'd woken up from her trance.

She'd realized what she was about to do.

And finally, I had to admit that this sort of thing, magic, was real.

I had seen it with my own eyes.

That all the stories, all the fairytales, legends... they might have been true too.

When I'd gotten home, I'd searched on the Internet for folklore stories about witches and all the other supernatural creatures. Some, I'd judged as rubbish but others sounded plausible.

And I had to smash my phone against the hard wall to prevent myself from texting her, from calling her and hearing her voice, to ask her about those legends or even to make sure she was alright.

I knew she must have loathed herself for what had happened in the school hall that day.

I just wanted her to tell me how she felt, to cy on my shoulder, to make her feel better. Safe.

I wanted to be there for her but I couldn't. Not after all the lies.

And I'd thought about her so many times I'd lost count. I'd passed by her house more often than I cared to admit, hoping to get a glimpse of her.

I must have a masters degree as a stalker by now.

I didn't see her at school afterwards, I'd heard she got expelled.

I was missing her presence so much, it was like the school full of the chattering of many students, seemed silent and empty without her. They were all just a white noise in the background.

I'd gone completely crazy and I knew that very well.

And those feelings for her were so deep and strong, I'd even thought for a second, that she'd played with me recklessly, making me care for her with her special abilities.

That's what I'd desperately tried to convince myself of.

But then she'd said that, *'You can't say I haven't tried to warn you'* and I'd realized that my theory, my hopes were completely and utterly wrong.

140

Jayne had indeed tried to tip me off. She'd rejected me many times, she'd made clear she was to be left alone, that it was for both our sakes.

But I hadn't listened and I'd been the one to insist so constantly for her to give it a try...

That girl had tried to protect herself, and make me aware that it was a narrow path that neither one of us would be willing to walk.

But I had been so very stubborn and blamed it on her. Thinking *she* had made me do all that, made me pursue her when she'd always been the one on alert, the one who had always refused to give in.

How could she be accused after that?

Because it was easier, some voice in my mind said.

It was simpler to convince myself that what I felt was fake, that everything, all the pain would fade away with time.

It was indeed easy to blame her for those feelings I couldn't understand, to pretend they were a mere game and they would soon go away. I lied to myself.

I sighed, I'd been so nasty and mean, and so very mad.

When I'd seen her in that shop, with that beautiful dress on... Heaven, she'd looked stunning and something had moved inside me.

I'd wanted her to understand the suffering she'd caused me, the disappointment in me, but then she'd spoke courageously, and all she'd said was undeniably true.

"You can't blame me for not opening up to you, for lying to you. I saw your reaction now and I'm glad I never did."

When she'd said that all of my stupid anger melted like snow under the sun, I'd understood her fully. Maybe for the first time.

All she'd done, it was to protect herself.

And I hadn't found the strength to blame her for that.

She was right.

She'd been right not to trust me, not to tell me anything. I showed exactly what she'd expected me to be. A coward.

And I'd grasped how her life had been so far, I'd witnessed it with my very eyes, the diffidence, the alienation and prejudice.

And I hated myself for being part of that, for being one of those who had hurt her badly.

In the end the joke's on me, I was the real monster.

I parked the car in our own personal parking lot, and walked to my room.

I was terribly wrong.

I sat down, massaging my temples. I was so tired.

A shy knocking at the door, our butler George popped in looking a bit guilty.

"What's up?" I asked tiredly.

"Something arrived for you, your father had left clear orders to burn to ashes anything that would come from..." he cleared his throat, "*her*. But I kept it nonetheless. I thought it was your decision to make."

From her?

"What are you talking about?" I asked confused.

The man handed a blue velvet box. I recognized it as the gift I'd bought *her* for her birthday ages ago. And a letter attached to it with my name written on.

"Thank you, George." I grabbed them gratefully.

"I'll leave you to it." George closed the door behind him.

I didn't notice my hands were trembling before having difficulties in holding the envelope. I muttered a foul curse and ripped the seal open. In irregular handwriting it said:

William,

There are no words to explain myself, to explain how sorry I am for lying to you. I can only tell you that everything I've done... hasn't been for malicious purposes, even if it may look like it. I had to build a wall between myself and the world; I learnt that since I was a toddler.

I am a coward, you have no idea how many times I thought about telling you the truth about myself, perhaps you would have understood, maybe we wouldn't have been at this point.

But I don't regret not doing so, as much as I try, you're better off without being mixed with me, without being in the middle of all this entangled mess that I call a life.

Nevertheless, I did enjoy the time we spent together and I will cherish the memories to my last breath.

Take my word for it, I've never cast a spell on you. It's amusing how I feel you've instead cast a spell on me, making me care, making me think there could be a different... something for me.

But magic never lasts.

With this letter I hope I find you well.

Love,

Jayne

I read the letter what seemed to be a million times, how could I have been so utterly blind?

What would you have done in her shoes, William Michael Black?

I thought I would have probably hidden the truth to the world like she did. I would have lied and cheated and run away. I just wasn't sure I'd be selfless enough to reject someone I liked, not even for their own good.

And I understood how noble that girl had been, all the warnings she'd somehow dropped for me along the way.

I stood up, ready to run to her if it was necessary.

I had to see her, to talk to her. Apologize for being such an arsehole.

For being stupid.

And frightened.

I just wanted to hold her in my arms again; the rest of the world could go to hell.

I was hers and she was mine, nothing else mattered. We belonged together.

I was ready to run to her place when on the way out, I met Doctor Kim who called me back to the house. My mother was asking about me desperately.

I sighed following him, thinking that I would go to see Jayne tomorrow, first thing in the morning.

I woke up with a bad back; I'd slept on a not too comfy chair close to my mother's bed.

Looking around me, I noticed the doctor had done the same on the other side of the room.

I was grateful for the attention and care that man was giving her; he was a good man and a great doctor. Even though I suspected there was more than he'd let on, I thought he somehow shared some kind of bond with her.

It's none of my business, anyways.

I checked the watch on my wrist; it was half past eleven in the morning.

I'd missed school, not that I was planning to go anyways, but I had to hurry to go and see the girl. My girl.

I went for a refreshing shower, picked my clothes not too carefully, black jeans and a white polo, and left for her house.

The drive seemed to take ages, when I finally knocked at her front door, I found my own stupid heart beating like crazy in my ears.

Look how pathetic you've made me, girl.

I sighed.

It was the same woman who'd answered the door the first time I'd been here, Maisa. She faced me, with an utterly confused and severe look on her face.

"What do you want now?" she asked as a way of greeting.

I will have to get used to her savage and rude behaviour.

I knew I would do it for her.

"I'm here to see Jayne." I tried to look behind the woman, tried to get a glimpse of her.

"You're too late, she's gone."

Probably, if she'd punched me in my stomach, I would have felt less pain.

"What?!" I almost shouted. "Gone where?"

She can't be serious.

"Your timing is the worst, boy, has anyone ever told you that?" She sighed. "She left for the airport an hour ago. She's leaving the country," she explained.

What the heck?!

No! She can't do that!

"She can't be!" I cried out, stressed.

It seemed to me that I was destined to run after her all the time. I sighed.

"She said it was time for her to move on, there was nothing for her here," she said slowly.

"I am here!" I touched my hair nervously.

Now what?!

I had to stop her, no matter the cost.

I turned to leave, when her voice called me back. "William Black?"

Please, please tell me it's a bad joke now.

"If you go to her now, if you pursue her... there's no coming back, ever." Maisa warned me in all seriousness.

"She belongs with me," I simply said while jumping into my car, not thinking about it twice.

Wait, wait for me, girl. I'm coming for you.

The airport was south, the traffic was unbearable. it seemed to me that the Universe was working against me.

I didn't care about the speed limits, about the traffic lights turning red. I just felt like I was running out of time. I just had to stop her from making a big mistake.

I parked in front of the main door, a police man shouted after me that I couldn't leave my car there, that it would be taken away and I had to pay an expensive fine for it.

My careless answer was, "So be it," before I ran inside.

The airport was big and crowded; I really did need a miracle to be able to find her.

I checked everywhere, shops, ticket desks... no trace of her.

I didn't even know what flight she was on, in the panic of the moment, I'd forgot to ask her Aunt Maisa.

I cursed myself mentally for smashing my phone, I could have called her, tried and reach her...

I sat down, discouraged, what if she was already airborne? What if she was going far away from me?

Think, William, think! Any hints of where she would go.

I tried to remember any phrase or detail that could help me with my search but no use, she never mentioned anything like that.

I looked around me, and an idea hit me.

This airport was big. Huge.

The last time I travelled, they recommended to come at least three hours before departure because of...

Yes!

She had to be somewhere here still!

There was one last place to check. I ran to the security door and finally saw her behind the glass door. As I'd thought, she was queuing to go to her gate.

I tried to kick off at the security guy, but he threatened to call the police.

I started shouting her name, but no use, she couldn't hear me.

I sighed and rushed back to the ticket desk, to gain access to the Terminal. I had to have a pass, so I bought a random flight ticket. This was the only way I knew I could pass through security to get to her.

And for some reason, her aunt's words came to my mind *"If you go to her now, if you pursue her... there's no coming back, ever."* I noticed that I was well aware of that, when she'd told me, I knew it already. I wanted it.

To never let her go.

"The next available flight is for Glasgow, it departs in one hour," the hostess said to me from the Ticket Desk.

"I'll take it!" I was in a hell of a rush.

"I'm going to need your passport and..."

"Credit card, yes!" I put everything on the counter in front of her.

She didn't look bothered by me or my clear need to get everything done fast. She took her time checking my passport picture, making the transaction and all.

I glared at her, her eyes were hidden by big red glasses, her brown hair collected into a ponytail. She was wearing an airline uniform without the wings. She was not allowed to fly as a cabin crew then.

Just work your magic, woman. Quickly.

After a time that seemed to be endless, she handed my passport with my ticket inside of it.

"Your seat number is..." she started.

"That's fine." I ran away.

The guy that stopped me before looked at me warily, but he let me pass. I was tempted to give him the finger.

I queued impatiently, and when I was finally able to race to her freely, she was the next to embark.

"Jayne! Don't!" I cried out, panting.

The girl turned in shock; she couldn't believe her own eyes.

"What are *you* doing here?" she asked me, when I'd finally got to her.

I almost couldn't breathe. "I don't... want you to... go."

"What?" Her pretty face looked astonished, her light green eyes so wide with surprise it made me want to laugh.

I need to catch my breath first.

"Don't go, please," I pleaded. "I can't... I'm not ready to let you go. I don't want to," I confessed a bit embarrassed.

The girl looked speechless, so I continued. "I'm sorry, about everything. And I don't care, Heaven, there's nothing I would change about you, not one single thing." I sighed.

Great, I'm evolving to a new level of pathetic. But I don't care.

"Stay," I whispered.

Amazement written all over her expression. "I don't know, I can't get you involved in this whole mess."

"Let's just talk, stay for a coffee and then you can decide whether to go or not," I pleaded offering a hand.

Jayne looked at it undecided, "I..." she started.

"Kiddo?" A tall woman with dark hair and a grey woman suit was calling her.

She was still looking at my hand, I insisted, "I will make it right, I promise. I don't care about anything else."

"You have no idea what it means to be with me, my condition, my curse..." she tried, her shiny eyes pleading me.

"I don't care," I repeated confidently, "I'm not letting you go."

Please, I can make you happy. There's nothing else I wanna do, I vow to protect you from anything and anyone. Just give me the chance to show you how our lives could be together. Just one shot.

"It's a matter of… I can't ask this of you. I won't." She seemed more determined now.

I was losing ground.

Why did she have to be this stubborn?

"And yet, you're still here," I realized after a few seconds.

She was trying to send me away, but did she really want me to go? Jayne looked uncomfortable.

It was time for the final knock out. "Stay for a coffee and tell me all that I need to know. If I think I can't face it, I will pay for the next flight to wherever you were going to go."

I knew it wouldn't happen, I would have gone to hell and back for this girl. I was ready to gamble it all.

A smile lit her pretty face. "One coffee," she offered and took my hand.

And that gesture, that smile was all I needed. I held her tightly against me, not caring about everyone's glares.

I breathed her perfume in. It was roses, and I thought it suited her; she was a red vibrant rose, strong and fragile at the same time, also so immensely beautiful.

"Let's go," I whispered in her ear.

Jayne nodded and turned to the woman, she apologized to her and the other smiled sweetly waving, and then left to catch her flight.

With some difficulties, we succeeded in leaving the Terminal building. Still holding hands tight, we jumped into a taxi.

There was so much to talk about, so many things left unsaid, but we stayed silent in the car, that was not the place to talk about it. We simply enjoyed each other's company, still with our hands joined together.

The cab left us in front of the narrow road that led to my secret place. I paid the fare and we walked slowly there.

She was the first one to break the silence. "What do you want with me?" she asked shyly.

"Honestly? I don't know, but whatever it is, you're part of it."

"Doesn't it bother to touch the hand of a witch?" she questioned softly a few moments after, without meeting my eyes.

"I would spend my life touching the hand of *this* witch." I saw her hiding a smile.

"Why?" she asked in a whisper.

"Because you're special, because you're not evil. You're this charming little beautiful girl who seemed to have cast a spell on me." I saw her opening her mouth in protest, I chuckled. "I'm joking."

"I'm different from you, all of you," she admitted.

"How is that a bad thing?" I sighed. "I wouldn't care even if you told me you got a third eye between your shoulder blades."

I knew I was in too deep to even bother about anything. There was no way out now, no matter how much I had tried to forget about her.

"And you don't care I'm a freak? That I'm not *normal*? That if you choose me, you'll be an outcast too?"

"I don't care about any of those things, 'cause for the first time in my life I feel like I am where I'm meant to be," he confirmed, then a twitch of lips, "with my little personal freak," I teased her.

She showed me her tongue, and I remembered what George had mentioned, about my father wanting him to burn any correspondence with this girl, to make him encourage me to give her up.

I clutched my free hand into a fist. I would have to have a word with my dear parent soon.

When we arrived at my special place, we both removed our shoes and walked on the cold sand, until we sat on the sea shore.

"Are you sure about this? Once you're in… there's no way back." She studied me. Probably looking for doubt but she couldn't find any. I was confident it was the right thing to do.

"If you go to her now, if you pursue her… there's no coming back, ever."

Totally fine by me, Maisa.

"How could you have changed your mind? I thought you hated me, despised me." She was wary.

"Yeah, I would have liked that." I sighed. "Truth is, I've tried so hard to. But to no point, I always ended up thinking about you, worrying about you," I touched my hair with a nervous gesture, "and I've literally been a piece of shit to you, and I'm sorry."

She looked so astonished by my apology, it almost made me burst out laughing. *How I missed her...*

"Are you certain you feel okay?" She made sure.

"I've never felt better." I opened my arms and looked at the sky, thanking whatever God there was for giving her to me.

"I see. I'm going to kill Sybil," she declared, her face darkening while she stood up.

"What are you talking about?" My eyebrows narrowed. I grabbed her hand.

"Have you drunk any strange tasting tea? Or something?" She sighed. "The effect of the love potion will wear off in a few days." She looked away, trying to break her hand free from mine.

I didn't let go. "I do not drink tea, I drink coffee and only the one that George makes with his good old hands. Ask him how fussy I am with drinks." I gave her a half smile.

"Are you sure?" She inspected me.

"Positive." I gave her a sweet smile.

"But it's so..." she started.

"Bloody Hell, Jayne Frost, do you want me to sign a declaration with my own blood?!" I interrupted her, snorting.

She seemed to be studying me for a bit, then whispered without looking at me, "That's not my real name."

I nodded, I had suspected that too. "What is it then?"

"Vivi Hope Grimm. Vivi."

"That's a horrible name." I nodded, teasing her.

"Oh yeah, and William Black is better?" she asked all smiley.

"So, so much better," I mouthed and smiled back at her.

Staring at her red cherry lips, I couldn't resist the temptation to lean and kiss her. How much had I desired to do it again?

Jayne-Vivi was the first to interrupt the contact, she kept her eyes closed and spoke softly. "This is technically not a coffee."

"You're just as delicious." I smiled amused. Then brushed a loose strand of hair behind her ear thoughtfully. "You're my privilege and my damnation."

She grinned, opening her eyes to look at me brightly. "I have no idea what that means but... you too."

"So tell me more about your abilities," I encouraged her after a few moments, I was curious. "Like can you teleport? Read minds? See the future?"

Vivi chuckled. "None of them. I've never learnt to teleport, it is very dangerous. If you don't focus or train correctly you could move just half of your body and stuff like that, definitely too scary for me. I know loads of people who have lost limbs because of it."

I almost flinched.

"Read minds? It's not something you can do that lightly, the human mind is insurmountable, it takes years and years of constant training, and the other person must give permission or have a weak will. I think the last person able to do that, a Reader – as they are called – died a few years ago. He was a friend of my father's, he always said that it was a dangerous ability, you could get lost and stay anchored to someone's mind for eternity," she continued.

"Do not expect my permission to stroll in my mind," I warned her.

She giggled. "I couldn't, I'm not trained for that and anyways, who would want to see around your peanut sized brain?"

I pushed her in to the sand as a punishment. "What about the future readers?"

"As in for seeing the future, it's an ability you're born with, it's not something you learn, you either have it or not. And I'm glad I don't, it's a great responsibility, you constantly need to make sure you don't interfere with someone's future," she explained.

Something snapped in place inside my mind, I remembered about the first time I went to her house, I recalled the odd sensations I'd felt when that bizarre woman had touched my hand.

"Your aunt has this gift, doesn't she?" I asked curious. Then remembered she had like three aunts so I had to be more specific, "The little hippy one."

"My Aunt Sybil is a Seer, yes, the ability's in the family but it skips a few generations usually." She nodded surprised, probably wondering how I'd guessed it right.

"When I went to your house for the first time, Sybil was very nice, she introduced herself and shook my hand… I think I felt it then, I felt odd but I knew she'd done something. And the other woman, Maisa told her off, she said she wasn't allowed to interfere," I remembered.

"Interfere with what?" Her eyebrows narrowed. "Anyways, well done. Very clever of you to click everything in place." She looked quite impressed. "Only strong personalities feel when she reads them," she explained.

"I *am* clever," I gloated, "but how does it work?" I asked curious.

"She has to touch your skin, she says that with relatives the images are clear and vivid, but with strangers it's like a blur sometimes. Every detail is very important to understand."

"She shook my hand." I nodded.

"Sybil saw your whole life then, to your dying day." I must have made a face because she giggled. She can't reveal anything important though, don't you even try. It's a waste of energy. Seers cannot say things that might change the course of the events," she clarified before I could ask.

"Then what's the point in even seeing the future?" I asked a bit annoyed. She shrugged.

Having all that power and not being able to use it to change people's lives for the better, I thought it was very selfish.

"Do you want to see what I can do?" Vivi asked me enthusiastically after a few moments of silence.

"Surprise me." I half smiled to her.

"Brace yourself." She grinned.

Vivi pointed high above and from her fingers, like bullets, colourful fireworks were shot in the grey sky, then she started drawing circles with her finger; the sand around them swirled around us like a hurricane. As her closing number, she snapped her fingers and two big bowls of ice cream appeared in front of us.

"You almost impressed me." I smiled. "What about those?" I asked with a risen eyebrow.

"I'm famished." She chuckled and tried one of the bowl's contents.

You're unique.

"So magic really does exist. All the folklore, the legends...," I asserted after a few minutes of silence.

"Apparently," she just commented.

"What about all the other creatures? Like werewolves, vampires, fairies, zombies and stuff?" I asked curious.

"All real," she nodded, "except for zombies, I'm pretty sure that is just fantasy."

"How are you a witch? Like how can you have magic and stuff?"

"I come from a dynasty of witches and warlocks, I was born with it. It's my heritance." She shrugged. "I see you Googled it." She smiled amused just to ease the tension.

"I had to know, but you can't find much on there."

"Well, do you think we are stupid enough to write the truth about us and our secrets on the Internet? For anyone to know." She seemed amused.

Yeah, fair enough.

"How did you manage to disappear that night at the bar? You said you can't teleport," I remembered.

"I just caused a little explosion of glass, then quickly ran away. No need for teleporting, I'm a fast runner." She winked, still enjoying her ice cream.

"What about the bartender? He didn't even remember about you," I pointed out.

"I might have altered his memory a bit," she declared all innocent.

"But you said you couldn't control people's minds." My eyebrows were narrowed.

"I can't indeed, it's just a little emergency spell we use sometimes," she explained, "it only works on a few people at time. It's just in case of immediate danger."

"Danger? I wouldn't have done anything you wouldn't have liked." I smiled lustfully just for the pleasure of seeing her blush. "Oh dear! You look like a tomato right now." I couldn't resist but tease her.

"Shut it!" She avoided looking at my face.

I never knew she was so prudish.

"After a bit, you would have begged me to continue. I must admit it, I overdid it just for fun."

Vivi glared at me. You know, we don't need to be Aunt Sybil to know what happens if you don't stop laughing at me. She showed her tongue.

"You would have loved it." I winked at her, increasing her embarrassment.

"You wish. You're just an arrogant piece of..."

"For someone who lies a lot, you're the worst liar sometimes," I commented, interrupting her.

"Moron."

Then I realized something, she said the spell worked on a few *people* at the time...

"I was supposed to forget about you too." My words sounded as astonished as I was.

"Yes." She blushed.

"But it didn't work on me. Why?"

She studied me for a long moment. "I really don't know."

That was a mystery I was determined to uncover. But not now.

She was there with me, and I couldn't ask for anything better.

I smiled broadly at her. "Pass me your phone."

"Why?" she asked astonished by the bizarre request.

"I need to call George, so he can pick us up," I explained. "I'm starting to be cold here."

"Use yours then," she said like it was the easiest answer.

"I can't, I smashed my phone," I explained slowly like she was thick. "Long story." I smiled.

I wasn't ready to admit how much I'd needed to hear from her.

She nodded and gave me her cell.

George said he would pick us up shortly. I noticed she was a bit disappointed about leaving. I smiled and promised her to bring her back the day after.

We got in the car quietly, I held her hand tight for the whole trip, like I was scared that if I let go, she would just disappear into thin air.

When we arrived in front of her house, she looked a bit embarrassed and uncertain of what to do.

"You should just give me a kiss and wish me and George goodnight." I smiled at her, half teasing her.

"Don't you guys... well, don't you want to come in?"

"Maybe next time, it's late now. I will pick you up tomorrow around four." She nodded and did as I'd suggested.

We watched her open the front door and, after a last glimpse back, close it again.

"If I may say my opinion, she seems like a nice girl, Master William," George commented.

"She's amazing." I nodded.

"Now you just need to find a way to tell your father about her."

Oh yeah, that...

"My father is not entitled any power over my life, he's never even been home."

"I don't reckon he'll agree with that, unfortunately."

"I shall deal with him soon," I decided.

The butler nodded and drove off without saying another word. I thought that yes, I would have a tough nut to crack with dear daddy.

But I would have thought of it tomorrow, for now I just wanted to enjoy my moment of glory. And happiness.

SOULMATES

Jayne.

As soon as I'd closed the door that night, Aunt Sybil had trapped me in a bone smashing hug. Incredible how someone so little could hide so much strength.

"I can't breathe," I begged and was released.

"I'm so happy for you, girl!" she trilled.

"It's not like I won the jackpot or something." I giggled cheerfully.

"Even better, honey, better. He's an angel."

I literally just laughed at her face, even though William looked like one, he was more of a nice and funny devil than anything else. *An angel... him... pff.*

"Sweetheart," Maisa was standing not too far away from us, her face a weird mix of happiness and worry, I thought that only that woman could pull that expression, "are you sure about this?"

"I like him, Aunt. I really do." I smiled shy. I was a bit embarrassed to admit such a thing.

"Have you told him *everything*?" she asked inquisitively.

I almost flinched, but before I could say anything, Sybil answered for me. "Maisa, stop being boring! Just be pleased for our niece's happiness!" She snorted.

"I am, really. I just want her to be aware that..." the woman started.

But Sybil interrupted her. "Just shut it, Maisa, really. Enjoy the moment, will you?" She smiled

and the tall woman twitched her lips to hide her own smile.

"Fine." She nodded. "He's so *very* hot, kid! If only I was a few decades younger..."

"Auntie!" I cried out laughing.

It was not so unusual that my aunt would comment about someone like that, she always did it when it came to the plumber. And the milkman. And the shop assistant at the bakery.

156

Which was weird because she was always going out with not-so-good looking men.

"What? I thought you wanted me to be happy! I'm *delighted* you've found such a hottie!" She laughed.

"Finally! I will get the Prosecco out!" Sybil trilled.

"There's no need! Come on." My eyes were wide with surprise.

"Do not ruin my happiness, Vivi!" she threatened.

I raised my hands in a gesture of surrender. "Fine, but you must know it goes straight to my head!"

"We'll take that chance!" She laughed and disappeared into the kitchen. She came back a few moments later with a chilled bottle and three glasses.

We drank and laughed for the rest of the evening, I must have drunk a glass too much as when I got to bed I felt light-headed like I hadn't felt in a very long time.

Looking forward to tomorrow.

I thought of William before falling asleep. Of how he'd always found a way back to me, of how we both always ended up finding each other again, no matter how far we'd both pulled the strings. I clutched my pillow tight wishing it was him.

I woke up early with my head pounding; I could have killed my aunts for making me have that sparkling wine.

I dragged myself downstairs with more effort than I dared to admit. No one was in the kitchen, they must have been still sleeping, those lazy two.

I decided I was happy enough to make breakfast for everyone, a good breakfast was the cure for hangovers, or so I'd heard.

When scrambled eggs, sausages, bacon and beans were ready, and the bread was toasted, I put everything on the plates and brought them upstairs.

Sybil had thrown a pillow to me to kick me out. She shouted I should let her sleep a bit more, *very ungrateful*.

Maisa hadn't even responded, sleeping so heavily that, for a second, I had wondered if she was still alive. I actually had to check her pulse just to make sure.

Sitting on the table alone, bored, I paid attention to the newspaper.

During the years, I'd learnt how to distinguish natural causes of death of people and the supernatural ones.

A particular article caught my attention:

Death again in Edinburgh, Scotland. It had all the characteristics of the same serial killer, as a woman had been burnt to ashes.

The police hadn't yet identified the victim but she seemed to be middle-aged, judging by the clothes that had been found a few feet from her ashes.

Investigators asserted that she'd probably been raped before being burnt and murdered.

"He seems to be an international murderer, his previous victims had been all over the places," Captain of Police Shawn had declared. For now, the police invite everyone to exercise extreme caution."

My appetite suddenly vanished, it couldn't be possible...

It can't be him.

Just breathe in and out.

It's fine.

After I cleaned my own plate, I had a shower and felt like new, but I kept on thinking about that murderer.

Quit it, relax. You're seeing William later on, you don't want him to see you upset over a newspaper's article.

The rest of the afternoon went smoothly, I cleaned my room and the house a bit, I also read a few pages of my favourite book, always checking the time on the kitchen clock impatiently.

At four o'clock, I was ready.

I left my hair down for a change, I wore my favourite lucky jeans, a black tank top and my father's old leather jacket.

When the door bell rang, I literally ran downstairs and sprang it open with a radiant smile. I greeted him.

"Were you behind the door?" One of his eyebrows rose.

"Of course not!" I started pushing him out.

"Why don't you want me to come in? Do you think I could scare your aunts?" he teased me.

"They are frightening at the moment, they are hung-over." I smiled.

"Big party last night? Is it because of me?" He looked at me from tip to toe, probably checking if I was in the same situation too.

Do not think too highly of yourself, pal.

Are you not utterly right?

"They were happy I didn't leave for the USA," I replied cryptically.

I just could not admit all the raving from last night was because of him. Ever.

It would have sounded so pathetic, I blushed a bit at the thought.

"What's up?" he asked me inquisitively, noticing the colour change.

"I was thinking about the party, nothing important." I smiled. I always had been a bad liar.

"Let's say I believe you." He gave me one of his crazy-beautiful smiles and I almost melted.

How could he be so handsome? It must have been some kind of spell his mother cast on him, some magic I didn't know about.

Suddenly, I was hit on my harm by something metallic; the dinging sound of keys falling to the floor.

I cast a puzzled look at him, he just smiled, his grey eyes lit with amusement. "You're driving today, my dear little Alice in Wonderland, so you can stop daydreaming about me a bit."

To my credit, I can say I kept my poker face, collected the keys from the floor and walked like a queen to the driver's seat.

After hearing the roaring of the engine, I remembered a teeny tiny detail. "I've never driven here in the UK."

"You do have a driving license, don't you?"

"Of course I do," I snarled.

"Then I'm sure we'll be fine." The fact that he fastened his own seatbelt really tight, showed me just the opposite.

I smiled, he wasn't the only one who knew how play.

If he was the Devil, then I was a witch. And they are not less dangerous.

I started driving deliberately badly, watching him paling and holding everything that could be held tight in his grip. Saying that he was terrified was euphemistic.

"All good there, baby?" I smirked in his direction.

"Yes!" He was too proud to even admit what he was truly feeling. The fear he was experiencing while I was driving European style, on the left, dodging other cars just for pure luck... well, it was hilarious to watch.

"Vivi, you're driving on the wrong side of the road, for Heaven's sake!" he shouted at some point, trying to hide his frustration.

"Sorry." *Sorry not sorry.*

"Stop the car, Grimm. Now!" he ordered and, after checking there were no cars behind us, I pushed the brake all of a sudden, just there in the middle of the street.

Needless to say, he almost jumped out of his skin, maybe only the fastened seatbelt had prevented that.

"Just go and park there, Ghost Rider!" He was almost panting. I complied.

I smiled, the great William Black frightened of a stupid car.

"Are you okay?" I asked with a saccharine voice.

He glared at me. *If looks could kill...*

"Where the heck have you learnt how to drive?!"

"And here I thought you were after great emotions, passions and living on the edge," I mocked relentlessly. "Did I scare you?" I gave him the sweetest smile in my arsenal.

William studied me for a couple of seconds, then looked down at his feet and appeared to be sad, his features darkened. The arrogance and fear in his face were gone, he actually looked like he was indeed about... To burst out in tears.

"What the...," I breathed, "what's wrong?"

"My sister died in a car accident last year," he whispered, his voice feeble and broken.

Fuck. Fuck. Fuck. Fuck.

"I... I'm so... I'm sorry, William."

I thought of anything else, anything that could ease his pain, anything that might shake him from this damage I'd done.

"It's..." He hid his face between his hands.

Holy Merlin Father of all magic! He was actually sobbing.

And I felt like a little drop of dirty mud, why did I always have to be this stupid?

With a trembling hand I tried to soothe him by caressing his hair, whispering my apologies over and over. I then tried to remove his hands from his magnificent face, ready to confront his tears, the consequences of my silliness but... what I saw was nothing even close to weeping.

The bastard was laughing himself hoarse.

"You son of a— how dare you?!?" I pinched at his arm with all my strength.

He still looked like he was about to split his sides laughing. "Your face, Vivi. Honestly, girl, you should have seen your expression!"

"You're the worst piece of shit I've ever met," I mouthed, offended.

How could I have let him play me like that?!

Perhaps I was wrong, *this* Devil would always be a step ahead.

"I must have some sort of problem if I still want to kiss that foul mouth of yours." He smiled and leaned in to kiss me softly. "Ouch, you little viper!" He cleaned the drop of blood that my biting caused.

I bared my teeth at him, just so he could be aware of the danger.

"That's called revenge," I muttered.

"Oh, don't try and teach me about revenge, I've got a percentage of Italian blood in my veins." He smiled.

"Really?" That was new.

"Yes, my granma, my mother's mother, was Italian. Beautiful, passionate and heated like I imagine all Italian women to be. My father never liked her, he hardly ever allowed her to spend time with me. She trusted people too easily, her temper and Latin blood seemed to clash with the plans he had for me." His now darker eyes stared at something I couldn't see out of the car window, his mind lost in memories. "'Passion and hot blood will never take you far. Cunning and cold blood will, they are your allies,'" he mimicked what I guess his parent sounded like. "She died when I was eight, he didn't seem too grieve her too much." William finished his story.

And for a moment, I felt less alone, he too had his share of pain, once again I recognized that his life wasn't as perfect as it looked like.

I took his hand in mine, hoping that touch would express what I couldn't say with words. That he didn't have to face the world alone anymore, I was there ready to share the weight of it with him.

What about my own burden? Was I ready to share it with him?
Would it even be fair to do so?

"Where's your mind drifting to at the moment?" he asked after a few seconds of silence, and I wondered if he needed distraction from the dark corner of his memories, if talking or thinking about his own father was like hitting a nerve.

"I'm thinking that I'm lucky I have you and neither one of us has to be alone any longer." Close enough to the truth.

William seemed to grin from ear to ear while saying softly, "Yes, you are lucky."

I decided I would give it another shot at my driving, this time I promised him I wouldn't *"deliberately try to get us both killed"*, and after the first twenty minutes of him shouting commands at me, it went well, almost smooth.

I drove into the city and in the countryside for hours; we stayed silent for almost the whole time, his hand on mine, tight, drawing lazy circles on my jeans.

Just his presence, his being there with me, was like a balm calming all my worries.

My problems, my life didn't seem so bad and complicated, just as long as he was there with me.

And that worried me. A lot.

I realized I needed him more than he would ever need me. Ever.

That I was just entangling him into a web of danger and lying and... running.

And I was just being selfish. I was a piece of filthy rubbish for doing this to him.

"What's with that worried expression?" He woke me up from my cogitations.

I looked at him for a moment, and I thought I didn't deserve the concern written into his light grey eyes, so light it meant he was in a good mood. I stared back at the road, shuddering.

I thought I had to tell him, sooner rather than later.

"I wanna take you out for dinner," he blurted out after a bit, "like on a real date. You'll have to wear a nice little dress that will leave my mouth dry when I see it, I will have to focus not to look down at your boobs while consuming our dinner in a pretty restaurant you've never been before." He was looking at me expectedly, smiling at my heated cheeks at the mention of my boobs. "I will wear a tie and you'll think once more how lucky you are and how amazingly handsome I look."

"And also how modest."

"Hey, don't ruin my fantasy of our perfect date."

"I'm sorry, Barbie. Please, do continue." I smirked.

He elegantly ignored my comment. "Like a true gentleman I will gallantly invite you to dance with me, kindly ignoring your almost-permanent stepping on my feet." I suppressed a chuckle. Now *that* was likely to happen. "You'll kiss me and ask me softly to take you to a quieter place. I will take you to our official place and I will oblige to your request to make love to you all night long."

The steering wheel just slipped from my hands, the car veering suddenly before I gained control of it again, I could feel his burning eyes on me. My heart throbbing.

"You wish," I just managed to mumble.

He was studying me, and if he understood why I was so embarrassed I will never know.

Luckily his phone started ringing and he had to pick it up.

Saved by the bell.

William just listened without saying a word to what, whoever had rung his cell, had to say on the other side. In the light of the sunset I noticed his eyes darken, the amusement gone from them.

"I'm on my way," he just said and hung up the phone.

"What's wrong?" My voice filled with worry; it was rare to see him upset.

It did last a few moments, then he wore his best poker face and turned to me. "There are some problems at the manor, I got to run back." There was no emotion in his voice.

"Is everything alright?" I dared ask.

William looked at me, no, studied me like I was some rare creature strolling around, deciding whether to trust me with whatever had happened or not, then he gave a half smile that didn't meet his now dark grey eyes. "It'll be fine."

Perhaps he needed to hear it himself, maybe he had to say it and believe it. Perhaps he was not yet ready to open his heart fully to me, and that, *that* hurt like hell. But I nodded.

I drove back to my house and with a sweet kiss to his cheek, I headed to my front door.

No complaints for the chaste kiss I gave him, no words of goodbye.

Some crap must be really hitting the fan in his house in that moment.

When I went upstairs to my room, I debated texting him or not, then pride won.

I went to turn off my own phone but then left it on, I fell asleep looking at its screen.

Waiting.

DATE NIGHT

William.

I texted her early in the morning. The way I left her, I could feel her disappointment; it left a sour taste in my mouth that I couldn't quite explain.

When the doctor had called saying that my mother had had another of her crises, I went crazy and I wanted to shout and let it all out but I couldn't. She had been there, I wouldn't have let her see the beast inside of me. I had vowed to protect her from the darkness that lurked in my heart. In my life.

How can you even tell your girlfriend that your own mother is a drug addicted attention seeker?

How can you explain years of watching her helplessly consuming herself like that?

Lowering herself to be a slave of that shit.

And when she'd asked what was wrong, I hadn't had the heart to spill my beans. To tell her how screwed up my family was, and always had been. How screwed up I was. My family was a family of addictions, my grandfather to money, my mother to narcotics, my father was addicted by his job and his many younger lovers.

And I felt that sword of Damocles upon my head; would I be addicted to something too one day? Did it run in our blood?

The beep of my phone distracted me, her witty reply made me smile; she'd always had that power.

I'd sent her a message about tonight, that I would pick her up at seven and the requirement was to wear a nice little dress that would help me fantasize the whole evening about the after.

Her only answer was: *Dream on, pig!*

I didn't count on it, on wasting our first night together like that, I just enjoyed getting on her nerves so much.

In all fairness, I wanted to wait and make it special because I was almost certain that our first time… would be *her* first time too.

I had understood it yesterday, when she reacted that way at my mentioning of the night together, her blushing and the pure panic on her face.

And I had gloated like a peacock when I had realized the reason. No one had touched her before, no man had seen her hot and excited for him, no one had discovered that treasure that felt like it was mine alone.

If I closed my eyes I could imagine her in my bed, naked calling my name, begging me to make her completely mine, in every possible way.

Something awoke in me and I headed for a freezing cold shower.

But before that, I quickly texted her back: *can't wait to meet you in one of those dreams.*

I knew I shouldn't be telling her that, but hell, I loved the way she got so embarrassed at the mere mention of it, I just couldn't resist it.

My lustful smile died as soon as the cold water worked its magic on me.

Exactly at twenty past seven, I had to fight the impulse of texting her again, she was late as usual.

I debated getting out of the car and go and get her. The only thing that kept me from doing so was the thought of seeing her half naked, I didn't know if I could have such self-control not to jump on her like a dog.

I was only human after all.

And she – she was temptation and fire embodied.

I opened the car window, the cool English air on my face, I closed my eyes and breathed, tonight it wasn't about passion but about showing her that our life could be normal, that we could simply be happy.

Tonight it wasn't about the rich heir of a great fortune. Or about the misunderstood witch.

It was just us, William and Vivi. Nothing else.

And I decided to show her that I was to be trusted, that I was there for her not just because I wanted her but because this little eerie girl had made a revolution in my soul. In my heart.

She was my personal hurricane.

And Vivi had always desired normalcy so that's what I was to give her tonight.

A nice normal date.

I heard the front door opening and closing, I turned and if I hadn't had my pride and self-control... I would have gaped in wonder.

The girl, *my girl* looked absolutely breathtaking.

She was wearing a knee-long strapless dark green dress, the slim fit of it highlighted her generous curves, her hair was unbound, soft chestnut curls were falling on her back.

I realised it was the same dress she'd tried on when I met her at that shop.Then and now, there were no words to describe her, she looked *magic*.

As soon as she opened the car door and jumped in, she gave me a luminous smile. "Hello, stranger," she greeted. "Is my dress mouth watering enough for your taste?"

"So far you're playing your role right," I simply said 'cause I knew if I had tried to describe how she looked, I would have made a fool out of myself probably.

She didn't look too impressed by my comment, I half smiled and turned on the engine.

"So how are things at home?" she tried after a bit.

Are you asking me about my absent father or drug addicted mother, babe?

"All good."

"Yesterday..." She tried to push me.

And I knew she didn't do it out of curiosity or to have some succulent gossip, but I simply did not want to ruin our date night talking about my screwed up parentado.

She deserved better than that.

"Look, I know you want me to share my chagrins and all, but I'm not ready. I can't..." *show you that side of me yet.*

Not tonight.

"What are you afraid of?" she asked me, searching for my eyes, but I kept them on the street in front of me.

"I'm not much of a sharer," I muttered.

"Bull," she breathed and took my hand in hers, holding me tight. "I showed you my dark sides and for some reason, you didn't run away. Whenever you'll feel comfortable enough, I will be all ears."

"Tonight's not about me or my problems," I turned to her, "tonight's all about us and how beautiful you look."

I'll admit it, it was a cheap attempt to change the subject, to avoid the topic but she let me do it, maybe she understood my need to drop it.

She smiled and almost purred, "Thank you." Then her face became serious. "There's something we need to talk about," she said after a few moments.

Was she going to tell me that she was still a virgin? Was that the reason why she wasn't looking into my eyes now?

"Everything you want, girl. Wanna just wait to be in front of a glass of wine?" I winked and she smiled a bit.

"We aren't the age to drink."

"I can do whatever I want, boring pants. And you can tag along just 'cause I like you." I gave her one of my most charming smiles.

She chuckled, still a bit nervous. "I'm not boring!"

"Show me then."

"How?"

"Tonight is 'crazy night', you do the opposite every time your mind tells you to act in a certain way." I looked at her, she wasn't convinced.

"You just want to take advantage of me at the end of the night, that's your plan." She laughed, indignation written all over her face.

I smirked at her. "You're just scared."

"Of course I am!" she busted out.

I laughed. "Don't be, I will be there to catch you if you fall" I swore I would.

Vivi looked at me, her eyes were almost heart shaped. "That might be the most romantic thing you've ever told me." She giggled.

"Don't get used to it," I blurted.

I parked the car and we walked to the restaurant, it was in the countryside, an old little castle now made into a five star restaurant.

I took her hand out of habit, it was amazing how easily I got so used I got to this little routine. How used I got to her presence in so little time.

When we walked in, we were welcomed by an elegant waiter in a suit who walked us to our table. I studied the girl beside me; she looked like a child in wonderland.

Her light green eyes weren't missing any detail of that place she seemed to like a lot. "What do you think?" I asked, observing her and the surroundings as well. The golden walls, the ancient windows, all lit by the light of candles.

A big wall screen stood above what looked like a throne, showing videos of couples dancing other centuries' dances.

"This looks like a fairytale place!" She giggled enthusiastically.

"I knew you'd like it." I half smiled.

As soon as we sat down, the waiter brought us a bottle of white sparkling wine which was quickly served in our flutes.

She looked at me, ready to bring her point up again.

I sighed and remembered. "It's not even illegal for you to drink anymore, you're eighteen now," I reminded her while sipping my wine.

Vivi looked at me like I'd just kicked her guts and she nodded thoughtful. "You're right," she said flatly.

What was wrong with her now?

"William, there's something I need to tell you." She wasn't looking at me.

"I know you're a virgin, it's fine, I will wait all the time that you need. There's no rush," I said soothingly. I'd tried to speak like I was trying to calm a wild animal down.

It looked like someone had punched her in the stomach, she blushed and sweated. Comparing her to a sinner in church would be certainly reductive.

"I..." she started.

"It's fine, it's not a big deal." I was being honest.

"How did you..?"

"Whatever God there is, apparently not only he gifted me with the most handsome face and attractive body, he had to over-do it and give me the most brilliant brain." I smiled from ear to ear to prove my point.

I watched her chuckle nervously and torture her own hands. She didn't crack a joke as an answer. The fact that she wasn't being sarcastic meant she must have been really nervous. I put one of my hands over hers to try and soothe her mood, they were so cold.

"It's fine, honestly. I can wait as long as you want me to," I assured her.

For her I would have done it, I would have jumped off a cliff for this girl.

"I very much appreciate that," she smiled, "but it's not what I wanted to talk about."

Right, it had to be something big to make her act like that, or not?

"There's something I haven't told you, I" She was interrupt-ed by a familiar voice, we all turned around.

A different video from the dancers appeared there, it was the hall in school and Alex and Vivi were in it.

"Go, run to that lousy family of freaks you got! But remember, you'll all get what you deserve. Watch your own and their backs, Freak."

"You do not speak about my family. Ever."

Everyone in the video looked utterly terrified by her, even the blonde girl in front of her.

"Her hands..." someone whispered scared.

The camera shot her hands, where blue sparkles were com-ing out. Her chestnut hair was floating around her head and her eyes went pitch black for a few moments.

I remembered that episode, it was that day in school when she got kicked out and provoked by that Alex girl.

Who'd shot that video?

But, more importantly, who was playing it for the whole res-taurant to see?

Cold rage built up on me, I was going to carve up whoever had dared do such a thing, I rose and the video stopped.

The place was silent, people not understanding what on earth was going on, if it was a clip from a movie or what. But the main actress was there, sitting at my table, looking pale as a ghost and about to burst into tears.

With the corner of my eye, I saw something moving, someone was leaving the restaurant by the emergency exit door and I thought that shape was too familiar. I followed it.

"Benson, I didn't think you'd really be this stupid to do something like that." My voice was as glacial as the iceberg that sunk the Titanic. Just as I was about to take him down.

He turned slowly with a grin. "People have a right to know, that's why I'd called it 'freak witch in Angel Falling, UK'…needless to say it was a hit on YouTube."

Half of a sob, I turned, I was so blinded by my anger, I hadn't noticed the girl had followed me out.

"Do you have any idea of what you've done?" she asked horrified, her beautiful eyes full of tears and… was it fear that I saw now?

And all I knew was that I was going to hurt him really bad and I was going to take my sweet time in doing so.

Her frightened expression.

The tears streaming down her cheeks.

I saw red.

"*I do* know what he's done, he's signed his death sentence!" As soon as I'd finished my sentence I knew, *I knew* I could have killed him easily and I couldn't wait to do so.

I didn't care about the consequences, jail would have been like jam afterwards.

So I threw the first jab at his nose, my hand already bloody with his blood and my own, I charged again and again, taking blows too. But I couldn't feel pain, adrenaline flowing in my veins.

We ended up on the floor. I hit his nose again and felt the bone cracking under my knuckles. He screamed in pain but I didn't care, I wasn't me; I was an animal, the beast inside me was now free to roar its rage. And I enjoyed every second of it.

I punched his jaw and kicked his ribs, he elbowed my eye and I felt the pain of my skin tearing apart, blood blinding me and my head annoyingly whistling but I didn't care.

I was a shark, and I would have continued to tear this bastard apart with my last breath.

I went on to charge another punch, ready to hit his mouth so maybe this time I would have shut that foul hole who insulted my girl in so many ways for good, when like pushed by an invisible wall, we were both separated and immobilized.

I struggled, not understanding what had just happened. The only thing I wanted right now was to keep on avenging her, to keep on feeling the cracking of his filthy bones under my blows.

I wanted his blood on my hands.

"Enough." Vivi was standing just between us, keeping us in place with each of her palms towards one of us and I understood she was using magic.

"Let me go," I almost barked. The need to hit and hurt was still alive in me, the beast screaming in rage.

"I need to go home," she pleaded, "please, William. I've got to go home." There was something in her voice, in her eyes that calmed me down. All my homicidal madness melted like snow under the sun.

The blind anger turned into worry. I nodded and rose from the dirty floor, only noticing then the people around us, all of them utterly afraid. I heard the sound of police cars coming closer and closer.

I took her hand in mine and I started rushing to the car.

I could only see from one eye but she seemed to be too upset to drive, so I did. Praying that my other eye would be good enough to see in the dark.

She hadn't said a word for the whole trip.

I struggled to find some words, whatever I could to break the ice she seemed to be made of at the moment, but I couldn't so I opened my mouth and shut it again a few times.

How could I explain that I would seriously go to Hell and back for her?

That she had to trust me to fix everything… when she saw the beast inside of me?

My heart skipped a beat, did I scare her off?

Was that why she was now silently sobbing?

I stopped in front of her house, it was only then that she spoke. "You should go to a hospital."

Only then did I remember about the pain in my eye, my bloody knuckles were numb and full of cuts and bruises, my lips sore.

"I'm fine," I said confidently. "What's wrong?" I asked after a long pause.

Her facial expression, I will never forget it and her voice as she said, "I need to leave."

"Go home, get some sleep…" I started.

"No, you don't understand. I need to leave town, I have to disappear."

What?

"What?"

Her beautiful face was as pale as a ghost and as spooked. "You-Tube… he wrote my location, he…"

"Everyone knows about your power anyways and we can say that it was edited with a computer and…" It was fixable, I would have paid millions if I had to. Just to give her some peace of mind again. And then, I would have finished dealing with the bastard who'd done this. Softly.

She started sobbing, banging her head against the car window in frustration. "Just now that I felt … he'll find me … I … I can't stay … It's … I'm eighteen and … he … I need to leave."

"Stop it!" I tried to grab her shoulders but in a swift moment, she opened the car door and slipped out, falling on her knees.

Weeping.

"Vivi?" I got out of the car, got to her but she gestured me to stay away. "Vivi, please. What's going on?" I tried but no answer arrived.

The sound of a thunder, and suddenly it started pouring down, but still she wouldn't move.

She was shaking violently, her already wet hair covering her face, her hands flat on the floor.

And I felt powerless once again as I didn't know what to do or say. "Please." I quietly reached her, took her in my arms with a quick movement.

She held me like I was the only solid thing, like I was an anchor, the only thing that could prevent her for going adrift.

"It's okay," I whispered in her ear, "It's gonna be fine, baby." I kissed her wet head, she kept on sobbing.

She felt so fragile in my arms, so little and undefended, the sour taste of anger hit me again. Just let me find that Benson and not even his mother would be able to recognize him once I finished with him.

"Vivi?" I tried. "Vivi, please talk to me."

She was shaking her head, hiding herself in that spot between my neck and shoulder. "Please, I can't help you if I don't know what's going on." Nothing. "It really kills me to see you like this," I confessed and she rose her red swollen eyes to look at me.

"I'm... I'm sorry," she whispered, trying to dry her eyes.

"It's okay, it's okay. Just tell me what's wrong," I almost begged.

"I need to do it again, start over. Find a faraway place, change my name and..." She started weeping silently again.

"No, you don't have to. I have money, money can fix this whole mess in a second, Vivi. It will be like it never happened."

Vivi probably didn't know the power of *dinero*, but I did. I was ready to show her.

"No. No. You don't get it, I have to leave. If I wanna live, I have to flee."

"What?! Why?!"

"He's looking for me."

I was certain I didn't want to know the answer, I felt like in my heart I knew it already. "Who?"

"The man who killed my mother."

And I reckon, if someone had stabbed me in the heart there and then, I would have felt less pain.

GIUING UP ON MY PAST

I tried to collect as much stuff as I could, as quickly as possible; I couldn't waste a second, I had to get to her sooner rather than later.

After that revelation, after she'd told me that some psychopath was chasing her for some reason, she hadn't had the time to specify, I decided I would follow her to the moon and back if I had to. I wouldn't let her go.

When I told her I would go with her, she'd started screaming that I was being insane, that she couldn't get me involved me in this mess, that she'd lived her whole life "with shit up to her knees" and it was her own crap to face alone.

She hadn't understood, she hadn't known that I was already in too deep to let her go alone.

She'd been so naïve to think I would leave her that easily.

We'd discussed, she'd shouted that I was just wasting her time, she needed to pack everything and flee, but I told her she was never to run away on her own again.

I had to threaten her in the end, in order to make her agree for me to go with her. *"I will go gather some money to leave with you, I will return in a few hours. If when I come back and you're gone, I will go around, publish everywhere on the Internet, call the press to say that my girlfriend's name is Vivi Grimm and whoever is looking for her better get himself known to me personally."*

She had paled even more if possible, she'd started to cry and shout and even plead for me to stay safe, that *he* was dangerous, but she had to agree in the end. I was not going to change my mind about that.

She was my soulmate, I would have never let her separate from me.

"Do you even know what that means? What you'd be putting yourself into?" she'd asked.

"I'm coming with you," I'd said without a doubt.

"You'd be giving up on your life, on your family. You'd need to be on the run forever, I can't ask you that, the price is too high!"

"I am coming with you," I simply had said and headed to the car to go and pack my things.

Now, the question was: *what stuff would you pack and bring with you if you don't know where you're heading to?*

I opted for all kind of clothes, I was going to bring money anyways, so buying new stuff was not a problem.

A knock at my door almost startled me. I checked my watch, it was past midnight, who'd want to see me at this time at night?

Without waiting for my permission to enter, a tall man came in. I gazed at him almost in shock.

I hadn't seen him in over a year.

He was wearing a grey suit with a red tie, in one of this hands a small briefcase, his black hair perfect and neatly styled on his head, his light blue severe eyes were staring into mine.

"Father."

"William," he greeted me formally.

"To what do I owe the pleasure of seeing you after..." I pretended I counted on my fingers. It was just for show, I knew exactly how long it'd been, "...one year of absence?"

Stop it, William. You have no time for this, you need to pack and go to her.

"It's a pleasure to see you too, son." He observed me. "What happened to your face?"

By instinct, I looked at myself in the mirror, my reflection showed a face that was red and swollen, with bits of green and purple bruises. My left eye was huge and completely shut, all the dry blood around it. Shit, I forgot about that.

Not that I cared about what he could say, he certainly wouldn't start being a concerned parent just tonight.

"What are you doing here?" I turned to him again.

He smiled, maybe he'd remembered how I was, no roundabout talk, maybe he was like that too. I didn't know, I never got the chance to get to know him.

"I heard news in the wind. I heard you're being seen with in-appropriate people."

"Are you talking about my girlfriend?" I blurted out. I re-marked the word *girlfriend*, just to make a statement.

I was not going to back off.

I knew this was coming, I just didn't have time for it now. Vivi's life depended on it.

"Yes, I've seen videos and gathered some information about her." He entered the room and closed the door behind him, this was going to take a while.

"You unleashed your dogs to get information on her." My indignation didn't know an end.

"My trusted private investigators told me a rather bloodcur-dling story about her."

"So what's your point?" Useless to deny it , he probably had already seen the video.

"I want you to stop seeing her," he said simply.

"You're insane." My knuckles hurt as I clenched the bag I was holding tightly. "So you think you can do whatever you want, never be present in my life and then all of a sudden start giving me orders?!"

"I'm your father," he rattled off calmly.

"Are you?! Where have you been all my life?!" I shouted at him. "Where have you been for my birthdays, my soccer games, when Mum was having fits and drugs? Where the fuck have you hidden?!" I smirked. "Or are you only my father when it's con-venient for you? When a scandal could ruin your dearest polit-ical career?"

He didn't so much as blinked at my rage. "You'll quit seeing her or I shall disinherit you, no more money or power, I will block all your cards. You won't be my son anymore."

Fair game, Father.

But you have no idea how much I'm willing to sacrifice for her.

I shuddered. "I've always thought poverty would suit me bet-ter than being your heir does." I continued packing, a clear dis-missal for him.

His cold expression now showed pure rage. "What are you doing?"

He most certainly wasn't used to be dismissed like that.

"I'm leaving this shithole you call a city, if you really wanna know." I looked at him with the corner of my eye.

"No, you are not."

And it all happened in a second, one minute my passport was on my desk, the moment later it was burning in the lit up fireplace. I flinched.

He was laughing at my horrified expression. "I always get what I want, William. You're my son, the puppet in my own game and you'll do as I say."

There and then, I wanted to punch that face so similar to mine. I wished I could erase his foul grin with my already bloodied hands, hitting my own father but... That would have meant wasting more time than I could afford.

"I will see you in Hell, Thomas."

He cringed as I addressed him with his given name. I didn't care, I passed him, hitting his shoulder with mine and left.

He shouted my name over and over behind me.

•••

MY DOWNFALL

I jumped into one of our gray Mercedes, thinking that worst case scenario this would sell well, so we could gather some money if we needed to.

I had to think on how to fix the passport inconvenience. I supposed we had to leave the country therefore getting a new passport quickly was a pressing matter.

I remembered about one of my classmates who created fake IDs and sold them, his price was too high for my newly almost-empty pockets, but I was pretty sure I could pull some strings.

I looked at my watch, it was 3 a.m. by the time I reached her house, I texted her and she said to come in. As soon as I left my car, she opened the door for me.

Vivi looked pretty as usual, the picture was only ruined by her puffy red eyes; it looked like she hadn't stopped crying for a second. My heart shrunk at that sight.

"We need to fix your eye and check your wounds," she whispered, taking my hand and leading the way to the living room.

"We have no time," I tried to object.

"You're not losing your eyesight for me," and that closed the argument.

The house was small and overfilled with strange furniture. She made me sit on a orange couch and took what looked like a ceramic bowl in her hands.

"I made it while you were gone, it will help your wounds and bruises heal faster," she explained while sitting beside me.

She immersed a green tea towel in it and brought it delicately to my face. I observed every movement she made as if enchanted. No one had ever taken care of me like that, nobody had ever been so concerned not to hurt me, no one so carefully sweet in doing that.

And in that exact moment I realized the depth of my feelings for her. That moment I knew it wasn't a temporary crush; if I let her walk away alone I would regret it for the rest of my miserable life.

It wouldn't have faded out with time, I was utterly and madly in love with this girl.

And I wonder if my father had become like that 'cause he once too had loved someone, but never took the chance pursue that feeling, really.

I knew if that was the case, I might have forgiven him for what he'd done to me, to my mother, because this love would consume me if I ever decided to let it go.

My feelings for her would burn me and leave just ashes of me.

"I love you." The words, those little tiny simple words I've never spoken in my life, came out of my mouth before I could realize it.

Vivi looked at me in shock. She tried to say something but then closed her mouth, but what she gave me was the sweetest smile I've ever seen. "I love you," she said back to me. And in that moment I felt completely and utterly invincible.

Then her beautiful face darkened, she looked away.

And I understood.

"We'll face it together, no matter what I'm not letting you go." I repeated the words I'd said before but this time was different, I knew I could never for real. Mine was a promise.

"You have no idea..." she tried but I leaned and kissed her, the best way to shut her up 'cause I didn't care.

I didn't care what it cost me, I would be with her.

I tried to show her how much sure I was about it, how much I needed her in my life. And how much I would have fought for her.

"You'll tell me all about it, all about *him* while we're on our way to Mexico or wherever you wanna go," I said.

It didn't matter at the moment, we had other pressing matters like putting as much sea and land between us and that bastard.

And then I would have found a way to get rid of him *for real*.

"I've never been to Amsterdam and we could drive there."

"Isn't it too close? I don't know how this works." I passed a hand through my hair, frustrated. I've never run away from anything.

Vivi smiled a bit amused. "We'll change names, start fresh."

"That sounds good to me, I just have to find some important name for myself." I pretended to be thoughtful. "How about Frederick Van Hotten?" I smiled playful.

"Really William, Van Hotten?" She chuckled.

"Don't you find it very appropriate?" I winked.

"No!" She was laughing now and I was glad all the tension had gone.

"Cheeky beggar, it's more than perfect for me."

"Keep telling yourself that."

"We'll wait till the morning and I will meet someone who'll get me a new passport." I smiled at her puzzled look. "My father burnt mine." I was quite annoyed about it.

"He did what?" Her pretty mouth shaped an O.

"Long story short, he disinherited me and lit my passport like a ciggy."

"That's all my fault... I'm sorry." She looked like she was about to cry.

"I make my choices, and I chose to be with you damning the consequences, so your only fault is that you made me fall for you." I smiled, I didn't really mind being a cheesy bastard at that moment.

She spoke gravely. "William, once you're in... there's no coming out..."

Alive, she wanted to say. The word hanging between us.

And I knew she'd already surrendered to her destiny, but I had not.

"Let the games begin then."

And I was sure I would have found a way to make it pleasant for *him* too. If I was to go to Hell, I would drag him along.

Vivi brought a duvet from upstairs and a pillow; she arranged a bed out of a sofa. A ginger cat followed her downstairs; he stopped in front of me and started studying me.

"That's the ugliest cat I've ever seen." His hypnotic green eyes wouldn't leave mine for a second.

"Careful, he understands everything we say, and you wouldn't like him to be pissed off at you." She smirked.

"I just said the truth, he's ugly and creepy." As an answer, he hissed at me.

I heard her chuckle. "You better start befriending him because he's coming with us."

"No, he's not!" I was surprised to hear myself almost shouting.

I didn't like him, I wasn't a cat person and anyways, if we had to take a pet, I wanted a vicious pit-bull to guard the house we were going to live in.

"He's part of the family. Don't worry though, you won't see him too much. He comes and goes at his leisure, sometimes he leaves for days. He was once gone for two months."

"He's still not coming." I hissed back at the cat.

When she wished me good night and turned off the light, I lay in bed sleeplessly for a bit, thinking about this whole situation, trying to find a solution.

Tired of turning round and round in that sofa bed, I turned on my laptop, hoping to find something useful to save her.

Needless to say, I found nothing, just a bunch of wiccan crap too absurd to be even real.

As soon as my eyes started stinging, I turned it off and fell into a restless sleep.

I woke up in the morning trying not to think about the nightmares I had the night before. A face was haunting my dreams, I could not remember it exactly but I recalled a ginger beard and evil eyes. The cat was in my dream too for some reason, but it was all blurry like looking through dirty glass.

"Good morning," a cheerful voice greeted me.

I opened my eyes just to find Sybil's face looking at me from high above.

"What time is it?" I rubbed my sore eyes, and noticed that the left one was completely healed.

Magic. I almost smiled.

"About seven." She smiled. "She's still fast asleep."

We needed to get ready soon, there wasn't much time to lose.

"So you're going through it, uh?."

"I am indeed."

I wondered how much she'd seen when she'd touched my hand that day, if she'd viewed this too.

"Are you really sure of it? It's a dangerous game to play."

"I know, I know the risks and all." I nodded, tired of people thinking I was some kind of moody child who would back off at the first sight of danger.

"It is a life and death situation, William. Quite literally."

I turned to look at her, her young face was solemn, serious like I'd never seen it. And that moment I understood her words fully.

They were a warning, if I was to go through it... It would be the death of me.

The woman held my stare a little longer, maybe studying me and testing me, my limits, perhaps trying to convince me it was a lost cause, who knows. But she didn't know me, nor the old me or the new me.

"I don't care," I simply said.

It was true, I would rather live one day as a lion with her, than one hundred as a sheep alone.

"I don't care," I repeated more convinced than ever.

Bring it on.

"Good," she said. One moment later she smiled broadly as if our serious conversation never happened. "Make the coffee then."

When we were ready to go, we said goodbye to Vivi's aunts. I looked in the mirror of the car, that ugly cat of hers was napping peacefully at the back seat. I breathed, I didn't even know how she managed to convince me to bring him along.

"Ready to give up on your whole life for me? Your family? Money? Friends?" she asked me, fastening her seatbelt.

I breathed. "Still trying to convince me to stay behind, uh?"

"It's not too late yet, you know," she whispered, looking straight to my eyes with a pleading look in hers.

"I'm quite alright where I am," I confirmed.

Even if that would lead to my death.

Vivi breathed either saddened or relived, I couldn't tell. I took her hand and started the engine.

I drove to school, the radio was the only sound in the car, if not for the loud snoring of that ugly cat.

I parked and asked her to stay in the car, knowing that if she'd tagged along, we'd have drawn too much attention and wasted more time than we could afford.

I jumped out of the car and went for my locker, suddenly remembering the money I always kept hidden there. For some reasons, I always kept a couple of hundred pounds hidden between the pages of my chemistry book.

I thanked God for that, I knew how much we needed that money right now.

I closed back the locker, thinking that it would be the last time I ever did it.

What did I feel, sadness? No.

Fear? Perhaps a slight bit.

But change scared everyone, didn't it?

And the awareness of their own upcoming death wouldn't help, would it?

I just didn't manage to regret it, as much as I tried to think of a reason why I should. I wanted to be with this girl and for her I would go to Hell and back, if necessary.

With the corner of my eye, I saw the person I was here to meet, so I stopped wasting precious time in my stupid dark ponderings, and followed him to the male toilets.

He was washing his hands and didn't seem to have noticed me.

"John Cameron." I called his name, getting a bit closer.

He turned to me.

He was a slim and short guy, dark hair and dark blue eyes. His face was handsome but maybe too thin to be attractive to girls. His clothes buggy on him, I never noticed how skinny he was till now. Maybe I never really cared enough to pay much attention.

"William Black," he greeted me with half of a smile looking at me through the mirror, "the guy who lost it for a girl."

I had to bite my lower lip not to roar like a lion at him. I couldn't, I needed a favour.

We used to be friends once, or at least the closest thing to friends that I had. We used to go out, play soccer and chase girls together.

Now that my star was eclipsed and forgotten, what were we?

His large grin told me we were nothing close to mates any longer.

"I need to call in a favour," I said without ceremonies.

"Do you, now?" His grin was even wider now.

The hands I kept in my pockets trying to play it cool, were closed into fists.

"Yes, seventh grade. I saved your sorry ass when you got caught cheating on the history test. Not to mention the countless times I got you out of trouble for your 'illegal activities'." My voice was calm and cold.

"I see," he chuckled, "and what on earth could I do for the mighty William Black that he can't do by himself?"

I ignored the sarcasm, he was trying to provoke me for some reason, and I understood I lost some of my power over these people, that I lost my influence. If I was their king before, a God among simple muggles, what was I now? A man fallen in disgrace? A funny story to tell? A memory?

And I understood that they had feared me, they had needed me, but now they didn't anymore. So I was no one.

I didn't care. I was no one for them but I was *someone* for Vivi, and that was all that mattered to me.

"I need you to get me a passport."

He started laughing out loud. "What happened to yours?"

"That is none of your business. Get me a passport with any name and we'll be square." I kept my face straight, emotionless like I did countless times before.

He was still laughing while searching for something in his backpack, he pulled a passport out of it, he read while opening it, "Elliot Albert Clarke."

"Whatever," I extended my open hand.

He hesitated. "Why do you need that? What have you two done?" His face was serious now. Almost afraid.

It was my turn to grin now. "You'd like to know, wouldn't you? Do you wanna know if you're helping criminals leaving the country?"

"If I hear anything, William, I will turn you in. I don't care," he tried to warn me.

"Go ahead, go to the police and tell them how your illegal *activities* helped those lawless bastards flee the country. Since you're there have a little urine test, they'll be delighted to discover all that weed... and so will your family."

Finally, *fucking finally* I had my power back.

"Are you threatening me?" He was glaring at me now, ready to attack but I had no time for that.

"No, I'm just making things clear. You know how I am." I grinned.

"Whatever she did to you... you gotta wake up, that's not you."

And in a strange way, I kind of appreciated his concern, even though it was all wrong. But it also annoyed me at the same time that they all thought she'd done something to me.

Well, in all fairness she did, she made me fall for her.

"-I'm perfectly fine. Now, back to business, my passport, please." I once again extended my hand, waiting.

He hesitated again, his dark eyes undecided.

I was starting to lose my patience. "I don't have the whole day, you know."

Every second I was wasting, she could be getting more and more in danger.

A struggle of wills, our eyes, mine light like a clear summer sky and his dark like a pit.

Finally, he handed over the passport. I opened it and saw my new name.

No more William, no more heir of a great fortune, son of the king of the city. I was just Elliot now.

And I could be whatever and whoever I wanted to be, for the first time in my life I truly felt free.

I just needed my picture on it and all would be ready to start fresh, to save her.

I turned to leave when I heard his words. "You're still on time, William. This game will destroy you."

And he didn't know how true his words were, that down this path my downfall was waiting for me.

He also had no idea how much I didn't give a damn about it.

"You know I'm a player," I said closing the door behind me.

I would play this dangerous game till the end. My end.

Walking back to the car park I looked around me, trying to memorize every detail, every smell and noise.

It was true what they said, when you know you're about to die, things had another meaning. You notice and enjoy everything fully, 'cause you know that it might be the last time you smell those flowers in the hall you always neglected, or the cheerful chatting of the newbies, remembering when you were one of them.

I smiled, but it died when a nasty ominous feeling hit me in my stomach, it was like someone had stabbed me with an invisible knife. And for some reason, fear and an unknown feeling of danger filled me. I knew I had to run.

When I arrived where I parked my car, I saw Vivi out, standing in front of a man.

He was tall, with medium-long rusty red hair collected in a low ponytail, a long ginger beard perfectly trimmed. He was wearing a grey suit, his black tie the same colour of his empty eyes.

Again, that feeling in my stomach hit me when I recognised the man I dreamt of last night was standing smiling madly at my girl.

BYRON HILL

Vivi.

Saying that I was utterly terrified would be using a euphemism.

The man who had haunted my dreams and sleepless moments was standing there, a few feet from me, smiling with his crazy smile.

His empty eyes were hypnotic, a tunnel of damnation taking in all the details of me, from my hair to my hips, to my legs.

A shadow of desire showed for a moment into his eyes, but I could have just imagined it 'cause they soon went back blank and empty. Crazy.

"You've grown to be a beautiful young woman." His deep voice was pleased. "I've seen many of you, but you are the one who looks the most like her."

"Who are you?" I had to play dumb, I had to buy time.

I could feel William's presence behind me. I hoped he took the hint and ran away. He had to.

I hoped he wouldn't be stubborn for once, and thought of himself.

Take the hint, please.

Save yourself, we've always known I'm beyond saying.

So just go.

"Yes, who the hell are you?" William asked coldly.

I looked at him, my eyes pleading him to shut up and leave, but he didn't seem to listen.

He now stood tall now between me and the man, who seemed to be quite amused.

"I see you made a little friend. And what would your name be, dear?" he was looking at him.

"He's no one." *Just go!*

"My name is William Black, and I'm her boyfriend. Now, who the fuck are you?" He answered fearlessly.

"Boyfriend?" the man chuckled looking at me.

If someone had thrown an ice bucket at me, I would have probably felt less cold. My blood literally froze in my veins.

"He's not, he's just someone who's obsessed with me. He's no one to me." I saw William opening his mouth, ready to rebate but I slightly moved my hand. My magic shut him up, I had to keep him safe.

He looked at me like I just betrayed him; he understood what I'd just done.

"Aren't we all, my baby girl?" The man laughed.

"What do you want from me?" I cut him off, William was struggling against my spell. It was so tiring to keep him bound like that but I had no choice.

"I believe you already know the answer to that. Now, come with me, baby girl. There's no wasting time. With you it will be done." He extended a hand to me.

"Fuck you and your crazy psycho vendetta plan."

"You got the fire, I like that. She was like you too, she was a fighter. And so was your mother, you know." He smiled, seeing how much those words touched me.

"Don't you dare talk about my mother, you bastard, you know nothing about her!"

"Oh, but I know enough. And I will tell you all about her. Now, let's go." Again his hand. Again, crazy expectation in his dark empty eyes.

"Fuck you," I repeated. I had to find a way to save William, if I had gone with him, he would have killed him anyways for spite.

"Such a foul mouth for such a beautiful young woman." He shook his head in disapproval. William rose his middle finger to him. "Come with me or I will kill everyone you've ever met. Starting with your little rude friend."

As soon as he said those words, William fell to his knees, his hands gripping his white shirt against his chest.

An expression of unspeakable pain appeared on his beautiful face.

"Stop it, Byron. Leave him alone!" I couldn't help but shout.

"Come, baby girl, he's beyond saving 'cause I can see he wants you, he desires you. He touched you," his words filled with anger, "I can feel that. So he's already as good as dead but you can still save everyone else."

"I'll come with you but please, *please* let him go." I hated to hear my voice pleading.

"I don't like him so he'll die. Everyone else is safe if you come with me, you have my word."

I had to think fast, the man was holding William's heart in a grip, a few more seconds, a bit more pressure and he'd damage it beyond repair.

It was disgusting how he had understood that I cared about William, got that I didn't want any other casualties and he had used it against me.

I wanted to save everyone so Byron had leverage on me but I could have some on him, there must have been something.

He must have had too his own Achilles' heel.

Question was, what?

What did he want?

Oh, yeah. Me.

A gun appeared in my right hand, I quickly pointed it at my temple. "Leave him alone or I swear, I will pull the trigger."

He appeared to be amused but maybe slightly shocked; maybe he didn't expect this move of mine.

"Really?"

"Yes, let him be or I will end my life right here, right now."

I was not bluffing, to save William I would have done it even though I wasn't sure how my death would have helped the man I loved, it was still the only card I could play at the moment.

I had to gamble it.

"Is he really that important to you?" he studied me.

"Do it." With the corner of my eye, I could see William's reddened face; he was struggling to breathe. "Do it, now!"

Byron smiled, and released the pressure on William's chest, who started to cough blood to the floor.

I'm so sorry.

"I want you to leave now," I told him, still with the gun pointed to my head.

"I like you, you're the most clever of them all. The funniest." He clapped his hands and then put them in his pockets with nonchalance.

"Go fuck yourself," I said.

"Funny, your mother said the same before I fucked *her* mindless." His grin wider than ever.

And I just wanted to point that gun to him, to wipe that disgusting expression of malice off his face, to carve him up and cut him piece by piece. But I had to keep calm, that was what he wanted, a moment of weakness from me.

I had to do it for William and myself.

With the corner of my eye, I looked at the guy I loved, still on his knees coughing blood and trying to catch his breath. I could see the sweat on his forehead.

In that moment, I decided he would pay for it somehow even if it was the last thing I did.

"Are you still here?" I barked.

He chuckled. "You know what? I want to make a deal with you."

"What kind of a deal?" I tried not to look interested as I asked him that.

He smiled. "I give you three days, three more days of freedom."

"What? Why would you do that?" I was shocked.

Was he bluffing to make me drop my guard?

"Because I like your spirit, you remind me so much of *her*."

"Fuck you." I spat on him.

He smiled and cleaned his face with the back of his hand. "Three days of enjoying your life. Before I end it."

"You must have some guts to..."

Byron interrupted me. "I will come and collect you in three days, try and escape and I shall kill your dear relatives and then find you," he said to me, then he looked at William with disgust. "You try and keep your hands to yourself, and I might decide to be magnanimous and spare your useless life."

William muttered a curse at him, but then he was gone.

I quickly turned to William, crying and apologizing, touching his sweated hair.

"I'm okay," he whispered, he finally looked at me, "are you?"

His look of pure concern made my heart skip a beat.

I smiled between the tears, how could he be worried about me when he nearly died?

I hugged him tight, whispering I would take him to my aunt's house and give him something that would make him feel better.

"I'm fine." Not without struggling, he stood up, starting walking to the car.

Only then I noticed the crowd around us, everyone was staring at us, utterly silent and terrified, someone was even recording us but I didn't care. What mattered now was to keep him safe.

He drove in silence. If he was still in pain I couldn't tell, he never complained once.

When we arrived, my aunts were already out waiting for us.

"Are you guys alright?" Maisa asked us, concerned.

She handed a glass to William who drank from it without saying a word. "I'm fine," he repeated almost automatically when he finished it.

After a few moments, he lost consciousness.

Good, they put something in to make him sleep. God knew how much he needed to rest.

"Are you okay, princess?" Sybil asked me while Maisa lifted the guy with magic and placed him on the sofa.

"This is all my fault," I said, sitting down on the floor close to where William was knocked out. I started caressing his soft short hair.

"He chose to stay, princess. If there's anyone to blame, it's only him," Maisa said softly.

"He chose to be with me. He didn't choose all this," I glared at her, "all this mess, all this pain... it's all on me."

"He was aware of the risks," Sybil repeated.

Was he really?! I doubted it. "He saw him, he knows who he is. He will suffer because of my selfishness!" I shouted at them.

I would have preferred if they had screamed back at me, if they had pointed accusing fingers towards me, anything rather than this...

I didn't deserve it.

Like I didn't deserve him. Truth was, I never did.

I looked at him, his expression so peaceful. His beautiful face so relaxed, unlike I'd seen him just moments before, the excruciating pain he'd felt because of me.

I had to find a way to keep William safe.

I only had three days to do so.

"Aunt Sybil, what can I do?" I didn't turn to her, I was still focused on his angelic face. So handsome.

"I'm afraid there's nothing you can do." Her voice was thin.

Tears started rolling down my face. "I... I have to save him."

I knew I was as good as dead, but it didn't have to be like that for him. I knew I could save him somehow.

"It's part of his destiny to die, child," she admitted gravely.

And it felt like someone just stabbed me with a million hot knives. I led the man I loved to his death.

He was destined to cease to exist because of me.

"He... he cannot," I breathed.

"He must and he will." She nodded emotionless.

"I will not let this happen, I will fight or... I will find a way to save him!"

And I thought of all the time we spent together, so little time.

I remembered his sarcasm, his loving side, that wonderful gift that God gave me... I couldn't let him die.

He was only eighteen, no one should die at that age.

I wanted him to live a life full of happiness and joy, and sarcasm. I wanted him to make his own dreams come true, it couldn't end like this.

I would not accept it.

"Maisa, remember that spell we use when we are in danger... the confusion one?" I looked at her. "Can it be modified? Improved in some ways?"

He wouldn't have been here, at this point if it hadn't been for me.

"I don't know, kid. That would require advanced magic… and I don't think it would work on Byron's mind. He's too strong."

"Who said I want to use it on him?" I caressed William's beautiful face while a plan was taking shape in my head.

"What have you got in mind, Vivi?"

THAT THING WORTH DYING FOR

William.

I woke up on a familiar orange sofa, utterly confused.

My head was banging and my chest was slightly painful. I looked around me and I recognized Vivi's aunts' house.

How long had I been asleep? It felt like ages and looking outside the window, by the moon high up in the sky, I understood it had been hours indeed.

With more difficulties than I dared to admit, I stood up.

I still felt a bit dizzy, but I had to find her.

I wasn't sure which door was her room's, but I let myself be guided by the sound of female sobbing.

I opened the door slowly. Vivi was in her bed crying her eyes out, she hadn't yet noticed me.

She was still wearing what she wore that morning, a white tank top, dark jeans and that big vintage leather jacket that felt so much like her.

Her chestnut-red hair was spread on the white pillow, looking like flames against the light of the full moon outside.

"Hey." I closed the door behind me and sat on the bed beside her.

"Hey." She didn't look at me. Hiding her face from my sight, her hair fell on it. I removed it softly.

"It's okay, Vivi. Don't hide from me."

"I'm surprised you even want to see my face, right now," she whispered without meeting my eyes.

"Why would you say that?"

"What happened today..." Another sob.

"I don't care, Vivi. We'll find a way to defeat him," I said confident.

She faked a laugh. "You can't, no one can. He's ancient and strong."

I didn't care, I would have fought him to my very last breath.

"I will find a way, I prom…" She pressed her little finger against my mouth, I kissed it.

"Don't. Please, just don't," she begged.

I looked at her, her eyes were red and watery, the mascara all smudged under them, highlighting the brilliant green of them. Her hair savagely spread around her head and I never found her more – *beautiful*. I whispered, "You take my breath away."

"Perhaps that's the problem, maybe you should go and find someone who gives you breath," she muttered.

"Maybe that'd be a wise choice," I gave her a half smile, "but I've never been wise."

"William, you have no idea what you're dealing with."

"I don't care, can we just think about it tomorrow? I just want to be with you tonight, I just want to be the guy who's in love with a girl."

Vivi nodded and rose to kiss me, pulling me closer to her, pressing me against her. I was completely awake now.

I responded to that kiss with all the passion I was capable of, when her hands went lower and lower to the buckle of my belt, I stopped.

"Vivi…"

"I understand if you don't want to… I mean, he threatened you…"

"Can you please not talk about him while you're in bed with me?" I breathed, looking at her. "I was just making sure you really want this, and don't feel like you have to or you owe me or God knows what."

"I want you," she smiled shyly at me.

And there was no clearer invite for me. I leaned down to kiss her and let her unbuckle my belt, her hands were trembling while she was undressing me.

When I was left with just my black boxers on, it was my turn to unclothe her. I took my sweet time in doing that, kissing every inch of skin I was discovering, making her shiver and gasp and crave for more.

When I left her in her underwear only, I touched her knickers and I was pleased to find them wet for me.

You'll drive me insane.

I kissed her once more, then removed everything with a frenzy I'd never known before.

I only stopped a moment to admire her naked body. She was just perfect, so beautiful there were no words that could describe her properly.

She immediately used her hands to cover herself up, to hide her nudity to my sight but I objected. I would enjoy every single minute of it.

"Don't. I want to see you, let me behold you," I breathed into her ear.

"Why?"

"'Cause you're stunning." I removed her hands.

"You're killing me," she complained after a few seconds.

"Such an impatient little girl." I smiled while with my fingers I traced a path from her mouth, down low until my finger was inside her.

Beautiful beyond words.

Vivi arched her back suddenly, while I was moving two fingers inside her, preparing her for me. I watched how she moved following my rhythm, how she moaned softly and gasped for air.

When I felt she had her first orgasm, I could not resist any longer, so I removed my own underwear and made love to her several times.

When I woke up, it was still dark, I searched for her in the bed but I found it utterly empty.

I opened my eyes just to find her sitting on the window, her feet pending outside of it.

I was naked; I didn't care. I went close to her. "Already stealing my clothes?" I teased her, remarking on the fact that she was wearing my shirt. *Only* my shirt.

I swallowed hard, trying not to let desire have the best of me.

"Do you know what my name means?" She hadn't turned to me. She didn't wait for my answer to continue. "Many think it's short for Vivienne or Vivian… but it's not. It's just Vivi and it's Italian, it means *live*. My parents gave me that name as a wish, if you want to call it that." She made a sad chuckle.

"Who is he? Tell me the whole story from the beginning, Vivi," I said after a few seconds.

She turned to me and gave me a melancholic smile, she nodded. "It's only fair, you deserve that."

I sat down on the opposite corner of the large window, the cool breeze touching my skin, making me shiver but I didn't care, I had to know.

"What does he want from you?" I asked.

"He wants to kill me."

And if someone had punched me, it would have hurt less bad. My heart skipped a beat and my hands were shut in fists.

"Why?" I breathed.

"Vendetta? Boredom? Madness? … all of them combined? Who knows, he's a patsy."

"Tell me the whole story."

"His name is Byron Hill," she started, looking at the full moon. "He was my great-great-great grandmother's best friend, they used to be like brother and sister. Or at least, she loved him like a sibling but he didn't, he was madly in love with her." She stopped, maybe trying to collect the words to explain.

My mind was stuck in a detail, I did my math. "So he must be…"

"He's over five centuries old." Vivi nodded.

I had to clench my jaw not to open my mouth in surprise, she smiled softly and explained. "Witches, wizards, warlocks live longer than mortals, we can live up to two or three hundred years"

I frowned. "But you said he's over five centuries old."

"He is indeed. You'll understand once I finish the story." She nodded looking at me for the first time. "One day she met a man and they fell irremediably in love. When Byron found out, he went completely insane. He set a trap for the man, sending him a letter where he asked him to meet my ancestor, Feye at midnight in the forest 'cause they had to flee her father's rage. The man was so in love with the girl that he didn't question the letter for a minute. When he went there, waiting for her... he was bitten by a vampire and turned into one of them. Byron then cursed him and all his kind to live in the dark, the sun would now burn their skin. That was his punishment for having stolen his own personal sun, he'd said to him. He had hoped that the transformation and the curse would change her heart towards him but that did not happen, they got even closer if possible.

"Feye found out about the plot and to protect the man she loved, she cast a spell on him. He would now be impervious to magic, so that Byron would not be able to hurt him again. Needless to say, when Byron found out that his plan hadn't worked, he raged into the newly made vampire's grave one day and killed him in his sleep, delivering his head to her. Feye and him had a fight, and he ran away. For a century, no one heard from him. Until one day, when he went back to her.

"My ancestor had a daughter from the man, before he was turned into a vampire, but not many knew about that. When he found out, Byron... Raped Feye and then ripped her beating heart from her chest. Eating it."

That was a lot to take in.

"He *ate* her heart?" I asked without hiding my disgust.

"Yes, magic is in our blood, William. Our hearts are the centre of magic, when you eat our hearts... you get awfully powerful abilities, your life gets longer, you get all the powers the person had. And you have their souls inside you."

"She's in here," he had said to Vivi, talking about her mother.

So he'd done the same to her mother too...

"Right, I get it he's a sociopath but... I still don't get what that has to do with you."

"That day, when he murdered Feye... he swore to her dead body that he would let her bloodline spread just to wipe them all out. That was his vendetta to her, her daughter had a daughter who had a daughter who had a daughter... until my mother and then me. All of them raped and murdered like my ancestor was. Like I will be. That is his way to cope with eternity. But he told my mother before he killed her, that I would be the last one, 'cause he's tired of this game. That I was to complete the circle of revenge at the age of eighteen."

Hell no.

I remembered the night when she got upset when I reminded her she was eighteen, she knew her time was up.

Fuck no.

"I won't let him touch you, I will protect you." I swore.

Vivi gave me a sweet sad smile. "There's nothing you can do about it."

"I will find a way... I..."

I had to think quick, I had to come up with a plan, a solution or she would...

"It's okay, William. It doesn't matter, you gave me more than I could hope for, now it's time to finish though. Leave, change name and never look back."

"What?!"

How could she even think I could do that?!

"I'm not letting you go."

I was in too deep now to just let it go.

"You know, I thought of how easy it would be to just jump from this window and end it all," she said after a few moments, without looking at me.

And those words hit me like a punch in the guts. "What are you talking about?"

"How amazing would it be to end it all here, right now? With your smell still on me? I debated doing it for the last hour."

"Is that what you wanna do? Give up on your life like this? Be a quitter?" I asked.

My anxious voice too loud for that late hour of the night.

"Maybe I should." She was still looking outside.

I placed myself in front of her, ready to catch her in case she was going to jump for real. "Let's do it then, jump together."

"You can't."

"I won't let you go alone so if that's what you want to do… let's get it over with."

"-The whole point in me jumping out would be to save your life." She looked at me with pleading eyes.

"How can you be this selfish? Leaving me behind to deal with the consequences?" I couldn't believe my ears.

Leaving me alone.

"Don't you get it? He almost killed you because of me, he had your heart in his filthy grip!" She exploded. "You've got to let me go."

"Are you insane?"

"You're insane for staying but I know how to fix this."

I watched her starting muttering words I couldn't understand, while tears were rolling down her eyes.

Suddenly, my head felt light and heavy at the same time, I felt confused, my sight now blurry.

She was doing something to me, I could feel the goosebumps, I could sense the tickling of… magic?

Why was she playing with my head?

I was sweating, the world felt distant.

All my memories of a girl with chestnut-red hair were replaying in my head, then disappearing in a blur. And in a moment of lucidity, with more difficulties than I care to admit, I placed a hand over her mouth to shut her up, fighting against it, against what she was trying to do.

Vivi didn't stop, her eyes on mine, so hypnotic and beautiful. I couldn't stop staring at them but somehow I knew I had to, that was my only chance of freedom.

"Quit… it…"

My other hand felt heavy, but somehow I managed to place it over her eyes, she struggled and we fell on the floor, the carpet saving us from getting hurt.

Suddenly, all the fog in my head got wiped away, and I knew for a fact what she'd tried to do.

I beheld her, for once showing all my emotions, I felt so utterly betrayed.

"How could you?!" I shouted.

"How did you...?" She was in shock.

"How could you try and erase all my memories of you?!" I was literally raging.

I stood up, needing to put as much distance between me and her as I could.

"I did it for you! So you could have a long happy life without me." She braced herself.

"You had no right to do that! Only I can decide what's best for me." I looked down.

She was still on the floor, silently weeping.

"I can't... I can't see you die." She sobbed.

"It's none of your business, girl!" I shouted to her face.

I was taking deep breaths, trying to calm myself.

"You're bound to die if you stay with me, you are. I know that, it's a matter of fact. She wiped away her tears but new ones replaced them.

"Do you think I don't know?" My voice was flat now.

Vivi opened her mouth in shock. "How could you have hidden that from me? Why the fuck did you stay?"

"Because there are things worth dying for, Vivi!" I screamed at her face.

"Not me!" she shouted back.

I massaged my temples, I felt so betrayed for what she'd just tried to do to me. "My whole life I had someone always telling me what to do, I was never free to make my own choices until I met you. And tonight, you tried and take that away from me, tonight, you decided *for me*." I took deep breaths trying to calm myself down.

How could she do it?!

"I'm not going to apologize for trying and save your ass," she whispered.

"Then don't ask me to spend the night with you tonight, Vivi. You were playing with my mind, you had already made the decision for us. You already gave up." I turned my back to her and after wearing my boxers I left, slamming the door behind me.

Let them all be woken up.

I was so mad, I went downstairs and I started walking up and down, restless.

I couldn't believe she'd just done it.

Killing my trust so utterly and consciously.

I punched a pillow hard, I missed my punch bag right now. Or my swimming pool.

I remembered how I felt when she was casting that spell on me, the fog in my mind, the confusion, the stain of magic. I never wanted to feel that way again.

I envied the guy her ancestor loved, the vampire immune to magic so that he could never feel...

And to protect the man she loved, she cast a spell on him, he would now be impervious to magic, so that Byron would not be able to hurt him again.

Something clicked in my mind, like a knot now unlatched.

He had been invulnerable to magic, did that mean that all vampires...?

"Yes," a voice said behind me.

I turned to face Sybil, she was standing a few feet from me, her face solemn.

"Yes, what?" I asked half heartedly.

"All of the vampires he made are impervious to spells, no witch or wiccan or warlock or wizard can harm them that way. Magic would never be able to touch them."

"How many did he make?" My heart raced.

"One." She came a bit closer to me.

My own heart pounding in my ears, what were the chances I found him in three days?

"Is he... Is he still alive?"

"Yes."

I looked at her, waiting.

"And I happen to know who that is," she continued.

I swallowed. "Can you take me to him?"

She smiled at me. "Question is, are you ready to die for her, William Black?"

TO HELL AND BACK

More than six hours later, I was sitting on an economy class seat —
Heaven, I hated being poor — on a plane from Moscow to Bo-
gashevo Airport in Tomsk, Siberia where apparently the vampire
was living. Or was it even appropriate to say that?

Sybil was sitting beside me, fast asleep and I wondered how
she could sleep that soundly on a plane.

I've never been able to do that, I always needed to be alert,
awake and act in case of an emergency to save my own ass.

I laughed mentally, that hadn't brought me far, had it?

I was on a suicidal mission, I was about to look at death in
its dark eyes.

But I knew I was ready, for her I would have gone through it.

No regrets of any sort in my mind, I was almost looking forward to it. To free her.

Of course, I was still angry at her for trying to erase all my
memories of her, and we'd certainly discuss that once all this situation was solved. She had to hear me.

But nonetheless, I was there, ready to give up on everything
for her. We'd left in the morning straight after I told Sybil that
yes, I would die for her a million times.

I hadn't left anything for Vivi, no hints of my intentions. She
would have probably tried to stop me and I couldn't afford that.

She'd just texted me earlier this morning saying: *I'm sorry. I
do understand.*

Had she thought I left her for good? That I had chickened
out just now?

Could she really believe that?

I hadn't replied.

Now, I just hoped this plane would hurry up and take me to
my destiny.

My written fate.

"You knew that I was going to do that, didn't you?" I turned to the woman sitting next to me. "When you shook my hand, you knew it," I realized.

"I did." She hadn't opened her eyes.

"Why didn't you tell me?"

"Were you ready then? Would you have believed me?"

Probably not.

"You should have told me earlier, now I feel like time is pressing on me. We could have avoided loads of suffering and fear." I remembered how scared Vivi was when she'd met him.

"You people do not understand that some things need to happen, that as bad they may seem, they are important. They are part of life and I'm sorry to disappoint you but no, not even I am allowed to change that." She turned to me.

"But you already knew it all," I insisted and I felt like an obstinate kid.

"Some sorrows, some fears need to be felt, all the choices you make are strictly connected to what good and bad happened to you. Yes, it would be nice if there was no pain, no bad stuff but that would simply not be life."

It did make sense. If I hadn't seen and lived what I had, would I even be here now?

"I still think you should have told me," I said just to be stubborn.

"You had to realize it by yourself, you had to make sure you were ready to do that, that it came from the deepest part of your heart. Besides," she smiled mischievously, "no one likes spoilers." She shut her eyes again. Conversation over.

The rest of the trip proceeded silently, I tried to enjoy my last moments as a human, trying not to worry about how Vivi was coping.

The temptation to text her was too strong for me to resist, so I was glad I had no network either on the aircraft or when we arrived in Tomsk.

When we got off, it was so cold I could barely breathe.

One second after, I couldn't feel my face, it had gone utterly numb.

I tried to enjoy the feeling.

I guessed once I got turned, I wouldn't feel any of these things anymore.

Our hotel was just beside the airport, Sybil told me to go for a shower that we would meet a few hours later for a meal.

When I objected we didn't have time to spare, she reminded me we were going to meet a vampire and vampires live at night.

My room was small and cosy, the fireplace was lit by flames that reminded me of Vivi's hair as I'd seen them just the night before, when we'd made love.

I wish I could hold her right now, that I could smell her long hair, that I could just hear her laugh one more time. That would calm down my nervousness.

I had a long hot shower, trying to impress the feeling of water against my skin. I closed my eyes and imagined the future with her. The future I would give her.

We'd live in a big house with a white fence, dogs and her ugly cat.

She'd be beautiful and warm with me like she'd always been, we'd make love all night every night, we'd travel. I smiled, we'd be together and that gave me courage.

I was impatient now, couldn't wait for that future to become present.

My last meal was a rich chicken stew with warm bread and cherry pie. I enjoyed every bite of them.

When we'd both finished, it was already dark outside.

"It's time," she said, studying me.

Perhaps looking for fear or regret in my face.

"I'm ready."

She couldn't find any.

•••

AN OLD FLAME

We entered the car she'd rented, apparently it was a bit of a drive to get to this guy; he liked his hermit life in the mountains.

She drove in silence, silence that felt too heavy for me not to fill, so I asked her, "How do you know him?"

"I kind of dated him once."

I turned to her, shocked. "You what?"

She giggled. "A lifetime ago."

"Please tell me you didn't cheat on him or stuff."

What if he held a grudge against her? How would I convince him to help me?

"Oh no, I just dumped him 'cause of the nightlife. I'm a day creature, you know."

That was like a punch in my guts, what if Vivi was a day creature too? What if she couldn't live that life with me?

Well, I decided it didn't matter.

I just needed to save her now, kill that bastard and give her the opportunity to choose. Even if I wasn't her choice, I would have learnt to live with it.

"She's not like me, you know. She truly does love you", she said looking at me.

And maybe she'd said that to make me feel better, to make sure I was still going through it.

"It doesn't matter, even if she... chose not to be with me, I am going to give her the possibility to live long enough to get to make that decision." I looked outside the car window.

I was enchanted by the pure white snow that was covering the path.

"Here we are," she said after a bit. She parked. "Ready?"

"I was born ready." And I realized that maybe I was indeed. Perhaps every single step I made was to be here, at this moment.

Leading me to die to save the girl I loved.

The little wooden house looked old, more like a shed than a house. Some smoke was coming out of the chimney, melting the snow on the roof. My heart skipped a beat when I noticed that there were no windows in sight, just a big wooden door.

We knocked and waited.

Those seconds he took to answer the door seemed to be like centuries.

A low deep voice finally said something in Russian, I couldn't understand.

"Vasiliy, it's Sybil Grimm," the woman said cheerfully, like she was talking to her best friend and not the guy she'd dumped a lifetime ago.

The door sprang open. Боже, взгляни на это личико.

The man standing in front of us looked more like a bear than anything else. He was big with a muscled body, thick dark brown hair the same colour of his huge eyebrows now frowning at us. His eyes were the deepest blue I've ever seen, almost hypnotic if you looked at them too long.

He was dressed with black flannel trousers, and a red tartan shirt too tight for his way too muscled arms.

He looked in his early forties. But especially, he appeared utterly menacing.

"Hello Vasiliy." She smiled joyfully not at all impressed by his huge figure.

"If It's not Sybil Grimm." His deep voice filled with a thick Russian accent. "What do you want, мой дорогой?"

"Are you going to leave us to freeze to death out here?" she trilled.

Only then, did he notice me, took in every detail of my person, studying me, trying to understand whether I represented a threat or not. He decided I didn't, he moved aside and we went in.

The house seemed smaller on the inside, the only light came from the fireplace, there were no candles or anything else. A brown leather sofa was in a corner, beside it a huge massive library that surrounded the whole little house. Only a grey fridge stood where the library ended. In front of it an old iron table with four chairs.

Sybil went and sat down on the table, when she saw me hesitating, she smiled broadly as if to say "play along", so I followed her suit.

"How are you, my dear?" she asked after a few moments.

"Just like you left me fifty years ago."

Yes, he was definitely holding a grudge. I swallowed hard.

"Oh don't be a drama queen, we did not work together." She chuckled, not at all intimidated by his harsh tone.

"Who is he, your new toy boy?" He pointed one of his huge fingers at me.

I've got to admit, it took all of my self-control not to flinch.

"He's the reason why I'm here."

Oh right, Sybil, no dancing around it then, just ask a favour to the guy you left fifty years ago.

You go, girl.

If I hadn't been hypnotized by the man sitting across me, I would have face palmed myself in frustration.

"I knew you didn't come here to see me." He muttered something in his language that I didn't get, then turned his whole attention to me. "And who are you?"

I felt a tiny bit intimidated but I couldn't show it, not now. So I used the best poker face I had in my repertory and answered, "My name's William Black."

He, once again, seemed to be studying me. "And what do you want?"

"I want you to turn me into a vampire." I thought it would be difficult to say but it came out easy and smooth.

His sardonic smile didn't reach his eyes, he looked at the woman beside me. "Is that a joke, Sybil? You always had your own perverse sense of humour."

"Never been more serious in my life." I answered for her, his attention on me again.

"You told him my secret, you brought this boy here... Why, Sybil, why?!" He was getting angry now. His white fangs showing in all their magnificence.

"We need you." She was calm.

"*I* needed you and you left!"

"Leave our issues for ourselves, we'll sort them out in another moment. He needs you to turn him."

"Get the hell out of my house, now!" he shouted.

I glared at the woman and tried with my most soothing voice. "If you don't turn me, the woman I'm in love with will be murdered by a bastard."

"My condolences," he said calmly, fangs nowhere to be seen.

My hands were fists and I decided to play my last card. "If you don't turn me, the man who murdered the one who turned you, will kill my girlfriend and get away with it. And mark my words, I won't find peace until I see you dead too."

It was risky, it was a gamble, I wasn't sure the kind of relationship that bonded the two but I had to give it a shot.

His expression showed confusion for a moment, then a murderous look took place in his bear-like features. "The man who staked my friend, my father, my maker?!" He seemed to ignore my threat.

"Byron Hill." I nodded.

He swore in Russian, his menacing eyes looking somewhere in the room.

"The woman I'm talking about is his great-great-great granddaughter, just so you know," I added with nonchalance.

He looked at me with new eyes. "Will you kill him?"

"Believe me, once I'm done with him there won't even be a body to bury." I nodded.

With the corner of my eye, I saw Sybil smiling beside me.

I took it as I was in the right path.

"Turn me and I will avenge him." I piled it on.

He smiled mercilessly and stood up, he walked towards me, only stopping a few inches from my face.

My heart was pounding, every cell of my body screaming to get away.

"Boy, once you're in, there won't be a way out. You'll be damned for your whole existence, there's no forgiving for us. We are demons of the night." His voice was guttural, frightening.

I swallowed. "I'm in."

He smiled broadly, showing me his perfect white teeth. I watched breathlessly as two of them turned into razor-like pointy fangs.

I had once been stung by a huge wasp on my neck when I was little. I remember the acute pain like it only happened yesterday, I had thought it was the worst I would ever feel. I had to get injections and antibiotics for that, it hurt like hell for more than a week. The terrible ache I felt now so intense and unbearable that that memory almost faded in my mind.

I felt his fangs leaving my neck, the pain was still there though. I felt weak, sloppy like I've never felt before. My blood was flowing down my throat, I had a hard time to breathe like I was always on the verge of choking but never quite.

Was this what it felt like to die?

Then someone opened my mouth with force. I wanted to fight it, wanted everyone to leave me alone but I couldn't, I was too damn weak.

A warm iron-like tasting liquid was in my mouth, it was so sickening that I had to try to cough it all out but they didn't let me, they only left me alone once I'd swallowed it.

As soon as that liquid reached my stomach, I felt like an explosion inside, immediately a million incandescent needles were piercing my skin, my organs, my guts.

I couldn't breathe, I couldn't move, couldn't even think straight, the pain was just too much to bear for me.

I was having several convulsions. I just wanted to end it all here.

Someone then lit me on fire, I was burning alive, maybe I was Vasiliy's personal vendetta for being dumped by Sybil half a century ago.

Perhaps, he only pretended he would turn me just to torture me, then he would have killed her only for spite.

I tried to move but my muscles weren't responding, I opened my eyes but I was blind.

I heard someone screaming far away from me, only to realize it was I, screaming for pain.

I was still burning. I wondered how long I would have to endure this agony before the fire would consume my body.

And I saw images of girls being burnt alive on a stake, screaming and crying. *A pretty girl smiling at me before the fire turned her body to ashes.*

I cried out in pain, again.

I saw the face of a man, a handsome friendly man before I begged him to turn me so I could beat my illness. I was going to die either way.

Utter agony, was I still being tortured?

Then Sybil, she was half naked in my bed, so beautiful and peacefully asleep. I'd woken up before her sensing the sunset around the corner, I had to let her go but I did love her so much.

The fire was still alive and scorching my very soul.

No more images, just nausea now, after having fits, I puked all I had eaten before for my last meal.

I tried to focus on my breath, the fire still consuming my skin.

I imagined the only thing that could ease my trespass: her pretty face, her light green eyes on mine, her long chestnut hair with red flecks under the sun, not quite red but not quite blonde either. Such an unusual colour.

I tried to think how I got lost in her body, her hands on my shoulders while she was asking me to make her mine.

Then her chuckling and laughing, and the colour her eyes were while she was crying.

The honesty in her voice when she'd said she loved me.

Breathing was not so painful now, I just felt so dizzy. If the fire was still on me I couldn't tell, I just couldn't seem to register things.

Perhaps, that was the dumbness of death, even the most sorrowful and violent of ends had to stop being an agony at some point. Maybe that was my moment.

Probably, my mind couldn't cope with all the distress and physical suffering that released some substance like morphine, clearly my time would soon be up.

Never mind, I could not think of any better way of ceasing to exist than trying to save my girl.

Maybe, I could have helped her as a ghost as well, no one could stop a feisty poltergeist. That was something to consider.

"William," someone said from very far away, someone with a foreign accent, "let it go."

The idea of getting some rest was not bad, I felt so tired and numb, I needed to just let it go he'd said.

So I did just after I felt my neck cracking.

•••

I BURNT FOR YOU

I jolted awake, my head was throbbing, I tried to open my eyes but there was so much light, that I had to cover them with my hands.

I felt so nauseous but when I tried to vomit nothing came out.

What happened to me? Wasn't I supposed to be dead?

"It's normal, it's part of the transition," a loud accented voice said.

"Stop shouting!" My hands were in my ears now.

"Open your eyes, boy." The voice was just so close to me. "Open your eyes," he repeated. "Slowly."

So I did it, I gradually started to see the world again. When I was comfortable enough, I looked around the room in wonder.

I was in the same place, Vasiliy's house.

Everything seemed somehow different.

The colours brighter and more vivid, I saw the man, Vasiliy, I could spot every detail of his face like he was standing two inches from me and not on the other corner of the house.

His blond eyelashes I had not noticed before, what once had been freckles now faded and replaced by pale alabaster skin.

"How do you feel?" he whispered but it seemed like he'd screamed it.

I tried to speak but my throat was hoarse, nothing managed to come out.

Vasiliy nodded as in an apology, went to the fridge and threw a ruby little sack at me. I caught it without any effort, my reflex more perfect and coordinated than ever.

"Drink, you'll feel better."

I didn't dare imagine what was inside that, but with a bite I opened it and gloated myself.

The taste was strange, it was like cold iron but elderflower like, it didn't taste amazing but I just could not manage to stop.

I saw a baby, my baby *when I was holding it for the first time, it was a girl... I was so happy about that, I've always wanted a baby girl. She seemed to read my mind as she smiled at me and I was her mother and I was completely hers.*

I opened my eyes again, cleaning the drop of liquid streaming down my chin, was I starting to go crazy?

"Did it... work?"

He smiled at me sarcastically. "What did you just drink, my son?"

Stupid question.

"What did you do to me?"

"Bit you, gave you my blood and then killed you. Just the usual protocol."

That was the liquid burning me, his blood. His blood had turned me.

"You had to die with my blood in your system to be reborn," he explained.

He snapped my neck after feeding it to me.

"How do you feel?" a female voice asked from the other side of the room.

I turned to look at Sybil, her young face filled with concern and something similar to... guilt? And I remembered seeing her half naked in bed, the love I'd felt for her...

"I saw your memories," I realized turning to the man.

"*Da,* my son, you did. When you drink a person's blood you always do, feel what they felt, think what they thought." He nodded. "Very clever of you to click it all into place."

"What did you see from his blood?" Sybil asked me, her voice filled with curiosity.

I looked at Vasiliy, maybe it wasn't my place to describe the affection he had felt for her. That he might still feel.

"Just a bunch of people, very confusing. I saw Feye's lover, I saw you begging him to turn you."

"He was my best friend, my brother from another mother. We wanted to live forever together and then I got mortally sick. He saved me just before being murdered." He looked melancholic.

"I will avenge him," I promised solemnly.

"I know you will, my son." He nodded.

"Why do you keep calling me that?" It was getting a bit annoying.

"Isn't that what you are now? My offspring, my legacy, my son and I'm your maker and father now."

I was speechless, one dad was enough, wasn't it? The last thing I needed was two.

"There's so much I need to teach you, but now it's not the time. Come back, my son, once you've done what you came here to do, and then I shall show you our world."

I nodded, I needed to know how to adjust and survive this new life, but first I had a place I needed to be, some people I needed to see. I felt my teeth turn into fangs, I almost panted.

"First lesson, learn to control your emotions or it won't be safe for you to show your face around," he said amused.

My fangs retracted.

"You'll teach him eventually but this is not the moment." Sybil's eyes were absent. "You slept for two days, her time will soon be up. He's going for her, now."

And those words made my dead heart bleed.

THE CAT AND THE MOUSE

Vivi.

I looked outside the window, watching one of the best sunsets I've ever witnessed, sipping a warm flavoured tea.

Maybe it was the most beautiful 'cause I knew it would be the last one, things have a way to be spectacular in your last moments.

I wasn't scared, I honestly just wanted to get it over with as soon as possible.

There was nothing keeping me here now, William, my love, had left.

Not that I could blame him.

Wasn't that what I'd hoped for?

I'd tried to play with his mind, and I knew he could never forgive that, not in a million years.

And maybe it was better off this way.

Wasn't that what I wanted? To save him?

I succeeded in that at least.

He was gone, ergo he would live.

Wasn't that victory enough?

Could I not die happy now?

He would go on with his life like this whole entangled mess never happened, perhaps someday he would remember me and say a prayer for me to grant me Heaven.

He didn't know that people like me couldn't afford Heaven.

I took a sip of my tea while stroking distractedly my cat. He was sleeping so peacefully on me and I envied him, I wish I could sleep through it till the end.

Like Maisa.

I'd given her a strong sleep potion. I couldn't afford her getting hurt for fighting for me. I would never forgive myself otherwise.

Sybil was nowhere to be seen, she'd left without a word three days ago and never came back.

Maisa had gotten so mad at her, she'd tried to call her but to no use, phone was off.

Aunt Maisa looked so disappointed and distressed.

Again, I couldn't blame her either.

I was a lost cause, I've always known that.

It was okay, though, I was ready to leave this world, I had no place in it.

There was no room for a teenager with the gift of magic and the curse of a vendetta.

The noise of steps on the gravel outside, I knew my time was up.

Good. I was ready.

A slight knock on the back door, I stayed still. The door opened and Byron's smiling face appeared.

"Are you ready, baby girl?"

I rose my tea cup to him as in cheers to him and drank the last few sips. I stood up.

"Good girl, we don't want anyone else to get hurt." His smile was wider, he was pleased.

"Promise me, no one else will be harmed," I whispered, "not my aunts nor the guy you almost killed the other day. This ends with me."

"What's your relationship with William Black?"

I almost jumped at the mention of his name, I had to make an effort to keep my face straight and calm, how could he remember his name?

"He used to be a friend," I said cryptically.

"Do you roll in bed with all your friends?" he blurted.

I blushed and looked elsewhere, I didn't expect him to know that. But yet, I should have known he'd keep an eye on me for those three days.

"It's none of your business," I muttered.

"Where is he now?"

"You scared him off, I don't know where he is."

"Well, if he doesn't try anything stupid, he can live," he shrugged, "same as for your dear aunts. If you co-operate everything will go smoothly and they'll all be fine."

"Let's go then." I walked to him.

He was smiling, expectant.

I stopped a few inches from him; he grabbed my chin, observing me, studying every single detail of my face.

"You are the one who looks the most like her," he said distractedly more to himself than to me.

I stayed silent, *let's get it over with.*

When he leaned to kiss me, I felt what it feels like dying. And it all went dark.

I woke up in what looked like a warehouse, I was wearing a white corset and an ivory lacy undergown. I blushed when I noticed I was not wearing any knickers. He must have undressed me and dressed me again.

What else had he done while I was unconscious?

I didn't dare imagine.

I looked at my hands, they were chained together.

I almost burst out laughing, as if I could fight him off.

I looked around me, it was a huge place with no windows or doors, the white neon light was bright, a pile of boxes around me.

The only escape route was a garage door but it was sealed.

In that moment, I understood he was not done playing with me. He wanted me to try to run away, just to play the mouse and the cat.

And I was certainly the mouse.

I stood up and ran to the garage door, the high-heeled sandals he placed on my feet so uncomfortable, I could cry.

But if he wanted me to play, I would play along.

There was a control panel on the left of the garage door, a switch with the word UP written on it. Did he want me to press it?

I did.

The door started to go up making loud noises, my heart was pounding in my ears. Where was he?

After a few moments, the door got stuck on something. The space was not big enough for me to walk out but I could try and limbo in.

Was that what he wanted me to do? Try and run away?

He said if everything went smoothly, he would let people I loved live, so I shouldn't risk it.

On the other hand, he wouldn't have left me alone there with the chance to escape if he didn't want me to try. What to do then?

After a moment of hesitation, I decided I would try, maybe he wanted me to find him?

I lay flat on my stomach, starting to move legs and arms to get out from the tiny space in between. The cold air almost left me breathless.

I was almost halfway out, when I heard his amused voice. "The apple doesn't fall far from the tree, does it?"

My heart skipped a beat when he grabbed my arm from the inside of the warehouse, he dragged me back inside with violence.

I raised my head when he pulled my hair, his face a few inches from mine, I just wanted to spit on him.

"Why did you leave me here like this then, if you didn't want me to try and escape?"

"That, my dear, was a test. All the others had failed and so have you." He made me stand up by pulling my hair harder.

I could have screamed for the pain.

"So I failed, now what?" I barked at him.

"If you had stayed where you were, I might have considered sparing you. Making you my queen," he sighed, "but sadly, bad blood flows in your veins, doesn't it?"

"Fuck you and your sick games, you psycho"

I'd rather die.

He grabbed me by the shoulders and shook me violently, I felt nauseous. "You don't understand, all this time I've been trying to find her. A better her in all of you, her descendants. I just wanted her love, is it asking too much?!" he shouted at me.

"You can't force love, she didn't love you and no one else will, you're just a sicko!"

His hand hit me before I could see it moving. I knew my noise was bleeding when I tasted the savoury taste of my own blood. I cleaned it up with one of my long sleeves.

"It's good that I already decided to kill you, your mouth is too foul for me to ever love you." With one hand he grabbed my chin again. "But that does not mean I can't have my fun with you." He again kissed me.

And if earlier I let him do that, if earlier it wasn't a violent kiss, the invasion of his filthy tongue in my mouth was too much for me to bear. I bit him.

He hit me again, with such a violence that I fell to the floor this time.

My ear was ringing but I could still hear him screaming at me, talking about how hateful my bloodline was, that I had mud flowing in my veins.

In a sudden rage fit, he moved a hand and an iron hook hanging from the ceiling appeared. He then grabbed me from the chains that bound my hands and secured them over my head, on the hook.

"You don't want to co-operate, fine. I'll be the bad guy," he whispered in my ear before starting to kiss me everywhere.

One of his hands was in my hair, keeping my head straight for him to kiss my mouth every now and then, the other was exploring my body. His filthy touch, so violent, so different from how I'd been touched just a few days ago. The way William, my William, had made love to me.

Warm tears were streaming down my face, my eye sight was blurred.

I felt sick.

It was like living a nightmare.

I just wanted him to stop, to kill me already.

"Slaughter me, please. Just stop this," I begged, sobbing.

"I promise you'll like it," he said distractedly, focused as he was in kissing my neck.

"No! Fuck you!" I cried out. "I hate you! You disgust me!"

Then suddenly, he was off me, knocked out on the far wall.

I raised my head astonished.

In all of his magnificence, William was standing there looking at me with a pair of fangs out.

THE AVENGER

William.

"How dare you?! I will..." Byron started but then stopped and stared in shock at my fangs.

Surprise surprise, bastard.

"Has anyone ever taught you that when a girl says no, it's no?" I said all smug.

I could not worry about Vivi now, I had to annihilate him first, I couldn't let him run away from me.

"What did you do?" she whispered.

With the corner of my eye, I noticed she was silently weeping.

"So, Byron Hill, the vampire ate your tongue? You were using it so well on my girlfriend until a few moments ago." I acted as I was confused, almost thoughtful.

He had to pay for what he'd done to her, for what he was about to do.

The man moved a hand in my direction, probably to use magic on me, maybe the same he used when he gripped my heart, but nothing happened.

He walked towards me, still not believing what he was seeing. "That's not possible..."

"You forgot to kill off *his* baby vampire." His face was a mask of shock. "He did it under your nose just before you staked him. Now, you cannot do anything to me." I smiled.

But I can and I will *do indescribable things to you.*

He had his usual psychopath expression now, he grinned. "You may be impervious to magic but it's fine, I shall finish you off the old fashioned way."

And it all happened in a blink, a wooden stake appeared in his hand and he was on me, trying to stab me in my heart.

We fell on the floor, he was punching me with his free hand, while the other was blocked by mine.

Vivi was trying to get free, a moment of distraction from my side and he stabbed me in my stomach, so very close to ending me.

I felt queasy, it wasn't quite painful just uncomfortable., I just couldn't worry about it now. I wasn't my priority now, she was. I had to save her.

I knocked him off me, hurling him against a pile of boxes and in a moment I was on him, my hands around his neck, about to strangle him.

Then a female scream pierced my sensitive ears, Vivi was crying out in pain.

I froze.

A dagger was in her skin, on the side, she was sweating and weeping.

"Funny how you were leverage for her at first..." he punched his way out of me, I was kneeling on the floor now, "...and now, she's yours." He chuckled, coughing a bit.

"Leave her alone or..." I threatened, not able to take my eyes off her.

I was still on the floor, my hands clutched. This couldn't be happening..

"Or you what? What can you possibly do at the moment?" He was laughing, a crazy laughter that would have made me shiver if I were human.

"I will find a way."

I still have my hands wrapped around you, you stupid bastard.

"You know, even magic proof vampires have an Achilles' heel, you know. And that is *blood*." His smile was sinister.

The dagger was immediately out of her body, ruby red liquid was flowing down her body, staining her white undergown.

And I wasn't me anymore.

My fangs reappeared, I automatically relieved my grip and stood up.

I took a step towards her, the smell of her sweet blood filling the air.

It was like calling my name, begging me to be tried.

And I wondered what it'd taste like, if that woman's blood tasted like elderflower, what would hers be?

Another step towards her, it was like I was enchanted.

Her blood like a siren singing for me.

"William, please," she mumbled.

I hadn't noticed how fast I'd walked to her until I was mere inches from her face.

The sweet smell of her blood filled my nostrils, her pleading eyes were red and puffy.

I put a hand on her wound. Touching her, the red liquid almost sent me to madness. I couldn't think straight.

I just wanted her.

Her blood.

Just a taste.

Before I realized, I was leaning on her neck, my fangs were out. Her skin smelled so good, fear was coming out of every pore.

Fear and something else.

But what?

I put my free hand on her neck, feeling her crazy heartbeat under my fingers.

What was the other thing I could smell in her skin?

I just couldn't wrap my head around that one.

Looking for answers, I raised my head and met her eyes.

"William," she simply said. My name.

And I got lost in the abyss of her sad eyes.

Just by beholding me, she was telling me that was not me, that I could fight it. But how could I?

The smell of her blood stronger now, the dagger had cut a gash on her chest, I almost immediately leaned to lick it.

"Don't let me go," she whispered almost faintly.

I only heard that because of my super hearing.

"I will not let you go," I'd promised her ages ago.

I meant it then, but now her blood was calling me.

I meant it then.

What had changed?

I had changed.

I met her eyes again, they were waiting, expectant.

What do you want from me?

What you promised her, a voice said in my head.

To never let her go.

And then, only then, I understood what the other smell was: love.

Vivi loved me so much, her skin was stinking of it.

Suddenly, I was awake.

The smell of her blood didn't bother me that much, not anymore.

I had changed for her.

I had died for her.

I was here to save her, because she was the love of my life.

Her eyes were still On mine so I winked at her. using all my supernatural speed, I was in front of the man I hated the most.

He blinked, confused at the sudden change of situation.

I smirked, before my hand ripped his heart out.

THE FAULT OF THE SAVIOUR

Vivi.

I could never forget what happened next, Byron's heart was in William's bloodied fist, his shocked and sorrowful expression while he fell down his knees.

And I saw transparent shapes of women all around him, smiling.

Between them, I recognized my mother.

Every other woman was looking at their saviour, but not her.

She floated to me and put her transparent hand on my wet cheek. It felt like the caress of the wind.

Then they disappeared.

"He had their souls trapped inside him," I said more to myself than to him.

I watched William drop the man's heart on the floor and squash it with his foot, then turn to me.

He broke the chains that bound my arms, never meeting my eyes.

"What's wrong?"

I called his name but he gave me his back.

"William, please." I put a hand on his shoulders but he shook it off like I'd burnt him.

"Look at me," I ordered. "Look at me," I mouthed.

When he turned to me, his expression was devastated.

"What's up?"

"I was about to... I wanted to..." He sighed.

"But you didn't." I understood what was tormenting him.

"I almost lost it, Vivi. For a bit of blood, I almost killed you." He swallowed and looked at me, his eyes were sad and angry at the same time. "I wanted to." He looked away, ashamed.

"You didn't, William. I'm still here, I'm alive." I caressed his face and he closed his eyes.

"Until the next time you cut yourself," he whispered.

"Please, let's not think about it now," I begged and he looked at me. "You saved me."

He gave me half of a smile. "I told you I would."

"Yeah, but... you gave up on your life for me."

"I couldn't let you go, I would have ceased to exist. I can eat, talk, sleep without you... but it's just a lie, it's just surviving."

And I wondered if any *I love you* in the world could express the density of our feelings for each other, if any *thank you* would ever be enough for what he'd done for me. For what he'd given up to save me.

"I'm so deeply in love with you it almost hurts," I said, going on the tip of my toes to kiss him.

"We better find you something more appropriate to wear, I don't want any stupid doctor seeing you in that attire." He smirked when we stopped kissing.

I smiled, only he could say something like that in that moment.

He gave me his jacket. "Let's get you to a hospital."

I had forgotten how badly my wound hurt, but it didn't matter. My superhero was there with me, there was no darkness or sorrow I should fear.

EPILOGUE

I was staring out of the window, watching the sun going down, I had been waiting for the whole day for this moment. The moment William would come back to me.

He left me begrudgingly that morning before sunrise at the hospital, promising me he'd come to me after sun down.

At the hospital, they stitched me up good while William was asked what had happened. He had somehow convinced them we'd had a car accident and the police needn't be involved.

I guess he used one of his brand new vampire powers.

I still could not believe what he'd done for me.

The many ways he'd saved me.

Would I ever be able to repay him?

Would I ever be grateful enough?

"Are you still on that window?" A voice behind me.

Heaven, I hadn't heard him walking in the room, he'd become so silent with his movements.

"The last time I was sitting here, I contemplated suicide," I admitted reluctantly.

"And now?" He got closer and closer to me, until he sat just across me.

"Now, I'm trying to imagine the rest of my life."

"What do you wanna do?"

I took his hand, started playing with it, it was as cold as an ice cube.

"I've never thought of it, I never believed I had a future," I said honestly.

"Now you do." He smiled at me.

"Thanks to you. Because you killed yours." I sighed.

The sacrifice he'd made for me...

"I do not regret anything, Vivi. Not a single moment, not a single choice." He leaned to kiss me.

With that kiss, I tried to show him how much I loved him, how grateful I was, how much he'd changed my life.

"I don't know what I want to do with my life, the only thing I'm sure of at the moment is you." I smiled at him.

William looked out of the window, lost in thoughts. "Maybe there is something that I regret, actually."

He looked melancholic.

My heart skipped a beat, he couldn't...

He noticed my panic and smiled amused. "Not that, not *this*." He placed a hand on my chest, just where my beating heart was. "I just..." he took a deep breath, "... I almost killed you, Vivi. That's my biggest regret."

"It doesn't matter, you didn't and..."

He placed a finger over my mouth. "I wanted to. I wanted to taste your blood so badly." He closed his eyes and took a deep breath once again.

"I have to learn how to deal with my new condition before I can be safe for you to be around." He said after a few moments, "I need to learn to control myself."

And it killed me inside but I said, "Okay, if that's what you want."

"It's not what I want, it's what I need." He looked at the moon. "If it was for me, I would just stay here with you for eternity."

"But you can't." I nodded.

"Not like this, not when I'm afraid I can lose control anytime."

"Go then, I'll be waiting for you," I declared.

"I don't know how long it will take me," he admitted. "I can't ask you..."

"You're not asking me, I want to. I love you and I will wait for as long as you need."

"You'll be my reason to come back, my anchor to my human part." He caressed my cheek.

"I will never let you go," I repeated the words he often said to me.

And there were no more words to be said.

We kissed and made love several times that night. I just wanted to stay awake, I wanted the night to stretch and last forever but, as a mere human, I fell asleep.

When I woke up, the sun was already up and shining in the strangely clear English sky.

He was gone.

On the pillow next to me, I found a note with my name written on it.

I opened it and read:

Now it's time for you to just live.

Adesso Vivi.

EIN HERZ FÜR AUTOREN A HEART FOR AUTHORS À L'ÉCOUTE DES AUTEURS MIA ΚΑΡΔΙΑ ΓΙΑ ΣΥΓΓΡ.
HJÄRTA FÖR FÖRFATTARE UN CORAZÓN POR LOS AUTORES YAZARLARIMIZA GÖNÜL VERELIM SZÍV
CUORE PER AUTORI ET HJERTE FOR FORFATTERE EEN HART VOOR SCHRIJVERS TEMOS OS AUTO
SZÍVZOÏNKÉRT SERCE DLA AUTORÓW EIN HERZ FÜR AUTOREN A HEART FOR AUTHORS À L'ÉCOUT
CORAÇÃO ВСЕЙ ДУШОЙ К АВТОРАМ ETT HJÄRTA FÖR FÖRFATTARE Á LA ESCUCHA DE LOS AUTOR
AUTEURS MIA ΚΑΡΔΙΑ ΓΙΑ ΣΥΓΓΡΑΦΕΙΣ UN CUORE PER AUTORI ET HJERTE FOR FORFATTERE EEN H
YAZARLARIMIZA GÖNÜL VERELIM SZÍVZOÏNKÉRT SERCE DLA AUTORÓW EIN HERZ FÜR
VOOR SCHRIJVERS TEMOS OS AUTO CORAÇÃO ВСЕЙ ДУШОЙ К АВТОРАМ ETT HJÄRTA FÖR

The author

A successful author of online fanfics, this is
Jade C. Russel's debut novel. When not writing,
Russel loves to travel. To date, she has enjoyed
many European countries including the UK, Italy
and Germany and has also travelled further afield,
to Canada.

The publisher

He who stops getting better stops being good.

This is the motto of novum publishing, and our focus is on finding new manuscripts, publishing them and offering long-term support to the authors.
Our publishing house was founded in 1997, and since then it has become THE expert for new authors and has won numerous awards.

Our editorial team will peruse each manuscript within a few weeks free of charge and without obligation.

You will find more information about
novum publishing and our books on the internet:

www.novum-publishing.co.uk